TO **JEKYLL** AND **HIDE**

MARTIN L. WILSON

GOLD—BUG MYSTERIES
COLUMBIA, SOUTH CAROLINA

Produced in the Republic of South Carolina by

Gold-Bug Mysteries
An Imprint of SHOTWELL PUBLISHING, LLC

Post Office Box 2592
Columbia, South Carolina 29202

www.ShotwellPublishing.com

Cover Design: Hazel's Dream / Boo Jackson TCB

ISBN-13: 978-0997939392
ISBN-10: 0997939397

DEDICATED to my parents Grady Franklin Wilson and Lillie Grace Wilson

ACKNOWLEDGEMENTS

My gratitude to the entire Shotwell gang for their enthusiasm in bringing this book to fruition. I am indebted to Dr. Clyde N Wilson (no relation) for his editorial expertise and his willingness to present my work to a wider audience. My thanks to Ms. Alyce Hackney of the Pamunkey Regional Library at the Atlee branch in Mechanicsville for her aid researching the World War II era. Any errors and misinterpretations are mine alone.

TO JEKYLL AND HIDE

CHAPTER ONE

THOUGH HE'D GROWN UP on the mainland, Clarke Deveau had never been here to Jekyll Island. That's because he wasn't a millionaire and he needed an invitation to get on the island.

He still wasn't a millionaire. But he had an invitation and today he was crossing the channel.

Jekyll Island, Georgia, had been known as "the millionaires' club" since 1888 when a battalion of the nation's robber barons had chosen it for their winter retreat. From then until today in March of 1942, they'd allowed only their invitees and their servants to set foot on the island. Sitting in the Cris Craft easing up Jekyll Creek to the dock fronting the marshy side of the island, Clarke knew even the Spanish moss waved gently in the ocean breeze with quiet disdain for this mere commoner.

A driver in nothing more than one of Mr. Ford's Model A's met Clarke at the dock. The driver orally confirmed his identity, opened the back door and bade him enter. Within five minutes Clarke was on the other side of the island where the driver pointed to a man sitting in a director's chair under a huge spreading live oak at the back side of the white beach.

"That's Mr. Blandford," the driver said with disinterest.

Clarke exhaled a heavy sigh, glad his wingtips were scruffy enough for stepping through the sand to the man. When he reached the man he saw that another director's chair sat beside him. Between the chairs was a small table with a bottle of Scotch and a pitcher of water

"Mr. Blandford?"

The silver-haired man looked sideways at him, frowned and nodded toward the chair. Clarke sat down and shook sand from his shoes.

"Mr. Deveau?"

Clarke nodded that the chunky man was correct. He guessed Harold Blandford had once been muscular. His might still be strong, but he was no longer muscular. His face was square and a bulge at his neck betrayed a double chin coating his Adam's apple. Clarke knew his host had already been into the Scotch and water.

"Glad you could come, Mr. Deveau. Your Mr. Warren recommended you highly."

"Indeed." Clarke recognized a whopper when he heard one.

David Warren was county attorney. Even though they'd grown up together, David hadn't been overjoyed to see Clarke come back home. After law school at the University of Georgia, David had returned here to Glynn County to pursue law and his political aspirations, while Clarke had gone on to get his law degree from Princeton and then settled into the Justice Department in Washington, DC. Since then, David had succeeded at his ambitions and Clarke hadn't. Clarke knew David never would've recommended him with the idea of doing him a favor.

"What you know about me, Mr. Deveau?"

Clarke hesitated then went into the painful details as he knew them. "I know you're Erica Blandford's father. She died after falling from a horse several weeks ago on

Pineland plantation. The coroner ruled her death accidental, caused by the fall."

"Even though she'd been riding since her childhood. You didn't say anything about me, Mr. Deveau. But that's fine. This is about Erica."

Clarke exhaled slowly and wished Blandford would snap his fingers and tell the driver leaning on the Model A to bring another cup. He also knew Harold Blandford had publicly accused one Jeremy Mann of complicity in his daughter's death. To be blunt, he'd accused Mann of murder. Clarke silently thanked David Warren for bringing him together with a grieving father who was convinced his little girl had been done in by foul means out there on the plantation.

"What did you think of the coroner's ruling?"

"I have no basis to question it."

Blandford shifted in his chair to face Clarke. His face and eyes were tense and angry. "Erica didn't die in an accidental fall, Mr. Deveau. Mann killed her."

Clarke coughed. In truth, he'd thought the case strange, too. A well-to-do young woman ends up with a broken neck while consorting with a man recognized as New York City's premiere cad. On a plantation sitting on the banks of the Altamaha River, some twenty miles away from the island society she'd supposedly come to enjoy.

"With anything like competence, your Mr. Warren and the coroner could've gotten evidence on Mann. Maybe that's all I could expect of law enforcement down here. They haven't been open even to my offers to fund a proper investigation."

Ah, funds. Greenbacks. The barons on Jekyll Island had it for breakfast, lunch and dinner. They had so much of it they didn't need to talk about it. In this case, Harold Blandford's banking money was checkmated by the Mann family's chemical fortune. The elder Mann's membership at the Jekyll round table made his son Jeremy a de facto member, too. With the difference that Jeremy preferred to live--cavort, some would wink--out of sight on the plantation up there on the Altamaha.

"Just how can I help you, Mr. Blandford?"

"I want you to get the proof that bastard killed Erica."

Clarke thought he controlled his shock rather well. "I frankly don't know that I can deliver. I've no reason to question the coroner's report."

His voice rose an octave. "It's not obvious to you? Okay, I may be the only one who believes Erica was murdered. I want you to get the proof."

"With all due respect, I wouldn't know where to start, sir."

"You're a detective, aren't you?"

"Sort of."

"Sort of? You were with the Justice Department. Warren recommended you. He said your schedule is open."

"He knows less than nothing about my schedule."

"I thought of bringing in a detective from New York. But a guy with a Brooklyn accent would have trouble prying information out of the locals. It'll take somebody who speaks the language. Warren told me you're the only man available here on a private basis. I can guess there's not too much work here for a private detective. You grew up here. You talk the language, even if you did come back under somewhat questionable circumstances."

Uh, huh. You heard, too. Local boy makes good. Joins the nation's official law firm. Pulls gun on wife's, ah, consort. Gets canned. Loses law license. Comes back home to family plantation to find something else to do. Loses family plantation and still has nothing to do besides find other husbands before wife takes shot at them. Great prospects here in 1942.

Clarke moved to stand. "I appreciate your confidence in me, Mr. Blandford. But I'd be wasting my time. And yours."

"Both of us have all the time we need. Sit down, Mr. Deveau. Warren and the sheriff have sworn off this case. They think Mann's money is better than mine. You're the only local investigator I can find."

"I'm not one, either. Not for something like this."

"If you were good enough for Justice, you've already dealt with riff raff. Jeremy Mann's a felon with money."

Jekyll's full of such people, Clarke thought. "Did Warren tell you I don't even carry a gun? But you already know the one I used to have in DC was confiscated."

"I'm not after a hired gun. Just somebody to carry through an investigation that has to be made."

Clarke sighed. "With all due respect, sir, how could I, anyone, disprove the coroner's findings? Why do you think your daughter died from something other than a fall from a high horse?"

"Because Jeremy Mann was there. That's all I need to know."

"What did the autopsy reveal?"

"My wife wouldn't allow her to be chopped up and dissected like a frog in a high school lab. We shipped her home and buried her whole. My wife still visits her grave every day. Erica took the truth to the grave. She must've found out something on Mann."

"Such as?"

"Jeremy's a rotten son of a bitch. Even if his dad has been my friend for 40 years.

All the more reason I need you. Your investigation has to be discreet. I can't let his dad know I think his son's connected to the mob. Maybe even to enemies."

"So you don't want to ruin your business connections if I end up chasing some wild geese through the marsh."

"I don't believe you will. Jeremy's a stinker. I'm surprised you haven't heard the talk about him. Not just about his women. About the people he makes deals with."

"What kind of people does he deal with?"

Blandford allowed himself a crooked smile. "Some call it treason. He can deal with anybody. Has all that charm. Damn, I wish I'd shot him that day he drove up to my cottage and met her. She was so immature he ran right through her defenses. She was hardly out of college."

"But she took up with him."

"He had too much experience for her. But why did he have to get rid of her? What did she find out? You find that and you'll know why he killed her."

Clarke stared at this tense, angry man, his silvery hair rustling in the light ocean breeze. Desperate to pin something on Jeremy Mann. Anything. Just come up with something. There had to be something. His sweet little girl had to have been a victim of an amoral rogue, had found out something he would kill for. Maybe it was true. But Clarke knew that not all women of 24 were naive pawns, no matter what their grieving fathers might think.

"How can you figure that bastard?" Blandford said, as though speaking to himself. "Erica's in her grave and he's out there playing master on his plantation with a French whore."

"French whore?"

"Lives out there with him. Brought her down from New York after Erica died. I heard he met her in London his last trip over, brought her over and set her up in an apartment in New York. London was full of frogs. They've already surrendered to Hitler. Maybe Erica found out something about her. There have to be spies among them."

Clarke knew Blandford was reaching for anything to pin on Jeremy Mann. A French whore who just might be a Nazi agent? In fact, he recalled seeing the "French whore" a couple days ago riding through Brunswick with Mann. She was too far away for him to judge her moral standards. He couldn't pick her out of an FBI lineup.

"You get the goods on Jeremy and I'll see the Justice Department hears about it."

Ah, the man has influence in DC. Don't all rich guys? "Don't bother. For your sake and mine."

"Say you'll take this on, Deveau. Somebody has to."

No, in fact, nobody just has to go sniffing around trying to find clues that a rich man had murdered his lover when official opinion had closed the case. Was a fee worth it?

Clarke pondered the matter of fees. He'd had to sell off his father's property to pay off debts on it after going broke in the depression. That property had included the Pineland plantation that Jeremy Mann had bought with his pocket change. That was another reason he didn't want to see Mann again. Pineland had been in the Deveau family since the early 1800's, only to fall victim to a depression that allowed the likes of Jeremy Mann to scoop it up. Clarke had kept only 20 acres down river and the little house the manager had lived in. That's where he'd moved when he divested the Deveau heritage.

Yes, he was forced to admit, a fee from Harold Blandford would help. Now all he had to do was convince himself Erica Blandford's death had been more than just an accidental fall from a horse.

Still, he heard himself say, "I repeat what I said. You'd be wasting your money and my time."

"I have plenty of money and you have plenty of time. I'll start by buying you a gun."

Clarke stood up. "I'll be in touch."

The uniformed chauffeur was waiting under the spreading oak. His smirk said he knew his boss had gotten what he'd wanted. The smirk didn't say what Clarke had gotten.

CHAPTER TWO

CLARKE FOUND DAVID WARREN in his office telling two sailors he'd forget they busted up the Marsh Bar if they'd get back on their ship and never show their Norwegian faces in Brunswick again. Through a combination of gestures and broken English their captain translated the message to them. They smiled enthusiastically and got up. The captain touched his battered cap, reaffirmed that he'd cover the damages and left with his men before David could have second thoughts.

David looked at the doorway and called, "Got an appointment Clarke?" He wasn't due in court this morning, Clarke guessed, or he wouldn't look so rumpled in his blue suit. But David had a way of looking rumpled anyway because his salary allowed him to eat too well. "What brings you here to the inner sanctum?"

"Erica Blandford."

With a tired shrug Warren beckoned him into his office and closed the door. "She didn't send you, so I guess her old man did. What kind of tall tales did he tell you."

"The biggest was that you recommended me."

"Yeah, figured you wouldn't mind, if you have the time."

"For sure, I don't make as much as the county's chief prosecutor."

Warren glared at him and sank into the worn leather chair behind his cluttered desk. "What's his angle?"

"That she was murdered. Any reason to think he's right about that?"

Warren exhaled wearily. "It was a fall from a horse, pure and simple. Broken neck, severed spinal cord."

"And no autopsy."

"No. The old man and his wife were dead set against it."

"He wants proof of foul play, yet refused an autopsy that might've provided it."

"If proof exists."

"You sound certain, David."

Warren spread his hands. "No reason to suspect otherwise. Jeremy Mann's no criminal. If he is, I've no proof of it."

"You checked his record in New York?"

Warren's chubby face reddened up to his thinning brown hair and Clarke knew he hadn't. "Was it really necessary, Clarke?"

"Yet you recommended Blandford hire me to find proof you think doesn't exist."

"He was persistent. You can use a fee, can't you?"

"Did Henry Brogan conduct the inquest?"

"He's the coroner. Want to see his report?"

Warren pulled a file from his cabinet and handed it to Clarke. It was short and stated exactly what Warren had just told him. He handed it back.

"I'll drop by and see him."

"Suit yourself. Happy detecting."

Henry Brogan owned the drug store across from the court house. When Clarke entered, the ceiling fan was stirring warm humidity already prevalent this far south. Henry had just left the pharmacy counter to pull a soda for two ladies who'd come in out of the sunshine in need of refreshment. He served them in the quick jerky motions expected of a man as thin and wiry as he was. Just the opposite of David Warren, Clarke thought.

Clarke slid onto a stool at the counter. "I'll take one of those."

"Sure thing, Clarke. Haven't seen you around."

"I haven't needed anything more medicinal than bourbon lately. Henry, David Warren just showed me your report on Erica Blandford's death. Looks straightforward."

"David showed it to you? Well, why not. It was in the papers. What's your interest in it?"

"Harold Blandford asked me to look into it."

Brogan showed irritation when he set Clarke's cola in front of him. "Blandford. I know the man's upset. It was his daughter. But he can't let it go. You know what he said about the inquest?"

Clarke sipped his cola and savored its tingle on his tongue. "I read. I rather imagine the newspaper cleaned up his remarks."

"Like I say, I can understand him being upset. It's awful to lose a daughter with her life in front of her. But to name Mann a killer and call me an incompetent..."

"I take it you disagree with his opinion."

"Don't tell me you think he's right. The poor man's grieving. Don't encourage him to think there's more to his daughter's death than there is. How come you're looking into this? "

"I was recommended for the job."

"You?"

Clark knew the thinly veiled sarcasm conveyed Henry's disbelief that anyone sane would entrust anything to him. His banishment from Justice was common knowledge in Brunswick.

"Did you notice any other marks on her? Bruises? Any damage at all?"

"Why're you asking, Clarke?"

"I told you. Her father has asked me to look into her death."

Henry angrily wiped the counter. "No, I saw nothing out of the ordinary. She broke her neck in the fall. That was a powerful hunk of horse she was riding. Mann said she'd never ridden it before."

"Did he say why he allowed her to ride that particular horse?"

"He didn't. He said she got up early before him and took the horse without asking."

"Got up early?"

"That's what he said."

"When was she found?"

"After the manager got up and found the horse wandering around the barn. He went out and found her on a road leading from the house to the highway."

"Who's the manager?"

"An English fellow. Max Lewis. He met Mann in London and came with him to America to escape the bombing."

"So you found no unusual marks on her?"

"None."

"Wonder if a medical examiner might've found something else," Clarke said as though musing to himself. He enjoyed seeing Henry Brogan's gray eyes flash.

"He might have," Brogan said with obvious anger. "But her parents refused an autopsy. They put her body on the train to New York and he's been complaining ever since we didn't do the job right. I was willing to send the body to a medical examiner in Atlanta, but they said no. That's all I could do. I'm not a doctor."

"No, you're not a doctor. Wasn't there another female in the house at the time?"

Henry Brogan's tense face relaxed into a smile. "A French girl. His maid."

Clarke took the last swallow of his cola, letting the refreshing burn linger on his tongue. "Two women there with Mann. Did the mademoiselle see Erica leave the house?"

"I didn't ask."

Clarke allowed his eyebrows to register mock surprise. "You didn't? Did anyone? The police? David Warren?"

Henry Brogan threw down his towel and started back to his pharmacy counter.

"Wonder why two young women would be in a man's house at once. Does that seem strange to you, Henry?"

Henry Brogan pretended to fill prescription bottles. Clarke walked back to the prescription counter. "Well, does it add up? Would you keep two women in the same house at the same time?"

"No, Clarke. I wouldn't. But I'm not Mr. Jeremy Mann, am I?"

"You reckon both the women were sleeping with him? Or the Englishman?"

"Didn't give it a thought. You need anything else?"

"No, just some idea of why you or David didn't give some thought to the unique living arrangements and wonder if it had anything to do with a young woman's death."

"I don't speculate, Clarke. I can only tell you what I saw. The coroner's job is not glamorous. I do it the best I can."

"Even if you see something that doesn't quite add up? Like a love triangle?"

"No, triangles are your territory."

Clarke stiffened at the reference to his ex-wife. This wasn't the first time someone in Brunswick had drawn her like a gun, knowing he had no comeback. They pretended he had no excuse good enough to justify drawing a gun on her and her friend.

Clarke turned abruptly and left Henry Brogan to dispense drugs to the customer standing at his counter. Humidity was already creeping along the coast, so he shucked his blue-striped seersucker coat and threw it into the back seat of his Chevrolet. Okay. Fair enough. Since he was an expert on triangles, it was time to go talk to what was left of a triangle out there on Pineland plantation. Or had it been a foursome? maybe an expert on marital affairs could come up with some questions that hadn't occurred to non-experts.

CHAPTER THREE

CLARKE COULD'VE DRIVEN to Pineland plantation as blindfolded as the maiden of justice. On a hill overlooking the Altamaha River some 20 miles up highway 17 north of Brunswick, Pineland was a reminder of a past epoch. Made of tabby-- ground-up burned oyster shells mixed with sand, shells and water--past Deveaus had built it to last. It was so solid that Clarke thought it disrespectful that Jeremy Mann had re-bricked the original exterior.

Clarke felt discomfort bordering on resentment as the main house came into sight. The plantation had expanded to some 2,000 acres since the first Deveau had fled slave revolts on Hispaniola. Now all he had left of it was a small house and some 20 acres downriver. With his Justice career in tatters, he'd come back to Glynn County to bury his father. That's when he found how totally the depression had ravaged his family's fortunes. He'd had no choice but to sell the estate to a son of an industrialist with enough money to comport himself as a grandee. Clarke hadn't spoken to Jeremy Mann since signing the deeds of sale three years ago.

Clarke parked behind a Packard Darrin and an MG sport convertible. Jeremy Mann got up from a patio table and walked toward him in easy, confident strides. He recognized Clarke and put out his hand in greeting.

"It's been a long time, Mr. Deveau."

"I see the old house is holding up well."

"I've enjoyed it. I can understand how you felt so attached to it."

Mann led Clarke to the patio he'd added to the house. Clarke recalled the patio area had been a grassy lawn under spreading oaks when he was growing up here. He accepted Mann's offer of Scotch, though he preferred bourbon.

Over his glass, Clarke examined the smiling Mann, now probably a shade over 40 and still without visible gray in his dark hair. He looked comfortable in an open-necked blue shirt and gray pants. The early spring warmth made Clarke happy he'd left his coat in the car.

"What brings you out this way?" Mann asked pleasantly.

"Work."

"Work? You are...were...with the Justice Department?"

"Ancient history. I do private investigation now."

"Sounds interesting."

"Sometimes it is. Usually it's not."

"I'm surprised there's much demand for a private investigator in these parts. Are you working on something interesting now?"

"Perhaps. I'm looking into the death of Erica Blandford."

Jeremy Mann's relaxed demeanor tightened. "Erica? Yes. Tragic. I still can't get over it."

"I'm told your manager found her. An Englishman named Lewis."

"Who asked you to investigate? The local authorities?"

"I've been retained by Erica's father. He disagrees with the coroner's conclusion."

"You mean Harold's paying you to prove I killed Erica?"

Jeremy Mann started to stand, then relaxed back into the wicker chair and forced a smile. "And what have you found, Mr. Deveau? Do you believe I killed my wife?"

"Mr. Blandford believes you did."

"Poor man. He's overcome with grief. It has affected his judgment. You'd think we'd never done business together."

"What kind of business?"

"Doesn't matter." Clarke knew Mann was dismissing him. A mere busted Justice Department lawyer from Georgia couldn't possibly understand the financial complexities of the Manns and Blandfords.

"Explain it to me. I investigated more than one case of business fraud."

Mann's eyes hardened though he kept smiling. "If Harold wants to discuss our business dealings, he should talk to me and not try to pressure me through you."

Interesting that Mann and Blandford were business partners. More interesting that Blandford had failed to mention it. "Are you still partners?"

"That's confidential. You know that."

"What time of the morning was Miss Blandford found?"

"Around eight. Before I was up. Max found her horse in the stable. It was saddled and he knew Erica must've taken it for a ride. He found her when he went looking for her. We think the horse threw her against a tree and broke her neck. There was a noticeable bump on her head."

"The report didn't mention a bump."

"Probably because the obvious cause of death was her broken neck."

"She got up early and went riding? Were you aware she'd left the house?"

"No. She liked to go riding early in fresh morning air."

"You have another female guest, don't you?

The wicker chair squeaked as Mann shifted. He sipped his Scotch and smiled. "I imagine you mean Marie."

"Marie?"

"My housekeeper. Marie Cardiene. She fled France as the Germans rolled in. She came to England with her father. She drove an ambulance. He returned to France to help the resistance. Nobody's heard from him since. Poor fellow's probably dead. Her mother died of a heart condition just before the invasion."

"How did you meet her?"

"In London during the bombing. We were introduced in a club, just before the lights went out. When they came back on we were good friends. I persuaded her to come here with my family until the danger is over."

"As your housekeeper?"

"She has been a great help to me. It's far safer here than anywhere across the Atlantic."

"I wouldn't want to be there myself," Clarke said. "She was here the morning Miss Blandford died?"

"She was in the house helping fix breakfast."

"What did Miss Blandford think about your housekeeper?"

"She liked her very much. They got along well."

"Was there any resentment between them?"

"I don't want to be rude, Mr. Deveau, but my housekeeper has nothing to do with this wild goose chase Harold sent you on."

"Perhaps. I see a triangle here, possibly a foursome including your manager, and one of the participants ends up dead."

Mann's eyes narrowed. "You actually suspect a murder? I can't believe Harold sent you to badger me with his fantasies. Did you need the money that badly? The price I paid you for this old place should've put you in tall cotton."

"It put me in a small house down by the river. How did you meet Erica? Up north?"

"I met her last winter when I went to find see Harold on St. Simon's to discuss a business deal. He has a smaller home there to get away from Jekyll. Uses it for an office time to time. He'd come there for our meeting and brought her along. After we talked, he went for a game of golf. I had the top down on my MG and she went for a ride with me. Women can't resist convertibles, you know."

"Led to a happy relationship."

"Almost immediately. We ended up there at the marsh where the Georgians beat the Spanish and ran them back to Florida."

"Yes, the Battle of Bloody Marsh. July 7, 1742. It ended Spain's attempt to take over the British colonies."

"Well done. You're a walking encyclopedia, Deveau."

"It's local history. You were saying about Erica?"

"Bloody Marsh they call it? Bizarre. How colorful. What else can I tell you? We fell on the marsh grass and nature took its course."

Clarke looked toward the barns and stifled his disgust. How could Mann casually talk of taking Erica Blandford in the marsh grass and show no remorse that she was now dead?

"Where's your housekeeper?"

Mann pointed to the road leading up the river. Clarke saw the horse and rider emerge under moss-draped trees. They rode toward him and clattered onto the patio where the rider nudged the horse to rear, the way Gene Autry made Champion do it in the movies. In an easy fluid swing, the young woman dismounted and accepted Mann's peck on her cheek.

She patted the horse's sweaty neck. "He ran so well today. I think he deserves a drink."

"In a silver bucket?" Mann said, feigning seriousness.

"Why not? He deserves champagne."

Mann laughed. "Not after a hard run. For you, perhaps, but not for him."

"Oh, please, give him champagne."

For the first time she became aware of Clarke standing at the table. She took in his six feet of somewhat Gallic looks and looked questioningly at Mann.

"This is Monsieur Clarke Deveau. He used to own this house and the trails you rode today."

"Monsieur Deveau? Are you also French?"

"Old American. My name comes from my Huguenot family line."

She showed no sign that she knew anything about the Protestants who'd fled France for the western hemisphere. Clarke took her to be no older than mid-20's, putting her at roughly half the age of the man of the house. She'd grown to young womanhood the way men wished all women would grow, giving distinction to her jodhpurs and chemise. Her tan glow, he guessed, came from hours of riding in open Georgia air. Her green eyes crinkled in appreciation of his obvious admiration. She turned back to Mann and again playfully urged him to attend to her horse's thirst for champagne.

Mann smiled indulgently. "He's a good Southern horse," Mann explained. "Comes from Virginia."

Clarke nodded, recalling his acquaintances from the Old Dominion, in particular the thirsty scholars at Mr. Jefferson's University in Charlottesville. The horse stuck his nose toward Clarke's glass and got a playful pat. "Easy, fellow. Somebody's going to mistake you for a frat boy."

The horse snorted its frustration. "Monsieur Deveau, I must take Gravedigger to the stables. He is hot and tired."

"I'll go with you, mademoiselle."

Mann snatched the reins from her hand. "Max!" he yelled.

A tall muscular man with dark brown hair came walking toward them from the barn.

"Did you know Erica Blandford well?" Clarke asked Marie, seeing that Mann wasn't going to allow him to be alone with her.

Her laughter died and her face went serious. "Erica? Was she a friend of yours?"

"No. I'm trying to learn all I can about her accident. Did you like her?"

"You're out of line, Deveau," Mann said harshly.

The tall man with dark blond hair arrived at the patio to take Gravedigger's reins. "You must be Max Lewis. Did you find Miss Blandford the morning she fell?"

Max looked surprised, his eyes shifting from Clarke to Mann.

"He's investigating Erica's death," Mann said with obvious irritation. "Her father seems to think there was something unusual about the circumstances. Tell him how you found her."

"I found her dead," Max said in a British accent. "What more can I say?"

"Yes," Mann said. "She'd been riding this very horse. He's very spirited, perhaps too much for her limited experience. Had I been at the barn, I never would've allowed her to ride him."

"Yet Mademoiselle Cardiene seems able to handle him," Clarke said, patting the horse's neck.

"Marie is an expert horsewoman," Mann said. "She

21

grew up riding on her father's estate in France."

"Lucky her. Could I see where Erica was thrown?"

"I see no point in it," Mann said, visibly perturbed. "Please report back to Harold that I've had it with his absurd suspicions and accusations. I've indulged him only because our families are close. Tell him enough is enough."

Clarke looked at the three stony faces and knew he'd heard all he would today. He put his glass on the table out of the reach of Gravedigger's nose. "Pleasure seeing you again, Mr. Mann."

Jeremy Mann appeared to relax at Clarke's intention to depart. "Sorry I can't be of more help. I truly hope Harold gets a grip on his emotions."

"I'm sure he will."

When he figures out which of you killed her.

CHAPTER FOUR

JEREMY MANN WATCHED the dust of Clarke's car only for a moment before turning to enter his house. Was Harold Blandford mad? His obsession was jeopardizing their negotiations with Herr Albert Speer. Jeremy was sorry about Erica, too. She'd been a fine diversion. It was damned unfortunate that she'd died, considering what was on the line. The old man had to get a grip on himself.

Mann fixed another Scotch and water and went to his study to examine his response to Herr Speer at the German Ministry of Armaments and War Production. Deveau's intrusion reminded him of that day he'd gone to St. Simon's to talk to her father at his getaway home about their contacts with Herr Speer. They talked and Harold left to play golf. Being alone at the house, Erica had readily succumbed to his international charms and gone riding with him in his MG. They'd ended up at Bloody Marsh where nature had taken its course. When he got back to Blandford's house, he'd reached into his coat pocket for his gold cigarette case and found it missing. Had it not been a gift of pure gold from a baroness he'd met in London, he would've forgotten about it.

When he returned to the spot where he and Erica had tumbled in the marsh grass, the sudden sound of a voice startled him as much as the Spanish must've been surprised by the English attack two centuries ago.

"This yours?" the young woman asked. Jeremy smiled as he recalled the meeting.

"Yes. Thank you, Miss..." he said, taking in the shapely blond with liquid brown eyes and a healthy sea island glow.

"I'm Alicia Jackson. I work for Mr. Sanford up around the bend there."

"John Sanford? Yes, he's a friend of mine. I'll mention you did me a great favor."

"I'd appreciate that, Mr. Mann."

"You know me?"

"Everybody knows you. Especially the women."

He smiled appreciatively.

"I just saw you and the girl."

This could be bad. "You saw who?"

"You and that little girl. Right over there in the grass. I came into the parking lot to look at your little car. It's so cute. I heard you two giggling and then I saw you."

He laughed. "If you know so much about me, you're not surprised by what you saw, are you?"

"No, I'm not."

"Do you intend to tell my mommy what you saw, Alicia?"

She stepped closer to him. "Will you offer me a cigarette?"

He opened the gold case and she took a cigarette. He struck a match and lit it for her. The girl was beautiful, no doubt about it.

"She's not all you can handle," Alicia said coolly,

24

exhaling smoke.

"I won't dispute that. But don't tell it around. She'd be embarrassed."

"She should be. You'd be more satisfied with somebody who knows how to do it."

"I'll bet you know of somebody. Alicia, I have an appointment. I won't forget you."

"That's okay. I know you're spent. I was in the top five in Miss Georgia last year. Mr. Sanford says he knows people in Hollywood. He's going to get me in movies. Do you know anybody out there?"

"Yes, I do," he lied. "Maybe I can make some contact for you." He didn't know anybody in Hollywood and doubted if John Sanford did either. But John was shrewd enough to stoke her dreams and keep her close. So many pretty girls wanted to be in movies.

"Oh, would you?" she said with excitement. "Maybe I can come to your house and see you."

"Do you know where I live?"

"Sure. Everybody does."

"I'll be in touch."

He gave Alicia a ride to John Sanford's house where she got out giggling. Her giggle stopped abruptly when a huge man with a nose that looked broken threw down his rag and stopped waxing a shiny sedan.

"Know that fellow?" Mann said uneasily.

"That's Sam Betts. He's sort of my boyfriend. Bye."

As he drove away, Mann looked in his rearview mirror and saw Alicia and Sam in a spirited discussion. He'd seen her again over the winter and had considered hiring her away from Sanford to help around his large house. But in the meantime there was Erica Blandford. But now Erica was dead and her father was telling the world he had killed her.

Mann put Alicia Jackson out of his mind and turned his attention to Speer's contract. What a shame the Brits had survived the bombing and had started pushing back. He had hoped the United States would help negotiate a peace, but the possibility had exploded with the attack on Pearl Harbor that had led Germany to declare war on just about everyone. If only reason could prevail, he could work out deals that would let both the British and the Germans send over more of their cars to enjoy on American roads. Maybe even that nosy detective Deveau could afford one.

He frowned at the thought of detective Deveau. Why had Harold Blandford sent him out here? There was nothing to find. It was past time to have a frank talk with the old man. Perhaps he'd see him when he went over to Jekyll for dinner this evening.

Marie kept in stride with Gravedigger as the tall man with brown hair led him back to the barn. Marie still knew little about this man other than that he was from England and she felt uncomfortable around him.

"You're enjoying life more than your countrymen, mademoiselle."

"Were they here, I'm sure they'd live as I do."

"Of course. Let them eat cake, as another French woman once said."

"Why aren't you in England defending your country?"

Max laughed without mirth. "Do you require any other aid with your mount, mademoiselle?"

His use of "mademoiselle" irritated her, as though he used it to emphasize she was out of place here. "Non, merci. I'll rub him down. He needs a woman's touch."

"Like others here."

Marie ignored his implication and set to making Gravedigger comfortable. After half an hour of currying the horse and talking to him like a child, she heard Jeremy Mann's steps shuffling in the sand. He came into the barn and patted the horse.

"Do you feel up to dinner on Jekyll tonight?"

"I find it boring. Must you go?"

"I must speak with some business associates. If you don't want to come, Charlie will serve you dinner here. Max and I will take the cruiser to the island. When I get back we can make up for lost time."

To his surprise, she didn't smile. "Jeremy, what did Monsieur Deveau want?"

"He was asking about Erica."

"I feel so sorry about her. What did he want to know?"

"He was merely completing the investigation. He probably won't be back again."

"He seemed to be an alert man."

"Yes."

Jeremy Mann sipped brandy below deck while Max navigated the cabin cruiser down the Altamaha River into St. Simons Sound. The route took them across the sound and into Jekyll Creek where U-boats hadn't yet ventured. There was little about Brunswick to interest U-boats, though that might change if the great shipbuilding complex became more than a gleam in Representative Carl Vinson's eye. Perhaps Herr Speer could visit him here some day, he mused.

"Approaching," Max called as he guided the craft to a safe docking at the Jekyll Club.

Jeremy put down his drink and stood to look at the island, the nation's most exclusive resort for the wealthy during the cold months. It was a haven for men he knew, a preserve for men so wealthy they'd profited from the depression. It had been established in the 1880's by financial barons who wanted to be with others of their kind where financial empires could be divvyed up over dinner. The search for the world's most favorable climate had ended here at Jekyll Island, and they'd combined to purchase it from the DuBignon family who'd owned it since the early 1800's. The club members built spacious "cottages" and turned the island into a recreation park for themselves and themselves only. Unless invited by a member, visitors were met at the beach and sent back to the mainland.

The Mann family belonged here and no one turned Jeremy back. He walked onto the dock and up Riverside Drive to the club where he was to meet George Hertle for dinner. He waved away the maître when he saw Harold Blandford sitting alone at a corner table. The older man scowled when Jeremy pulled up a chair.

"Did anybody invite you to sit down?"

"I'm meeting George Hertle for dinner."

"Do you see him sitting here?"

"A Mr. Clarke Deveau came to see me today, Harold."

Blandford grunted. "So he's earning his fee. Good."

"What're you trying to do, Harold? We're in the final negotiations with Speer and you send a detective out poking around? What're you thinking?"

"I'm thinking he might get the goods on you."

Mann spread his hands. "Harold, surely you don't think I was responsible for Erica's death. In any way. I had no reason in the world to harm her. I loved her."

"I don't intend to discuss it with you, Jeremy. Unless you have a confession to make."

Jeremy Mann sighed. "Then business. You're still with us?"

"Perhaps."

"Perhaps? Look Harold, when I go calling on Herr

Speer, I need to be certain. We're not dealing with a small company we can gobble up and throw away."

Blandford glared at him. "I have my doubts about dealing with those people. Don't you? No? Of course, I don't have a criminal mind that lets me see all the advantages."

George Hertle waved from the entrance and came to the table.

"Does Albertis share your views on Germany?" Blandford said, his eyes boring into Jeremy Mann's.

"I haven't discussed it with dad. But he trusts my judgment. He realizes the importance of chemicals to both sides. The Americans are still relying on old fashioned armor while the Germans are pressing ahead with new weapons."

"Yes, they're hammering Britain to pieces and France has already given up," George Hertle said. "Ford's gearing up to produce tanks and jeeps, and I won't produce another passenger plane until this war is settled."

Jeremy struggled to stay calm even though he wanted to shout at these two old men. "Face it. France is gone. Britain's on the ropes. The rest of Europe has given up. I think we can see to it that we're on good terms with whoever emerges the victor."

"Victor?" Blandford's voice rose. "You doubt we'll win? We'll support our own county. We're not on the ropes. We're just getting into this thing."

Jeremy maintained his unruffled demeanor while wanting to punch out Harold Blandford. "The Germans know that, too, Harold. For heaven's sakes. You sound as though I'm proposing to call Hitler and get on his payroll. He doesn't want our industry blown all to hell. It's no good to him or us if it's destroyed. We still have an opportunity to build bridges between us and Germany. Good communications might even bring the war to an earlier end."

Blandford glared at Hertle. "How do you feel about dealing with Hitler, George?"

Hertle cleared his throat. He'd used his Wall Street contacts to negotiate contracts between German and American businesses while he was in the American embassy in Berlin. "There's some truth to what Jeremy says. Though we do need to be cautious. Hitler's not just another businessman looking for a merger. He has a habit of shooting competitors."

Jeremy smiled. "Sort of the way we do it. Did it bother you when Don Franklin committed suicide last year after he lost the Defense bid to you, George?"

Hertle looked across the dining room, shifting his eyes away. "Franklin had other personal problems."

"I'd feel better hearing from Albertis," Blandford said. "Hitler's invasion of Russia could backfire on him. That's a huge country to try to occupy. As for the Brits, they're like those palmettos out there. They sway and bend in the worst of storms, but they don't break. Unlike the French. You're familiar with the French, aren't you Jeremy?"

Hertle looked at Jeremy in amusement. "Yes, you are, aren't you?"

Jeremy showed a touch of anger. "She has little liking for the Nazis. She fled to England with her father when the Germans occupied France. Her father returned to France to join the resistance. She wanted to go back herself but he wouldn't allow it. So she stayed in London and did her part driving an ambulance. She was with a French officer at a casino when I met her in London. She's here waiting out the bombing."

Blandford slammed his hand on the table. "Oh, is she now? How fortunate for her."

George Hertle quickly waved for the waiter. Jeremy smiled with relief when the menus arrived. "What would the island residents recommend?"

"The catch of the day never disappoints," Hertle said.

"Roast beef," Blandford said in his growl.

Jeremy studied the menu. This confab wasn't going as he'd hoped. He'd have to tell Herr Speer's representatives to come here to Georgia after all. He'd have to warn them against wearing their uniforms.

In the cruiser Max Lewis adjusted the ship-to-shore radio and transmitted in the code he'd learned in Hamburg long before the invasion of Poland. So far the Americans hadn't found a way to intercept signals, especially in isolated areas like this coast. Except for industrial and military ports, their ocean patrols were erratic and ineffective. German U-boats had started the *Paukenschlag*--Operation Drum Roll--in late December 1941 after Germany's declaration of war against the United States. The *Paukenschlag* was designed to use U-boats to bottle up American shipping. So far the pickings had been easy, cutting off supplies the British desperately needed.

Tonight he signaled to confirm that a U-boat was offshore should he need to leave in haste. Satisfied, he went ashore and strolled along the sandy road that ran in front of the Jekyll Club. The mild evening air was pleasant, relaxing. No doubt his countrymen would find this spot a pleasant place to relax after the war. It was so unlike the cold, wet climate on the continent. It showed no scars from the pounding of planes and armies. Such places would be at a premium after the victory.

CHAPTER FIVE

CLARKE DEVEAU STOOD on the back porch of his frame house looking across the yard toward the trees that lined the Altamaha River. He was thinking he should do something today to earn his fee from George Blandford, but his first day on the case had left him stumped. First the grieving father had accused a man of murdering his daughter. But he'd destroyed his case by refusing to allow an autopsy on her. And the corpse was now securely interred in New York state.

A talk with the alleged killer had revealed business ties between the accuser and the accused. Further, the accuser had declined to talk to him and simply said the evidence was there if only he had the gumption to dig for it.

Without evidence and without cooperation even from his client, Clarke decided the only way to move the case forward was to get to know the residents of Pineland better. Easier said than done. He hadn't exactly endeared himself yesterday, so getting back on the plantation would be approximately as difficult as getting back on Jekyll Island for a heart-to-heart with Harold Blandford.

"You ready for your breakfast, Mr. Clock?"

"Coming," he called to Annie, his housekeeper and cook. She and her husband Jasper were the only remnants of Pineland's once large work force. He could afford to pay them little, but couldn't bear to ask them to leave in such hard times. They were willing to work for almost nothing, asking for little more than the old house by the river and the privilege of raising vegetables they willingly shared with him. He wasn't sure how long Annie and Jasper had been with the Deveaus, but he remembered them fondly for petting him when he was small.

Annie already had a full breakfast on the table--biscuits, ham, eggs, grits and coffee. Annie was determined to put weight on him.

"You going to town for some work today, Mr. Clock?"

"I'm thinking of taking the day off and fishing."

"Fishing sounds good. We could use more."

"Didn't Jasper catch some yesterday?"

"That man don't know how to put a line out, Mr. Clock. I hope you have better luck."

"I sure need a line onto something. Anything."

First he'd see about getting that little office he'd been thinking about in town. Maybe more clients would come if he set up an office instead of waiting out here for somebody to find him. After that, he could think about some fishing. And this case between Harold Blandford and Jeremy Mann. These guys should be partners, not enemies. There had to be a reason Jeremy Mann was down here in isolation on this plantation instead of livelier spots up north. Even to escape the dangers of invasion, the sea islands were quiet.

Max Lewis felt as confused as Clarke Deveau this morning. Standing on the dock at the bottom of the lawn that sloped from the big house to the water, he thought over what he'd learned of the river from the topographical maps in the Abwehr's headquarters in Berlin. The river presented no problem for craft headed downstream toward the ocean. But the voyage upriver was a tortuous tease for a pilot unfamiliar with eddies and sandbars. His dispatches would have to be very specific if he had to summon craft upriver. Still, at high tide, a U-boat skimming the surface under cover of darkness could make it as far upriver as Pineland.

When Max returned to the house at the top of the hill, he heard the sound of hoof beats, then the roar of the MG. The wolf and lamb are returning, he thought. Thus far the sprightly French girl had posed no threat to him. In fact, she'd been a help by holding Mann's attentions so completely that he paid little attention to Max. Still, Max promised himself, the rules of war dictated that the lively mademoiselle would experience more than one man before he departed this coast.

That departure was in doubt. He didn't like such doubt. His only order in England was to shadow the master of Pineland for a purpose to be revealed later. Easy. The vain playboy was the easiest target in London. By arranging for another Abwehr agent to attack Jeremy as he left a London club, Max pretended to make a daring rescue and reap the American's gratitude. Max let the grateful Jeremy Mann know that, in fact, he could use some work and that he was particularly good with boats and horses.

It was no lie. He'd learned about horses and boats from his father who'd been attached to the German embassy in London prior to World War I. His father had married Adrian Lewis, the daughter of a British socialist. Herr von Oster had left his son with his mother when he was recalled to Germany. The boy was raised and educated in England as a British citizen, taking his mother's family name as Max

Lewis. In 1936 after his mother's death of a heart attack, he joined his father on his Baltic estate. The reunion didn't last long. His father was killed in a street riot in Berlin in 1937. No one ever stood trial for his death.

But Max's British education had already gotten the Abwehr's attention. He had studied at Cambridge and was so thoroughly British he could blend into the population without effort. The Abwehr put him through complete training at their espionage school in the Wahldorf suburb of Hamburg, including weapons and hand-to-hand combat usually reserved for commandos and saboteurs. With the blessings of the Abwehr's wily little chief, Admiral Wilhelm Franz Canaris, Max returned to England. His Anglicized speech and manners kept him safe during the bombing of Britain when so many other agents were flushed out.

With the growing likelihood of America's entry into the war, Canaris ordered his prize agent to attach himself to a prominent American businessman with connections to an industry likely to be vital in the war. They specified Jeremy Mann, the prodigal son of an American chemical magnate whose firm was deeply involved in weapons research. From there it was a short step to the fake attack outside the London club and the trip to America.

But thus far Max had been disappointed in his lack of opportunity to fulfill his mission. In the beginning, he had radioed ship movements in and out of New York harbor for the benefit of U-boats prowling the Atlantic. Even that small service had been frustrated by the move here to the sea islands where nothing of importance ever happened. He'd heard talk of a shipyard to be built here, but that would be months into the future. Max knew he was under criticism in Berlin for the lack of information he was sending back. The time was near when he would need to make his apologies and move on to a new assignment.

Across the field Max saw Marie on the big thoroughbred Gravedigger, leaping an occasional hedge as effortlessly as a deer. Without a glance toward her, Mann got out of the MG. "Max. Zeus will return to Olympus. I'm to dine with him this evening at the club. Have the boat ready at five."

"Zeus?"

"Dear old dad. Recall your Greek mythology. Why the hell couldn't he have been there yesterday when I went?"

Max brightened. Albertis Mann controlled the Mann complex. If the company was getting involved in the war, the old man would know about it. He'd give the orders to gear up for war production. Perhaps soon he would have something for the admiral after all.

CHAPTER SIX

MAX BARELY LOOKED when Jeremy Mann waved to a man fishing from a small dock on the bank of the Altamaha. "There's Deveau earning Harold's fee," he said laughing.

Max waited until he had navigated into the Altamaha Sound before casually asking, "Will your father stay long?"

"Probably not. Perhaps he just wants to let me know how much gas he's going to sell to both sides."

Maxed chuckled mirthlessly. Jeremy's joke could be too close to the truth. Though forbidden, the manufacture of gas for warfare was quite feasible for Mann Corporation.

Jeremy lapsed into silence for the rest of the journey. When the boat docked at Jekyll, he got off and hardly looked back as he walked to the club. His father had already arrived and was seated with two strangers. From their pedestrian dress and downcast expressions, Jeremy knew they weren't club members. This evening, with the addition of Harold Blandford and George Hertle, the party would break the club's tradition of seating no more than four to a table.

"Jeremy," Albertis Mann said with scant civility to his son. "Harold and George have already met my guests. I'd like you to meet Dr. Neil Harris and Dr. Gunther von Richter."

"Do we need two doctors for a meal?" Jeremy asked. "Normally one is enough to treat everyone who gets sick."

"I've bought these two gentlemen down for some relaxation," Albertis Mann said, disregarding his son's attempt at humor. "You'd know that if you'd bother to come to check in with your office every six months."

George Hertle wanted to soften the tension. "Albertis, you haven't told us what these gentlemen do for you. Aircraft design? If so, I'll top his offer, gentlemen."

"They have little to do with planes," Albertis Mann said brusquely.

"I think I can guess you're involved in research," Hertle pursued. "Most likely with some connection to the war. If you're looking for a peaceful contrast to war, Jekyll's the place. Only Jeremy ever provides a break in routine down here."

Jeremy pretended to join the appreciative snickers about his non-business activities. "If my father insists on withholding your identities, gentlemen, let's at least toast the secrets you're hiding from us."

Jeremy saw that neither of the guests found amusement in his comment. Very serious men. He could guess that Dr. von Richter had already seen the European conflict closer than he cared to remember. He tried the direct approach. "Dr. von Richter, are you visiting from Europe?"

Dr. von Richter coughed and glanced at Albertis Mann. Dr. Harris answered for him. "Dr. von Richter comes from Germany. I'm here from Chicago."

Jeremy smiled quizzically. "I haven't been to Chicago recently. Mann Corporation is headquartered in Jersey City. Did you leave Germany unhappy, Dr. von Richter? Many have."

"Yes, I felt it necessary to leave," Dr. von Richter said in a noticeable German accent.

"Both these gentlemen are now associated with Mann Corporation," Albertis Mann said. "Their work is stressful and I've brought them here for some relaxation in the Southern sun."

Jeremy wanted to know more about Dr. von Richter but his father's tone told him he wanted the conversation to flow into other lines. Everyone at the table complied, talking around the two somber scientists who rarely smiled or spoke.

After dessert, the two scientists excused themselves and, soon afterward, Hertle and Blandford left for the comforts of their own cottages. Jeremy pulled out his golden cigarette case that reminded him of Alicia Jackson. He put it away when his father shoved a cigar at him.

"Cigarettes will help win the war," Jeremy said. "I just saw an ad in which Miss American Aviation said Chesterfield pays $2 million in taxes every week. What that means, she said, is that Mr. Roosevelt can buy thirteen destroyers. Or 416 flying gun boats. Or 5,200 anti-aircraft height finders. It seems tobacco is America's secret weapon. Perhaps I should cultivate a few hundred acres out at Pineland."

"That would be better than the wild oats you're cultivating. You're squandering resources at a stunning rate. Your gambling debts are the talk of the eastern seaboard. You've dropped two, maybe three, fortunes on women of dubious virtue. You've..."

Jeremy broke in on the recitation of his virtues. "You're

leading up to my current guest, aren't you?"

"Guest. There's a new one. Good grief. What did you offer this one, paternal guidance?"

"Not quite. In fact, I don't plan to marry this one. Or maybe I will."

"So soon after promising Erica? No wonder Harold barely communicates with me. His bank is a vital part of our proposal to the government."

"Then you'll be relieved to know my consort's Gallic honor is intact. As you might guess, that irritates me. But I'll strive to be a gentleman, just the way I know you'd want me to be. I realize that's much easier for you than me."

Albertis Mann's nostrils widened but he kept his composure. "Your mother and I shared an honorable relationship until the day she died."

"Then I'll strive to emulate your example."

"Is this one another dancer?"

"No, she's a French patriot. A refugee from our German friends. Her mother is dead from the shock of it all, her father's back in France, likely dead. I felt a duty to offer her sanctuary. She grew up in the country, so she has taken to life here rather well. I'll take her back to the excitement of city life soon. She was actually enjoying it in London."

"Touching. If you're also planning to offer her a stake in the company, hear me out. I'm past weary of your profligacy. I had hoped you'd prepare yourself to succeed me, but instead all you've done is leave a trail of debts and ruffled sheets in two hemispheres. Sometimes I actually envy your ability to enjoy yourself and shut out the danger we're in. But if you insist of remaining a wastrel, you're going to end up in the crapper without a pot. As best I can tell, the one solid investment you haven't thrown away is that plantation, though you'll have it on the block before long, I daresay."

"Why would you think that?"

"Because I know you. I'm not going to keep extending credit so you can maintain your harem. Don't think no one's noticed why you prefer to live out there instead of here on the island."

"Very few prying eyes out there," Jeremy agreed. "It's far more agreeable than going on these boring hunts, playing bridge with boring people, going to the beach with them. To think these dullards run the country. They even put the Federal Reserve together here in their spare time. Unless I'm misreading the signs, another momentous deal is in the making. Involving your two scared scientists. What're they doing for you? Am I right that you brought them along to keep government agents from contacting them? Even the United States government is forbidden to set foot on this island."

Albertis Mann ignored his son's probe. "You're probably aware there's been some discussion about expelling you from the club."

"What a tragedy that would be. Am I having too much fun for their comfort?"

"You're violating every rule of decency these people hold dear."

"You mean none of them gamble? None are adulterers? None fornicate? What a marvelous gathering of saints. Get out tomorrow and look behind a few bushes while you're shooting ducks and rabbits. Take a trip through the cottages right now. You'd find enough adulterous mergers to close Wall Street for a week if everybody stopped to catch up on the gossip."

"Dammit, Jeremy. The people here at least know enough to be discreet. You act like a dandy at Louis XIV's court."

"I'd be happy to fix you up with one of the wenches in my harem."

"Jeremy, get a grip on your affairs, financial and otherwise. Selling that plantation would be a good first step."

" I am getting a grip. I hope you don't mind if I make some deals on my own."

"Deals?"

"The war. Aren't we supposed to make a profit on it?"

"As long as you do your duty to the country."

"Duty and profits go together, don't they? Has it ever occurred to you that we might be on the losing side? You know the tides of history, don't you?"

"You mean deal with Hitler? Jeremy..."

"No, no, no. Nothing of the kind. The man's unstable. Germany would be far better off to dump him for somebody else. I'm simply suggesting that all our friends who expect to enrich themselves from the war pause to consider the aftermath. Members of this club know as well as anybody that Hitler may one day have dinner at the White House. His U-boats own the Atlantic right now. They've run torpedoes onshore at Atlantic Beach in broad daylight. I wouldn't be surprised if a couple of U-boats weren't cruising around out there in Brunswick Sound right now taking in the sights. Where does that leave you and the Jekyll Club if American forces never get across the pond to stop Hitler? What's more, can he be stopped?"

"The Russian winter is doing a fair job of stopping him. As for us, Mann Corporation would be vital to any regime."

Jeremy laughed. "Yes, I daresay it would. Yet, unless Hitler knows you, would he be inclined to allow you to continue to run our...your...corporation? That's what concerns me. Nobody is making any attempt to maintain communications with the richest country in Europe. I'm told this club's members own one-sixth of the world's wealth. Yet all they can think of is to come to this very room to enjoy ten-course meals and cigars and brandy. The Jekyll Club alone holds enough influence to effect a ceasefire that would benefit us all, before we destroy each other. Instead, we're letting the British drag us into a war to cover their own blunders. Perhaps Roosevelt could accomplish more if he talked to Hitler instead of Churchill."

Albertis Mann glared angrily at his son, his nostrils widening. He stood abruptly. "I'll go see that my guests are comfortable. We'll be heading back home tomorrow by train. Whatever you're hinting, I strongly advise you to do it in your own country's service. Please."

Jeremy watched his father walk briskly across the dining room to find the scientists he was shuttling back and forth to keep them away from government attempts to recruit them. He sat at the table for another few minutes before going outside where he found Max strolling the road that ran between Jekyll Creek and the village. He threw the cigar into the water and boarded the cruiser for the return trip to Pineland.

Jeremy ignored Max's attempts at conversation and stared out into the darkness. He told Max only that his father had introduced him to two guests he'd brought down from the company's headquarters. A Dr. Neil Harris of Chicago and a Dr. Gunther von Richter from parts unknown in Germany.

In his cottage at Pineland, Max opened the case that contained his radio transmitter. Pity, he thought, that this transmitter had led to the pretty woman's death. He had enjoyed Erica's company, and it might've lasted for both his and Jeremy Mann's benefit had she not been so curious. She was not nearly so innocent as her father thought.

He asked in code for identification of Doctors Neil Harris and Gunther von Richter. Within minutes came acknowledgment from the Abwehr radio complex in Hamburg, with the promise to provide answers on his call tomorrow.

The following evening, after a day Marie had spent on Gravedigger and Jeremy Mann had spent brooding in his study, Max put his call through to Hamburg. He had the answer to his query. "Doktor Neil Harris unknown here. Doktor Gunther von Richter defector from Kaiser Wilhelm Institute. Stand by for further instructions."

Max re-locked the radio case, his heart racing. He knew little of scientific research. But he knew the Reich was developing a new weapon, as were the Americans, including Mann Corporation. He had been assigned to Jeremy Mann to learn all he could of the research on the weapon.

Max unlocked the small room he had converted into a photo laboratory. Working with excitement he hadn't felt for months, he produced a microdot with information he'd just learned about Doktors Harris and von Richter. He placed the dot carefully on a letter, put a fake message of condolence to his friend , and addressed the envelop to the mail drop in Washington, DC.

CHAPTER SEVEN

THOUGH HE WANTED to hang a murder charge on Jeremy Mann, Harold Blandford refused to discuss his suspicions. To Clarke, this was carrying the old boy network too far. The man owed him more than a curt command and fee to poke around in the affairs of a Jekyll Club member.

But this was his only case and he couldn't pretend he had other business to attend to. He had worked out a lease on a small office in town in hopes more clients would find his door, but apparently marital fires were burning bright in Brunswick and no one came to hire him to get the goods on a wayward spouse.

The inactivity convinced him he would miss nothing if he skipped going to the office and took one of his horses on a ride through the pines that led up the river toward Pineland. The Spring air was a candy store smelling of wisteria, laurels, pine, magnolia mixed with the ever-pungent marshland. He rode through the acres he'd sold Jeremy Mann to pay off his father's debts. This was land his ancestors had treated as tenderly as a lover even as they wrestled a hard life from it. He'd given it up as soon as it had come into his possession. But most of the old plantations had changed hands, their fate uncertain with war looming.

Clarke allowed the horse to find its own speed, preferring to enjoy the air and smells and his Leica camera. He was so absorbed with his Leica that he didn't see the French horsewoman until she was almost on him.

"Monsieur Deveau. You ride the horses, too."

"One of my better vices, mademoiselle." He nudged his horse a few feet away so he could frame the woman and her horse with his camera. The horse appeared to understand his role and reared while the woman waved to the camera.

"You should be in western movies," he said. "And wear a western hat."

"What is western hat, monsieur?"

"The large hats women wear in western movies."

"Chapeau? Oui. I would like one very much."

"Ask Mr. Mann to get one for you."

"Perhaps. I see him little. He travels so much for business."

"It must be very important business to take him away from such a charming guest."

"I wish he could stay more with me. But he saved me from the bombs. It is so good to be here."

"Did you know you're riding over land once scarred by war?"

"This land? How can this be? It is so beautiful here. So peaceful."

"Yes, it's far from the guns of England and France."

She turned the horse and started riding away. Clarke clucked to his mount and trotted with her. "I'm sorry. I didn't mean to remind you of bad memories."

He saw the sadness in her green eyes. "I am sorry I ran from my country. France needs all her children."

"You had reason to leave. Who could want to be in war?"

For a time they were silent, the padding of their horses' hooves in the sand the only sound in the open air. "I know I should be in France. To avenge my mother. To fight with mon pere. I wanted to return, but he refused to let me come with him. Instead, I found an easy way to escape. Here the war seems so far away."

She went silent again as they rode slowly up the trail. "It is terrible to lose a parent and your country. Nothing can ever be the same again, even if France can defeat Germany. I am ashamed I came here and didn't go back to fight the Germans. Can you understand?"

"I can. I told you this country was once ravaged by war. My great-great-grandparents lost everything in that war."

"This war, it was long ago?"

"In some minds. In other minds it was like yesterday."

"Who did it? Germans?"

"Yankees. Your Jeremy's family."

"Jeremy? He would not do such a thing."

Clarke laughed. "No, not your Jeremy. His ancestors. His offense was to make me an offer for the land my family had lived on for generations. I had no choice but to accept."

"So he is not your enemy?"

Clarke laughed again. "Not at all." Unless he's harboring secrets about what happened to the woman the mademoiselle replaced. "Like you, I tried to escape this country, too. Just as you've escaped yours."

"Did Jeremy do things to make you want to leave?"

"No. My father owned the large house where you now live. But he could not afford to keep it, and I had to sell it."

"Did you love this place as your father did?"

"Yes. Pineland was started by a Deveau who moved here from Charleston, South Carolina, where he had gone after a slave revolt in Haiti. The estate there was burned by the slaves. So he came here and restarted his plantation and named it Pineland. His French children married among the English and Scotch settlers already here. That's how I have a Franco-Scotch name. During the war in 1864, the Yankee General Sherman's men burned Pineland and anything else they happened across.

"My great-grandfather rebuilt Pineland and passed it down to his children. It belonged to my father when the hard times struck in 1929. My father refused to believe he couldn't make it as his father and grandfather had done. He was wrong."

"Did you help him?"

He knew he sounded harsh. "No. I'd already left. He supported me through law school. After he died I found that he couldn't afford it. When I got out of law school, I went to work with the Justice Department in Washington instead of coming back here. I got married. Biggest damned mistake I ever made. My lady and I vowed to love each other until death did us part. The Department got upset when they thought I threatened to hasten her death. She'd fallen in love with another man."

"You must've been hurt."

"Not as much as my father. My mother died of a tumor while I was in Washington and my father died of disappointment. He was already fighting money problems and he seemed to simply give up when I was kicked out of the Justice Department. Most people think he died of the strain. I know better."

"Pardon? What did you know?"

He ignored her question. "I took your Jeremy's offer

and moved down to the house where the caretaker used to live. That's how I got out of debt. I suppress my urges to go back and talk to Deveau ghosts in the house."

"When you came, did you see any ghosts?"

"No. Unless it was the ghost of my former wife."

"Do not pity yourself so much, monsieur."

"Pity is not what my ex-wife arouses."

She detected the harsh tone in his voice and seemed to have nothing more to say to him. She said "adieu" and spurred her horse into a gallop. He automatically raised his camera and snapped a photo of her as she rode away. He took a second shot just as the horse suddenly swerved to avoid a truck that had turned from a side road. The sudden evasion sent her hurtling to bounce off the truck's hood. She landed on her back and didn't move.

CHAPTER EIGHT

INSANITY, MAX THOUGHT. Pure insanity. They had actually sent an SD captain to meet him here. Even as isolated as this town was, he would stand out more easily than he would in the multitudes of New York or one of the other cities in the north. The man was a fool, calling from the town and ordering him to meet him near the docks where foreign sailors were common, where the Americans had to be smart enough to have agents. Well, Sturmhauptfuhrers must be humored.

This man's appearance here confirmed Max's suspicion that Doktor von Richter excited the highest levels of the Reich. It must've brought a twinkle to Heinrich Himmler's dead-fish eyes to learn that herr doktor had turned up on the sandy, mosquito-infested shores of Georgia in the United States. Surely he'd been sent by Himmler, or perhaps Obergruppenfuhrer Reinhard Heydrich himself.

But why send him here? Why send this Sturmhauptfuhrer Volker here to risk exposing Max's cover?

Max told Jeremy he was driving to town for some horse supplies. He parked the truck at the feed store and then walked to the docks. He found the cargo ship flying the Argentine flag and began looking for the man wearing a red bandana and blue cap. He walked slowly among the men, listening to the polyglot of accents, suppressing his urge to stop a German-speaking sailor and ask if, indeed, the war was going as badly in Russia as the American papers reported.

He distrusted the American press. Just days ago some fool in the local newspaper had reported Stalin's disavowal of any malice toward the German people. "We only want to destroy Hitler," the paper quoted the Russian leader who'd joined the attack on Poland in 1939 to start the war.

Max approached a man dressed as he'd been told. "You ordered the pants?"

The man hesitated, then said, "Yes."

Max grunted, relieved the man hadn't replied "Ja." He nodded backwards toward the main town. "Walk to the church. I'll come in a black truck."

The tall unshaven man frowned, hesitated, then set off for the town.

Max first went to the feed store where bags of grain and blocks of salt had already been loaded into the truck for him. The store owner knew Jeremy Mann could pay his bills and wanted to be sure he stayed pleased with his service. Max circled the block, overshadowed by the spreading live oaks he admired, wishing such trees would grow in the Black Forest. Just now he had no interest in springtime scents in this fragrant, exotic country, so different from chilly damp Europe and the ice of Russia. Burned, bombed-out Europe and the stench of dead bodies too numerous for individual graves.

Volker was standing next to bushes in front of the

church, as though trying to hide. Max stopped the truck, let him get in and headed up highway 17 toward Pineland to get out of town.

"A fine day for a drive in the country, Herr von Oster," Volker said in German.

Max replied in German. "Why have you come?"

"To cheer you up. To bring you greetings from the fatherland. You are much in the Obergrupenfuhrer's mind."

"What a comfort. You must bring information too sensitive for radio transmission."

Max resented Volker's condescending laugh. "You sent a very interesting transmission. Ah, this is pleasant country, Herr von Oster. Perhaps the Fuhrer would enjoy having a villa here after we conquer America. It would be a welcome addition to his home at the Berghof. What's that odd growth hanging from the trees?"

"The natives call it Spanish moss."

"Spanish? Odd. All this swampland. Of what use is it?"

"You'll recall St. Petersburg was built on a swamp. You must know it is now called Leningrad where many of our countrymen have died in the snow. Of course, there's no snow here. I've heard that bodies disappear easily in these swamps."

Volker glanced quickly at his grim chauffeur. Obviously the strain of being so far from the fatherland had affected von Oster. Of course, von Oster felt the hostility between his Abwehr and Volker's SD. It was common knowledge that Heydrich intended to absorb the Abwehr's military intelligence operation into the SD.

"What is the urgent matter that brings you here on your pleasant visit."

"Doktors Harris and von Richter. The Reich is interested in them. Especially Doktor von Richter. He left the fatherland without official leave while engaged in vital research. Herr Heydrich wants to know why he is here and to know your plans to return him to the fatherland."

"Plans? I have no plans for him at this time. Herr Mann is my assignment. I'm to stay with him and learn all I can of American industry's role in the war. It's strange, Herr Volker. I merely ask Berlin for identification of these two men and then I get instructions to meet you on a dock in open daylight. Is this standard SD procedure?"

Volker ignored the implied insult. "So you have no plans. Then I'll give you some plans. The Reich intends to reclaim Doktor von Richter's services. Your assignment is to find a way to do this. If that's beyond your capabilities, I'll devise a plan for you. If the American Doktor Harris can be included, so much the better."

Max snorted his disgust. "And has the Obergruppenfuhrer suggested how this might be accomplished?"

"He proposes that you abduct the two and convey them to the fatherland. It would seem simple for a U-boat to come here and take them away to a vessel or a plane."

Max fell silent, his mouth dry. Could this dummkopf be serious? "They are only guests here for a few days."

"Then you must move quickly, Herr von Oster. You are attached to Herr Mann whose father employs these men. Is that not so?"

"Yes." How much did this unshaven lout know about him?

"I think it is normal to believe Herr Mann would know his father's plans for the doktors. You must learn this."

"The father and son are not on good terms."

"A pity. Fathers and sons are often like that. Were you and your father close, Herr von Oster?"

Max glared at Volker who was enjoying his badgering.

Volker smiled grimly. "You are aware Herr Mann has approached the Reich through Herr Speer, are you not? You didn't know? Are you truly the efficient agent we've been led to believe? The SD may not be so impressed with your services when we take over the Abwehr. You do know that's the plan, don't you? The fatherland is depending on you to learn who on this island of wealthy men is sympathetic to the Reich. Be thinking on how they can be evacuated with minimum attention."

Max drove in stunned silence. A mass kidnapping of the millionaires who control much of the world's wealth? With a couple of scientists thrown in?

"Think what a blow this would be to American morale," Volker said, striking a match under his thumb nail and lighting a cigarette. "Could America survive the shock?"

"Is this the Obergruppenfuhrer's plan?"

"It will be. I plan to recommend it. I thought of it as I was flying here to rendezvous with the ship. I feel certain he'll approve."

"It wouldn't be the first time someone misjudged his temper. And paid dearly for it."

Yet, Max marveled at the audacity of the idea. All this time he had been among these men, knowing their collective importance to America, and he had overlooked this possibility. In time, he knew, he would've conceived such a plan for Harris and von Richter. But for dozens of very wealthy men as well? Perhaps it took a mad man, like this Herr Volker, to conceive such a bold plan.

"Tell me," Max said as nonchalantly as he could, "what does atomic research mean to the Reich?"

Volker did not answer. He had heard only rumors about atomic research. He knew that the Reich's leaders discussed it in secrecy. He guessed it related to development of a new secret weapon. Few would be privy to such information.

Did von Oster know about it?

Max turned off the main road onto an unpaved sandy road. Suddenly he and Volker instinctively ducked when a large bay horse darted across the road and swerved just in time to avoid crashing into the truck. They watched in astonishment as a human body slammed onto the truck's hood and bounced onto the sandy road.

Max sat dazed, the truck's motor dead from its sudden stop. When the horse trotted a short distance away and turned to look back, he realized it was Gravedigger and the motionless body was Marie Cardiene.

CHAPTER NINE

BEFORE MAX COULD JUMP from the truck, the detective who had been at Pineland a few days ago rode up, hastily dismounted and dropped to his knees on the sand by Marie.

"Lie still," Clarke said, He took off his light jacket and bundled it under her head. To his relief, her eyes fluttered open.

Marie was dimly aware of the faces staring down at her. They must be confused, she thought. They look so fuzzy. One of the voices told her to stay still. She knew that voice, recalled it from moments ago, forced her eyes to open and focus. Yes, there he is. The detective. A rude man. He'd been nice to her but then said something rude about his wife. She forced herself up on her elbows.

"Gravedigger. Where's Gravedigger?"

"He's fine," Max said in his British accent. "How do you feel, mademoiselle?"

"You'd best take her into town to a doctor," Clarke said, looking into her glassy green eyes. "She may be hurt."

Marie grunted. Why was he staring at her like that? Was her hair such a mess? Was it sand on her face and clothes?

"No doctor," she said. "Max, help me up."

Clarke persisted. "Please go see a doctor. Injuries can be deceiving."

Max helped her to her feet. She brushed dirt from her hair and clothes. "No doctor."

"Mr. Deveau may be right," Max said. "I can take you in the truck."

"No. Come to me, Gravedigger. Let's go home."

She moved shakily toward the horse and Max steadied her with an arm around her waist. He turned to a man sitting in the truck that Clarke now noticed for the first time. "Lead the horse back to the house. I'll carry her in the truck."

For a moment the man in the truck stared dumbly at Max. He slowly got out of the truck and started toward the horse, only to see it trot a few steps away.

"I'll lead him back," Clarke said, going to Gravedigger and taking the reins. This man obviously was unfamiliar with horses. "I'll follow along."

Max nodded and the other man got into the truck bed and sat on a bag of grain. Max settled a groggy Marie into the seat beside him and cranked the truck. Suddenly Clarke threw up his hands and came quickly to the front of the truck to pick up something.

"Go on now," he called to Max, stepping back with the camera he had dropped when he had knelt by Marie. How ironic, he thought. His Leica camera, a product of Germany, had made images of a woman who hated all things German. He mounted his horse and took Gravedigger's reins.

Clarke arrived well after the truck reached Pineland and turned Gravedigger over to a black boy at the stable. Max met him at the edge of the lawn. "She's fine, Mr. Deveau."

"I still recommend a doctor examine her."

Max smiled. "I agree. But who can change a woman's mind?"

Clarke nodded, irritated by Max's dismissive manner and Marie's refusal even to allow him to see her. He remounted his horse and trotted away, noting that Max's friend was standing by the truck.

Max unloaded the truck and told the stable boys he had to make a return trip for more grain. He spoke tartly to Volker as he drove. "I'll demand an explanation for your presence here, Herr Volker. The incident today shows how easily you can be detected. Had you opened your Deutsch mouth there at the accident, you would've given yourself away. If the Obergruppenfuhrer distrusts me, I'll request a reassignment."

"This is an urgent mission. If the American industrialists can influence the American government to do business with the fatherland, all the better. If they cannot, certainly Doktors Harris and von Richter will be of great use. Don't waste your time complaining to Admiral Canaris. My orders come from Obergruppenfuhrer Heydrich. You know he has the full support of Reichsfuhrer Himmler. No, Herr von Oster, learn the habits of these rich men. Learn the contours of the coast, the depth of the channels. Soon you'll arrange a visit to Herr Mann from the fatherland."

"Visitors? From the fatherland? Are you mad?"

"Do you consider the Obergruppenfuhrer mad, Herr von Oster? You will be in my report to him. We're all vitally interested in winning the war. Aren't we?"

Max seethed in silence and let Volker out at a rooming house where he was staying near the docks. When he got back to Pineland, he went to his cottage and unpacked his photographic equipment. He imparted the essence of Volker's plans onto a microdot which he placed in an envelope addressed to a postal box in Arlington, Virginia.

CHAPTER TEN

ON JEREMY MANN'S ORDERS, Max took a protesting Marie to the Mann residence on Jekyll Island the evening prior to the arrival of Herr Albert Speer's emissaries at Pineland. Karl Meinkein and Oberstleutnant Heinz Bache took an Italian LATI flight to Bogata, then a U-boat to Jacksonville, Florida, where Volker collected them for the final leg of their journey up the coast to Pineland. That first night while Marie fretted on Jekyll, they joined Jeremy Mann for dinner and rest, then spent next morning hunting quail with him. After lunch, the two rested and waited for the important guests Jeremy had invited from Jekyll and St. Simons.

As late afternoon and his guests approached, Max watched with amusement as Volker and the two German visitors stared out at the Altamaha River, clearly enchanted with this unfamiliar environment. He smiled grimly to hear the two men commenting on the lush warmth of coastal Georgia, how it was so different from cool Europe and the brutal cold of Russia. Like Volker, they too mused upon the possibility that the Fuhrer and others might find this a pleasant retreat, especially if the spacious accommodations of Jekyll were of the scale they'd been told. Jeremy Mann assured them the Fuhrer would find the mild climate of Jekyll more delightful than the Berghof.

Oberstleutnant Bache was dressed in a gray green SD uniform, under the belief it would impress American industrialists as it had those in occupied Europe. The industrialist Meinkein reflected the influence of his British and American peers in blue pin stripes that would be at home in boardrooms on both continents.

With his background in the Ruhr steel industry, Meinkein presented the Reich's case to the guests who assembled in Pineland's spacious parlor with liquid refreshments and snacks that Jeremy Mann and his black houseman Charlie passed around. In English with only a slight German accent, Meinkein assured his audience that he felt certain the Fuhrer would very much enjoy a visit to such a pleasant clime. "In fact, I intend to recommend that he purchase a cottage here. If anyone wishes to sell, please speak to me before I leave."

His listeners chuckled and nibbled on hors d'ouvres of shrimp, oysters and ham with amber drinks.

Meinkein introduced Bache, noting his uniform. "Unfortunately, our countries are officially at war, a tragedy when we consider our shared interests. Our countries complement one another. There should be a free exchange of commerce between us. Such an exchange would benefit everyone. And we would be at peace with one another, instead of at war."

"I remind you," said Robert Marshall of National Steel, "that Germany declared war on us first."

"You are correct, of course," Meinkein answered calmly, ignoring the flash of irritation in Bache's expression. "I regret it happened, as do many in our country. I hope that soon the Fuhrer will be in touch with your President Roosevelt to discuss our mutual interests. As is so often in such grave matters, governments turn around the ship of state only with great difficulty. I believe there is every reason to hope that you could influence your friends in your government to accelerate the process toward peace. From my own connections to German industry, I know that we may well have the same kind of influence upon our government."

"What influence have you exerted?" Marshall persisted. "German industry is profiting handsomely from the war. Tell us how Krupp and Farben are working toward peace."

"Let us discuss them as we discuss your Fords and Rockefellers," Meinkein said with a smile. "In war, there must always be suppliers. Most of you in this room know that, and have already profited from it. You will continue to profit if the war continues. It is always so with great banks and industries. Of course, others--your countrymen and mine--will not be so lucky. Many will face the fire of battle, many will die. Homes and businesses will be destroyed. And for what? I humbly suggest your government is being led into this conflict by the British who are..."

"The British are fighting to survive," snapped Charles DeWitt of Southern Petroleum. "You can't justify the bombs Germany's dropping on the British."

"I should point out," Meinkein continued calmly, "that Britain and their prime minister Churchill have vowed to destroy Germany. Can we permit that? Yet, recall that, but a few months ago, Britain and Germany traded freely, to the benefit of peoples in both nations. Now, Britain has isolated itself, depriving each of our countries the benefits of free commerce. Even so, many Britons are sympathetic to Germany. They desire a cessation of hostilities which benefit no one except those in power. Besides, Britain's record of dealing with its empire is hardly exemplary. "

Marshall broke in. "The Brits are putting up a spunky fight against heavy odds."

"Britain's position is worse than you've heard," Bache said in an accent that clashed with Meinkein's English. "That's why Britain is so desperate to involve your country. You may have heard that your own former ambassador, Herr Joseph Kennedy, gives Britain little chance of holding out without involving America in the war."

"That's true enough," came a voice from the back. "The word I get is Kennedy thinks Britain would be better off with a change in government."

"Of course he does," Marshall said. "Just as long as Der Fuhrer lets him keep him keep shipping his liquor into the country. Say, I've heard Hitler doesn't drink. Doesn't even smoke. Can you trust a man like that?"

"Gentlemen," Jeremy Mann broke in. "Let's remember something else. The Russians. Right now Germany is going it alone against them. But you know Russia wants to export its revolution to every corner of the globe. Germany only wants to assure its own security."

"You're correct, Mr. Mann," Meinkein said quickly, grateful for Jeremy's intervention. "Should Russia prevail, America would face a grave threat from the Bolsheviks. In fact, they already have considerable influence with your government through their agents."

"I have a bit of a problem with that," said oilman DeWitt. "The war started when Germany and Russia signed their own pact and then divided Poland between themselves."

"And now we're at war with each other," Meinkein said, his eyes telling Bache to keep his heavily accented comments out of the discussion. "We knew, as you must know, that friendship with Bolsheviks is impossible. Our intelligence told us they were planning to attack Germany, and we chose to go on the offensive first. But we're a much smaller country. Now we also face the threat of war from your country which would be catastrophic for both our countries. If we weaken each other, what can either of us do to restrain the Bolsheviks?"

"I see little difference between Nazis and Communists," said Henry Hamilton whose cargo fleet had already suffered U-boat attacks. "I see damn little difference between national socialists and international socialists."

"True, Germany practices socialism," Meinkein said. "Yet, our socialism has produced a far better life for our people than the Russian kind where there is constant hunger and poverty, even great famines that have killed millions. Russia is a country that must take from others to survive."

"And Russia offers no markets to us," Jeremy Mann said. "If any of you doubt it, I challenge to put together a deal with the Russians that they will honor."

Silence greeted Jeremy Mann's challenge. Meinkein thought this a good place to add, "I know most of you have already dealt with Germany before war separated us. You know our record for honoring our contracts. You know the quality of our goods, just as we appreciate good American workmanship. You know you could count on our commitment to a contract."

"Just what sort of contract are we talking about?" Marshall said, waving his glass to Charlie for a refill.

"You know our needs," Meinkein said. "We'd even be willing to broker contracts through third parties to avoid any misunderstanding with your government. Who knows? Perhaps good men can then prevail upon our governments to find peace. In the meantime, Germany still must deal with the Bolshevik threat. Just as you must. Herr Stalin is as great a threat to you as to us."

Marshall had his fresh drink from Charlie. "I find it hard to believe you're trying to do us a favor."

A slight weariness crept into Meinkein's answer. "We treated each other as friends before this conflict began. We should understand that we can be partners again. That will be impossible should Russia succeed in its mission to destroy Germany."

Not even Marshall protested and Jeremy Mann nudged the group to move about and engage in more informal discussions with his guests from the fatherland. He felt pleased that so little open hostility had greeted Meinkein, though he frowned to hear Bache denounce "British lies" that Russian citizens were happy under Stalin. "Why does not your press report that Stalin has eliminated entire classes of people? Where are the farmers of the Ukraine today? Millions of them?"

The informal talks got past that minor bump and eventually the guests from Jekyll and St. Simons began drifting back to their cars and boats.

"An interesting exchange," Meinkein told Jeremy Mann. "Hardly the outpouring of support you promised."

"They're naturally reluctant to make commitments at this point. I believe you made a very favorable impression on them."

"I sincerely hope so, Herr Mann."

The two Germans were eager to be on their way back to the fatherland and declined Jeremy's offer for overnight lodging. They got into a sedan and began the drive to the craft that would convey them to a rendezvous with a waiting flight back home. Watching them depart in the dusk, Jeremy said to Max, "I think we can do business with those gentlemen."

Max smiled and started to dismiss himself. He had a report to commit to microdot. "Max, take the boat to Jekyll and get Marie. I feel a strong need for her tonight."

Max cursed to himself at this delay, but left Jeremy and walked down the sloping lawn to the dock. The microdot could wait for a couple of hours.

Clarke Deveau put away his binoculars when Volker drove away. From this distance he had been unable to learn much about the guests. From growing up on Pineland he know of this oak and its spreading branches that allowed him to view the house without being seen. The congregation of rich men made little sense. They had stayed only a short time. He guessed they'd come for a meeting, not just an afternoon drink. But that didn't fit with their habit of doing as little as possible, and doing all of it on the island. Normally they did little more than golf and hunt. And fornicate.

What made even less sense was a man in what, at this distance in twilight, looked to be a uniform. A German uniform at that.

Clarke slipped down from his perch and went to his car hidden among bushes off the road. One way or another, he thought Harold Blandford owed him an explanation of why he'd come to see a man he'd accused of murdering his own daughter. And was that a German officer present at the meeting?

Chapter Eleven

THE NUMBER OF GUESTS at Jeremy Mann's conference with Bache and Meinkein meant there was little secret about them on the islands. Marie learned of it before she left Jekyll and greeted Jeremy with an angry torrent of mixed French and English when he met her at the Pineland dock. He understood little French but he had only to hear her screams, see her flashing green eyes, to feel the heat of her outburst.

"You're angry," he could only say.

She stopped her tirade long enough to wonder at his interruption before spitting another furious stream of French at him. He endured her anger in hope of calming her down at dinner and making up in the master bedroom. Her plan for dinner was to stalk up the hill to the house.

"Where are you going?"

"For a ride," she said in her first English sentence since disembarking.

"Let's have a glass of wine together."

She ignored him and disappeared into the house. His

house, he thought bitterly. Shortly he saw her leave the house by a side entrance and walk resolutely to the stables. Gravedigger was in a pasture, so she took a big black stallion, saddled him and urged him into a gallop across the field of straw to a tree-covered road that ran downriver. Mann saw the amusement in Max's eyes as he tied up the craft that had brought her back here to what he had thought would cap his triumphant day.

Clarke arrived back at his house and waved to Jasper at the barn. Jasper, his white hair rimming his head from under his cap, waved back and continued feeding the cows and two horses, all that was left of the stable of a dozen prized horses that were the last of Pineland's glory days as a working plantation. Even before he reached the front door, Clarke smelled the mullet, greens, potatoes and corn bread Annie had fixed for supper.

This old frame house needed a coat of paint that neither he nor Jasper had ever found time to apply. But the house was always here when he came home, and he could always count on Jasper and Annie to take care of the garden, milking, even slaughtering a beef or hog. In fact, he was relieved they could stay with him. Mann had no need of them and, with their children spread from Atlanta to Detroit, they were content with the son of the man they'd worked with all their lives.

"Smells good, Annie. Did you catch the fish yourself?"

"Got it down at Sims Market in town, Mr. Clock." She smiled, showing worn-down teeth in her sweaty face. "You give me the money, remember? Got two pounds of fish for twenty-five cents. Taters cost a quarter for ten pounds."

"Did you pick up eggs, too?"

"Yes. They come for a quarter a dozen. I'm sorry my hens too lazy to lay enough for both of us. Maybe they'll do better when the real spring comes."

"I know Jasper needs lots of eggs."

"I seen they was selling two loaves of bread at Big Star for fifteen cent, so I got some extra in case I don't bake enough."

"Good. Maybe I'll make a sandwich for tomorrow instead of going to the Oglethorpe to eat."

"You just let me know and I'll fix them for you. No sense spending so much for dinner. Supper's ready when you want it."

"Thanks, Annie. Just leave it on the stove to keep warm. You and Jasper go on home when you're ready."

"Soon's I fix it for you," she said.

As he started down the hall leading to his office at the back of the house, his eye caught movement through the front door. It was the French woman. Why was she riding across his yard up to the house? She reached the steps and sat there on the horse, looking as though she expected him to serve her wine.

"Mademoiselle. What a pleasant surprise to see you again."

"It is you, monsieur."

"Oui, mademoiselle. Won't you come in?"

She hesitated, as though recalling her previous unpleasant encounter with him which had resulted in her collision with a truck. She slowly dismounted and came up the creaky plank steps in boots and riding pants. She began smoothing her long auburn hair, though it was hardly disheveled. She tugged the reins of the black horse which was showing interest in the horses snorting in the barn. Clarke took the reins and tied them to the porch post.

"I don't believe you've invited me to your home, Monsieur Deveau."

"We didn't part on good terms, mademoiselle."

"Then perhaps we can make a new start. I do not know yet the ways of American women. They have fewer problems than women in occupied countries. That is fortunate."

"It is indeed. Have you read *Gone with the Wind*? Un roman. It shows how women struggled when we had war here."

"Yes, now I remember. Mademoiselle Scarlett. She was French, I think, in her power with men."

"The book is set here in Georgia."

"Here?"

He decided it would be useless to try to explain states and capitals to her. "The people in Scarlett's time experienced what France is going through now. Do you read our local newspaper?"

"No. I had rather ride. It is so pleasant to ride here."

"The Brunswick *News* had a photograph of...let me see...yes, here it is. A photo of Margaret Mitchell disarming a bomb."

"A bomb? Is she in England or France?"

"In Atlanta. She's in a class of air wardens, just in case the Germans or Japs get as far as Atlanta. Mademoiselle Mitchell wrote *Gone with the Wind* ."

"Mon dieu! She lives out her book. Oh, I do hope Monsieur Rhett is there with her."

"I'm sure she'd like that, too."

"I am going to read it again. I had no idea I am so close to the place that awful war happened. Oh, just to dream of Monsieur Rhett."

"He's a hard act to follow," Clarke said, opening the screen door for her.

Her eyes swept the hall and the sparse furniture in the parlor. She walked to look more closely at the portraits on the wall. "Your famille, monsieur?"

"No home is complete without its gallery of saints and rogues. That's Jacque , the first Deveau. He called his estate in Haiti Chateau Deveau. He escaped to Charleston during the slave uprising in Haiti. One of his brothers was killed before he could escape. Jacque set about re-building the chateau here on the Altamaha and named it Pineland. It was too much to accomplish in his lifetime, so my great-great-grandfather there completed it. He saw it burned again by General William Tecumseh Sherman. My grandfather, Charles Deveau, was fighting in Virginia at the time and couldn't help. He likely would've just gotten himself killed if he'd been here when Sherman showed up. That's his sword and scabbard there under the crossed flags of his unit and the Confederacy.

"Grandfather's first wife died of starvation during the war, so he married Mary Hunter and set about re-building Pineland after the Yankees left. They produced my father in 1870. Both my father and grandfather concentrated on lumber and naval stores. It went well enough until 1929 when the depression wiped out my father. It was as though Pineland had been burned again.

"And that's my mother there. Pamela Clarke. She died of a brain tumor in 1933."

She listened silently, glancing at him at the slight catch in his voice when he spoke of his mother.

"And Pineland is lost again?"

"Yes. Dad's debts were greater than I'd ever imagined. I had no idea how much the depression cost him. I had to sell the plantation and the house to Jeremy Mann"

"And now I live in your family's house."

"Yes. Families like his profited from the Depression. Unlike my family. I came home without enough money to support an old mansion. This little house is all I need."

Her eyes swept the dim parlor again. "Pardon me,

monsieur, your house could use the cheerful care of a woman."

Before Clarke could explain how cheerful his last woman had been, Annie said from the kitchen doorway, "That's so, honey. I've told him a thousand times. Needs him a woman here. Mr. Clock, your supper's on the stove. Be back tomorrow."

"Thank you, Annie. Mademoiselle, would you care to join me in my evening meal?"

"I'm expected back," she said, her wiggling nose indicating some concern about the smells coming from the kitchen. She hadn't yet acclimated herself to the local cuisine which she found too heavy in oils and smells.

"At least have a drink with me. I have bourbon."

"Borbon? What is borbon?"

He went to a cabinet and took out a bottle of the amber elixir. "It's almost like a liqueur. Looks like Jasper left some for me. He prefers to make his own."

"Does Monsieur Jasper have a winery?"

He thought of Jasper's moonshine and laughed. "You might say that."

She took the glass he offered with an inch of the brown liquid, sipped, and grimaced. "Magnifique!"

He took it from her hand and added water. Tomorrow he'd find local purveyors of spirits and stock up on a wider variety. He might even find some French wine, though its supply had dwindled to nothing under the country's occupation.

"I really must learn the local customs, especially the cuisine, " she said.

"I missed it so much when I was in Washington. I should learn to cook it myself."

"Perhaps if you had a wife."

"I've tried that already. Once was enough."

She heard the bitterness in his tone. "I'm sorry if I offend you. It is sad when two people fall out of love."

"It happens when only one loves. We were too naive to realize how different we were. Well, I was. She was an exciting woman, in her way. Not my way. She was the kind of woman your Jeremy might appreciate. She liked fast company."

"I wonder what company he keeps," she said, recalling why she'd stormed out of Pineland an hour ago and ridden down this strange road to this strange man's house. "Do Americans still do business with the Germans?"

Clarke tensed, guessing her meaning. She knew about the German officer he'd seen through binoculars while trying to carry out his investigation of Mann, only to find his employer with him. Do business with them? Was that what the meeting had been about?

"Some do. War is a profitable blessing to some men."

"Does your government frown on it?"

He took a breath. "Yes, if I still worked with the Justice Department, I would likely be prosecuting such people."

"Prosecuting?"

"I'd be trying to put them in prison."

"Prison?" Her eyes widened. "Will someone put Jeremy in prison?"

"Is he making deals with Germany?"

"I do not know, monsieur. If he is, please do not tell anyone."

"Don't tell anyone what? Is your... is Jeremy making deals with Germany?"

Her face went sullen. "I told you I do not know. I know only I do not like the people who came to see him today."

"Those who met with him today?"

She nodded and started for the door. He didn't want her to go. He needed an excuse to delay her.

"Did I show you the photos I took as you bounced off the truck?"

"No." Suddenly her mood changed to glee.

Clarke led her to his photography room. "I started doing photo lab work when I was in Washington working with the Justice Department. Now, look at this."

"Oh, no!" She laughed, looking at the photos of her posturing for the camera, and the last of her just before Gravedigger swerved to avoid the truck.

"I'm sorry I didn't get you in flight. That would've been a lucky shot."

She laughed again. "What would mon pere think if he could see me now."

She stopped and bit her lip. She stifled a sob that Clarke knew was for her father, now supposedly somewhere with partisans in France. Still alive, she prayed.

"You were fortunate that you weren't injured," he said, showing her the photo.

"Yes." She smiled slyly. "What did you say to make me so angry I ran from you?"

"You don't remember? Then I won't remind you."

She laughed again and looked back at the photos. "I like these."

"I'll enlarge some copies for you."

"Merci, monsieur."

A whinny reminded her that her horse was tethered to the porch post. "I must return home. And leave you to your meal."

He watched her ride out of the yard, aware that she had aroused him more than anyone since he left Washington. She'd also aroused intense interest about Jeremy Mann's visitors. So he was right. Those visitors had been Germans. They'd been at Pineland, on his family's ancestral grounds. Germans visiting a man who'd been accused of murder.

He went into the kitchen and put his supper on the table. He wondered if a Justice Department ex-lawyer was up to some nighttime breaking and entering. Yes he was.

CHAPTER TWELVE

JEREMY MANN WAS STANDING under an oak on his front lawn when Marie came riding up his driveway on the big black horse. He put down his glass of Scotch and walked to the barn where she was unloosening the girth.

"It's late. I was about to send Max to find you."

"I know the way through your forests," she said coldly.

The frost in her tone surprised him. Normally she returned from a ride in good spirits, as though the jostling of the horse between her legs had aroused urges he could exploit in an intimate way.

"Let one of the boys rub him down," he said.

Marie ignored him and continued to curry the horse while it happily munched oats. She looked over the horse's back at him. "How can you deal with people who have destroyed my country and intend to destroy yours."

Her outburst caught him off guard. So she was upset about the Germans. "Peace is impossible unless we talk. If we find mutual interests, peace is more likely."

"Peace? Like the peace in la France now?" He

suspected her voice suppressed a shriek. "In my country peace means you're dead. Monsieur, I wish to return to my home."

He spoke slowly, gathering his wits. "Home? France? You can't be serious."

"I want to go home and help my country fight."

"Marie, what's come over you? You're happy here, and safe."

"I miss my home. My famille."

"You can't go home. It isn't possible. I'd miss you terribly. I brought you here because I love you. And because this is where you can make friends who can help France."

She continued to curry the horse. "I believed I loved you, too. Now I question why."

"Marie, you know why. I can show you why. Leave the horse and come to the house with me."

"I plan to leave, monsieur. You may find some other woman. I know you can."

He pretended amazement. "What's this, Gallic morality? Your France developed the bordello to an art form, and here you are spouting off like a Southern preacher. Did you acquire your sense of morality consorting with officers in London?"

"I've known men well, as you yourself know. But I cannot desire a man who gives himself to me and talks business with men who destroy my country."

"If you could love me as you love horses, I could accept your complaints. Now I understand why French men are so keen for mistresses. Don't make me feel that way. Come to the house with me. Unless you prefer love here in the hay."

"I am not finished," she said, continuing to lavish her affection on the horse.

He stepped around the horse and took her arm in a strong grip. "James," he called to a black boy, "see to the horse. Tuck him in for the night."

She dropped the brush, bewildered by his grip and coldness. Instead of leading her to the house for his idea of love, he pulled her outside to the corral where her favorite Sandpiper was prancing and pawing the ground. "Good, they're still here. Pay attention, Marie. I want you to see natural passion in action. Perhaps it will inspire you. Max!"

Max came around the barn.

"Max, has Sandpiper been through his session yet?"

"No."

"Excellent. Bring Gunboat out. Marie is curious about the process that produces these wonderful beasts that she loves to have between her legs all day."

Max nodded, barely suppressing a sneer. With military briskness he marched into the barn to a stall where a big bay stallion neighed and pawed on his gate. Max led Gunboat into the corral where Sandpiper pranced restlessly. Jeremy leaned on the white board fence, his arm wrapped tightly around Marie's waist.

"See how anxious they are, darling? The old boy wants to get it on. But the lady, well, she's not quite in the mood. Maybe she has a headache. She's had other studs, but she's not quite sure about him."

Her attempt to break his grip only brought more pressure from his strong arm around her waist.

"There," Jeremy said soothingly, "she's showing more interest in him. Seems to understand what he's here for. See? Now he's stalking her. That's the male's role, you see. She's pretending to reject him, but he knows she's just playing hard to get, leading him on. Now, there, up he goes! No, she's moving away again. Watch Marie, you really must watch. See, there they go again. They're beginning to understand each other now. She's just teasing him a bit. Whet his appetite. There, they're closing again. Doesn't seem to bother her that Sandpiper's been with other fillies. It's part of the game. There, up he goes! See?"

She turned her head, but Jeremy's other hand cupped her chin and forced her eyes back to the two horses.

"See how effortless it is, Marie? How much they enjoy each other? Gunboat had her doubts, but now she's just plain enjoying herself. Beautiful."

She closed her eyes though she'd been around stables all her life and had seen this act many, many times. But until now it had been like a ceremony, a beautiful ceremony of love. This was ugly. Just as ugly as those men Jeremy had entertained here.

Jeremy's hand shook her chin. She opened her eyes, too exhausted to resist. She felt his body shake with chuckles in appreciation of Gunboat and Sandpiper in their final shudders of passion.

"Ah, now they're happy and satisfied with each other, despite their doubts. Perhaps we just saw the procreation of another champion, from a purely natural act. I'll bet both of them will remember this day with pleasure. Even if they have other mates. Dear, you simply must see Countess do this tomorrow. Good old Sandpiper gets the honors. He has all the luck. You'll be up in time, won't you?"

When at last he turned her loose, she sprinted away from the corral. She paused briefly, out of breath and nauseous, to look back at the barn where the men were leading the horses to their stables. She stumbled down the walkway to the dock where the boats were tied. At the end of the pier she stood panting, bathed in sweat, looking out at the Altamaha, muddy and red from the wash-off of snow and rain. She held her hands against her stomach to control her nausea. She stared at the boats bobbing in the water, wondering if she could drift downstream and trust whoever she met.

But the islands were at the mouth of the river. On Jekyll or St. Simons they would treat her like a runaway child and send her back to Pineland in a chauffeured limousine.

No, the river ran nowhere she could find refuge. She allowed herself an inner scream before turning and reluctantly climbing the hill to the house. Jeremy was waiting for her at the top, his hands in his pockets, his expression wooden.

"Wine?" he asked nonchalantly.

"No, merci, monsieur. I wish for you to transport me back to England. I want to return to la France to fight against those men you do business with."

His expression tightened. "Don't be so dramatic. No matter what you think of me, I do care for you. You're far better off here than dodging bombs and bullets in London or back in France."

She brushed past him, stifling a scream but not tears. Before she was out of earshot he called, "Don't forget. Countess gets her turn bright and early tomorrow."

Her warm bath soothed the knots in her body. But she could do nothing about the knots in her mind and heart. When she dried and went to her bedroom, she locked the door and uncorked a bottle of Burgundy. French wine. She sipped it, incredibly sad to know the land that had produced this wine was under the heel of men who were honored guests in this house. Did la France even exist anymore? Poor France. It had a government at Vichy openly collaborating with its conquerors. Conquerors who had killed her mother and likely her father who had returned to wage hit-and-run warfare.

She found the book Monsieur Deveau had told her about. The book about Mademoiselle Scarlett and

Monsieur Rhett.   The book Monsieur Deveau had recommended. He seemed strangely resistant to her.

CHAPTER THIRTEEN

WHILE JEREMY MANN TRIED to keep Marie from leaving, Max stealthily went to the study and took photos of the contracts Meinkein and Bache had left with the master of Pineland. He went to his cabin to commit them to a microdot, then returned to the house where Mann had gone to the study. Max found him sullen.

"I came to learn your plans for tomorrow," Max said.

"Tomorrow and tomorrow and tomorrow. Recall those lines, Max? Oh, hell, of course you do. You're a Brit. You're weaned on Shakespeare. Tomorrow. Tomorrow I want you to go to St. Simon's and find a Miss Alicia Jackson and bring her here. She works for John Sanford. Our diplomat bootlegger who smoothes our way with the Reich."

"You want me to bring her here?"

"Here. Miss Jackson possesses charms that will undoubtedly offend the mademoiselle. Let's see how she reacts to the challenge."

"What reaction do you expect?"

Mann laughed bitterly and sipped his whiskey. "I'm fed up with Marie's dismissal of me because I'm willing to do business with the Krauts. You'd think I ordered her father's death. I saved her from the bombs in London and now she thinks she was born to ride around the plantation like a Southern aristocrat. Perhaps the earthy Miss Jackson will jolt her back to earth."

"A shrewd plan," Max agreed.

"I must move fast, Max. Before I and these island demigods move back home to New York in a couple of weeks, I must know if Marie is a keeper, or whether I'll leave her to the mercies of these crackers down here. If she would play her role, she would greatly enliven life in the city. But if I left her here, her knowledge of my deals with the Reich could be dangerous. She seems to have taken a liking to Deveau, and I have my own reasons to stay clear of him. If she got close to him, there are lots of beans she could spill. Ah, she's a vexation. Do I really need to rid myself of her?"

"Perhaps not," Max said, containing his anxiety at the mention of leaving here before his mission was complete. He said as casually as he could, "We'll be moving back to New York soon?"

"You didn't know? Of course, this is your first season here with me. The first weekend in April. That's the custom. Our compatriots here can weather the fires of burning each other over millions of dollars in business, but they can't handled the heat and mosquitoes of the coast in the summer. Just another couple weeks and we can go back to the excitement of the city, and the wonderful women who make it so special."

"No sir, I didn't know the seasonal custom." Two weeks. And still nothing from Berlin about the scientists.

"When we leave, Southern ghosts can have back these

islands and plantations until the fall when it all starts again. Frankly, I don't know why we come. Somebody started it years ago and now the Social Register ends up down here every winter. Guess it beats the snow and ice up north. Max, I want Joan of Arc burned at the stake before we leave."

"I'll keep the matches ready."

"Yes, do that. It has to be soon. My contracts have been finalized and I expect my down payment soon. Incidentally, Dad will be coming back down here for a couple of days. I'm going to enjoy showing him how to do business."

Max's heart thumped with excitement. "Your father?"

"He's bringing along the two scientists again. Harris and von Richter, I think they're called. He's trying to keep the Washington crowd away from them. They want these fellows to work on weapons for them. Dad wants them to do research for him so he can sell it to the government. If they're on Jekyll, even Roosevelt wouldn't disturb them."

"He's wise to keep the politicians away from them," Max said. His heart pumped furiously. Doktors Harris and von Richter would be here!

"Our Kraut friends tell me they might be interested in talking with these two guys. Maybe I can broker a deal for their work. Of course, there's no way Dad would allow them to work for the Germans, any more than he'd let those dunderheads in DC. He would lose too much control over their work."

"I should think not."

So Mann's German contacts were interested in dealing for Harris and von Richter. He had told Meinkein and Bache about them, and the two Germans had expressed their interest. How did they know the value of the scientists? From Volker. Volker knew about them, knew their worth to the Reich. Who had told him? Of course.

Volker's superior, Obergruppenfuhrer Reinhard Heydrich, sitting in Berlin, controlling the world like a puppet master. Jeremy Mann didn't know, if indeed he cared, that his business partner was the SD. Heydrich and Himmler's SD, the counterintelligence unit that had spawned the Gestapo. Volker's involvement meant the SD planed to abduct Harris and von Richter, and anyone else of value.

With shaking fury, Max knew Volker and his masters in Berlin didn't intend to include him in their plans. The bastards meant to leave him here to face the hangman's noose alone when the U-boats pulled away from Jekyll with their cargo. He took several deep breaths to calm himself and make a suggestion. "Perhaps you should invite your father and his friends here for dinner. They would enjoy the picturesque setting away from the stifling club."

"Splendid idea, old chap," Jeremy said in the mock Oxford accent he loved to affect. "Leave it to you chaps to think this coast is just a big pub. I like it, Max. Let the old buzzard see me as master of my plantation making contracts with the strongest nation in Europe."

"Depend on me to make all the necessary arrangements."

Max could barely keep himself to ordinary steps when he left Mann's office as though he had no more to do than stroll by the river. He wanted to sprint to his cottage in the evening breeze that reminded him of early summer days in Berlin and London. Albertis Mann was coming here--here! Coming with the two doktors in tow. He moved briskly, humming as he unpacked his camera and transmitter.

Max smiled grimly later that evening when Volker called and brusquely told him they must meet at a spot on the highway north of town. Splendid. The meeting would be easy to arrange during his drive to pick up Mann's new love.

"Tomorrow. Gute nacht, Herr Volker."

Max whipped Mann's MG off the road where he found Karl Volker waiting. The SD man scowled when Max got out of the MG and leaned against it, showing no intention of getting into Volker's car and submitting to his territorial claim.

"The U-boats are approaching the coast," Volker said. "You must prepare the doktors for departure."

Max showed no mood for pleasantries. "Why aren't the U-boats waiting for my signal?"

"Herr von Oster, people more important that either of us want this operation to move forward with all haste. What do you know of these men?"

Max met the SD man's hard stare, considering the pleasure he'd feel to flatten his hawkish nose. "The elder Mann will be on the island tomorrow. He will bring Doktors Harris and von Richter with him."

"Tomorrow! Why wasn't I informed?"

"I learned of this only yesterday. I transmitted the information to Berlin." Max chuckled at Volker's anger to know Max had left him out of the loop. "I thought it best to let my superiors know immediately."

"I am here, Herr von Oster. Don't let your family's prestige blind you to your position. I am not your inferior. You serve the Abwehr. You know, of course, that you and your Admiral Canaris will soon be under the command of Obbergruppenfuhrer Heydrich. When we take the scientists, I will assume command. At that time I will wear my uniform so that both you and your American servant will understand who has responsibility."

"I advise you to keep your beautiful uniform out of sight. Unless you'd care to have it filled with holes spurting your blood. I don't care what happens to you, but I won't allow you to jeopardize this mission. Even Herr Heydrich would agree with me. Stay out of sight until you get my signal. I will know more about the scientists today. I'm planning the abduction to move through the sound to the U-boats offshore."

"Why couldn't the U-boat itself come into the harbor under cover of darkness?"

"Bring a U-boat into the sound? Madness."

"The channel is deep enough."

"Yes. But the chance of getting in and out without being seen is nonexistent."

"The river is deep at the estate where you stay."

Damn! The bastard wants a stage for his grand finale. He would get a promotion out of it. Bringing a U-boat up the Altamaha to Pineland? It could work when Albertis Mann came there for Jeremy's reception. But to have Volker already thinking about it? Damn!

"The water up the river is deep but dangerous. Very dangerous."

"We live in constant danger, Herr von Oster. The charts show the U-boats could come up the river to the estate. What you call a plantation."

"The charts?"

Volker smiled smugly. "The Reich has complete charts of every milliliter of this planet. Even of this forsaken spot."

"You have seen these charts?" Max struggled to control his discomfort with Volker's ever-ready information. No doubt his information came from the SD in Berlin.

"I have seen the charts. The depth is adequate." Volker smiled grimly, like a wolf. "Cheer up, Herr von Oster. When we complete this mission, the Fuhrer himself will reward us for bringing him two valuable researchers and several worthless American businessmen."

A reward from the Fuhrer. These scientists must be

exceedingly important to the Reich. He pondered their worth and his reward as he continued on to St. Simons to collect Miss Jackson.

Jeremy and Marie sat tensely at a table on the veranda overlooking the river, a light lunch of soup and vegetables between them. He pretended to scan some work papers while she gazed silently at the muddy river. At the sound of a vehicle approaching, Jeremy put down his papers. "There's Max returning from town."

He left Marie at the table and walked to the front of the house. Marie heard the sound of feminine giggles and saw Jeremy leading the pretty blond girl to the veranda.

"Marie, please meet Alicia Jackson."

"Enchante." Marie noted that Alicia had already dressed in riding pants displaying the kind of proportions Jeremy liked.

"Alicia came over from the island to spend the afternoon with us," Jeremy said with obvious pleasure. "I thought she'd enjoy a ride. Have you had lunch, Alicia?"

"I'm not hungry, but I'd love some champagne," Alicia said giggling and sitting down in the chair Jeremy pulled out for her opposite Marie.

"Charlie," Jeremy called.

Charlie materialized within seconds carrying the champagne bucket. Marie realized Jeremy had had it on ice awaiting his guest.

"Don't you love living out here in this old mansion?" Alicia said to Marie after sipping from her champagne. "Here with Jeremy you must feel like the mistress of an old plantation. Like Scarlett O'Hara."

Marie stiffened at the name of the heroine Clarke Deveau had talked about, that she'd read about.

"Marie doesn't enjoy everything about life here," Jeremy

said.

Max came up the lawn leading two horses. Marie suppressed a squeal when she saw that one of them was her favorite.

"Ah, here we are," Jeremy said, looking at Marie. "Shall we go, Alicia? Are you steady enough to ride after a sip of champagne? No, don't finish the glass. There will be plenty after we return from touring the plantation."

"That's Gravedigger," Marie said numbly.

"What's that, dear?" Jeremy said to Marie. "Gravedigger? Oh, yes. Of course. He's easily the best of my stable. Alicia will enjoy riding him. Remarkable how Southern girls ride so naturally."

Marie stifled her protest. Gravedigger belonged to Jeremy, not her. His perky friend could ride her if the master pleased. When she and Jeremy mounted, Marie said in a subdued tone, "Please be careful, mademoiselle. He's very spirited. One woman fell from his back and was killed."

Jeremy suppressed his rage at the mention of Erica's death. "Don't worry about Alicia. She grew up riding horses. Fact is, I'm thinking of taking her out to Hollywood and putting her in Western movies. Just look at the way she sits on a horse. She'd be a great cowgirl, don't you think? Have a nice afternoon, Marie. We'll be back in time for dinner."

Marie brushed past Charlie on her way to her room, ignoring his question as to whether she'd like some more lunch or maybe some champagne. If there had been another horse in the stable as spirited as Gravedigger, she'd have saddled him and challenged Jeremy's movie queen to prove how well she could ride.

In her room she wondered how she had ever thought Jeremy Mann was the courtly lover she'd taken him to be as they'd ignored the Luftwaffe roaring over London. But she frowned to recall she had met him in a club where soldiers and citizens went to find some relief from daily confrontations with death, not during her duties driving an ambulance rescuing the victims of the bombing attacks. While she was driving, he was out of the line of fire until the clubs awoke to merry making that relieved tension before a new round of raids.

She found the huge novel about Mademoiselle Scarlett and started it again. She read all afternoon until she realized the sun had set and it was time for dinner. Charlie persuaded her to come out to dinner where she endured the laughter of Jeremy and Alicia until they retired to another part of the house. The little shouts of glee told her they'd camped in his bedroom.

She heard their squeals until midnight before they faded away. Marie slept fitfully, listening to creatures that came out when humans were trying to sleep. She got up early and went to the stables and saddled Gravedigger. The silly young woman sleeping in Jeremy's bed would not ride him again today. When she returned in early afternoon, Charlie told her that Max and Jeremy had left with Alicia to meet with Albertis Mann on Jekyll.

"Why did she go with them?"

"Mr. Mann, he likes to keep her close."

Relieved they were gone, she asked Charlie if any white French wine was left. He smiled and produced a fresh bottle within the minute along with rolls, cheese, boiled eggs and meats. She sipped and ate on the veranda looking toward the muddy river, wondering if there was another casino where she could go meet another man as she had during an air raid in London. But not another man like Jeremy.

Another kind of man. Perhaps one like the quiet detective in the little house downriver.

CHAPTER FOURTEEN

MAX DELIVERED JEREMY MANN to the Jekyll Club dock where a man in a blue blazer, white pants, and white hair met the boat. Max knew it was Jeremy's father, Albertis Mann, impersonating an admiral.

Max left them and took Alicia to St. Simons to enjoy a seafood meal, ignoring the pretty blonde's incessant chatter about her plans to go to Hollywood and get in the movies. Not that he would've kicked her out of his bunk, but just now he had U-boats and a Sturmhauptfuhrer on his mind.

"Your deals are the talk of the club," Albertis Mann said as they walked from the dock to the Jekyll restaurant.

"You sources sound reliable."

"Nothing's a secret here."

"The truth is, I've been rather fortunate in some deals I've put together the past few days."

"Perhaps too fortunate. I know you haven't been dealing with the salt of the earth."

"On the contrary. Several members of this club have

collaborated with me."

"All the more pity," Albertis Mann said. He said nothing else until they were seated in the restaurant.

"Did you bring your friends with you?" Jeremy said.

"Friends? You mean Harris and von Richter? Yes, they came with me. They're dining over there at the far table. I hope the sunshine and sea air will help them relax. Their work is taking a great toll on them."

"Just what sort of work do they do?"

"I can't discuss it."

"Because their research is war related?"

Albertis Mann silently sipped his wine.

"Chemical warfare?"

"Drop it Jeremy. Don't ask. And don't pester them either. Those fellows have enough on their shoulders. Look at them. They can't even enjoy a good meal without looking around like someone's stalking them."

Jeremy watched the two cautious men with the disquieting feeling that he knew less about them than the Germans who had requested he arrange an appointment with them. He raised his glass to his father. "Here's to full mobilization and its profits."

"We're sure as hell mobilizing. Heaven knows if it'll be in time. Our best hope is that Hitler exhausts himself fighting on two fronts. The news is that the Russian winter's doing its job on Germany, just as it did to Napoleon."

"If Germany's defeated, can we do business with Russia?"

"Sure. The Russians are on our side, remember?"

"I keep trying to remember. Just a few months ago Stalin and Hitler agreed to carve up Europe between themselves."

"True. So?"

"So I detect some hostility because I'm dealing with German customers. Why no reservations about dealing with the Russians?"

"Because Russia's our ally now. Besides, they've learned a lesson about dealing with Hitler."

"Yes, take while the taking's good, then get the U.S. of A. to come in and save their Red asses."

"Russia's fighting Germany, just like us."

"And if our side wins, what will we sell to the Russians?"

Albertis Mann smiled broadly. "We can sell them anything. Our government and banks will loan them the funds to buy our products."

"We have customers who can pay now, without loans from your neighbors here on this island."

"I know what you're saying. Be careful. War changes rules. If you look like you're collaborating with the Germans, you could end up in serious trouble. So could I and the corporation. You saw what happened up there in that Senate hearing last week. They outright accused Standard of helping Germany develop synthetic rubber without making it available to the United States. That Senator Truman character accused Standard of treason right there in the hearing."

"I know enough to be discreet. I don't care if we deal with Germany or Russia. Makes no difference to me. All they have to do is honor their contracts a damn sight better than they honor treaties with each other. They may be enemies now, but they teamed up to start this war. No reason we all can't make a profit from it."

Jeremy started to remind his father again of Mann Corporation's business dealings with Germany in the past, but the old man suddenly asked, "Is the French woman still, ah, working for you?"

"Marie? She loves America. Really enjoys riding around

the plantation pretending she's Scarlett O'Hara."

"A French Scarlett? The Scarlett in the book could be a real pain. I know she's a valuable employee, but do you intend to marry her?"

"I hope to. She'd fill the void I feel from losing Erica. Her crazy father still thinks I had something to do with killing her."

"Sad. I have problems communicating with him, despite our ties. He makes me uneasy."

"You need to relax. So do your scientist friends. Say, perhaps you could bring them out to Pineland. You could all relax. I could show them some real Southern hospitality."

"Not a bad idea. I'd almost be willing to leave them with you, hide them out there. I've had some direct hints that the government might actually draft these fellows. There's talk of consolidating weapons research into one big project, supposedly under some general named Groves. It may just be a rumor, but I can't discount it. It would be just like the government to grab these guys, after all I've invested in them and all they could do for the corporation."

"Come over on Saturday."

Max deduced his boss had had a pleasant evening with his father. Very out of the ordinary when the two met. Jeremy was suspiciously jovial. When he came onboard he took the giggling blond below deck for champagne, stopping just short of doing what they'd do later anyway. Max smiled, looking forward to the haughty mademoiselle's reaction to her rival's return.

Finally Jeremy disengaged himself from Alicia and came on deck while she continued to giggle with her champagne.

"She's lively, just as you said," Max said.

"She should be a great education for Marie. I'll keep

her a couple nights to teach the mademoiselle some humility."

"She won't like this."

"That's entirely the point. I don't even care if she likes me for a few days. I want her to make up her mind to prove she's more woman than my friend below. If Alicia does her job, I may just help her get that trip to Hollywood she wants."

Max let Jeremy congratulate himself on his shrewdness before asking nonchalantly about his father's health.

"Disgustingly fit. He brought the two gloomy professors with him. I wish I could get him to tell me what they're working on. He acts as though the war depends on them. I persuaded him to bring them to Pineland on Saturday. Maybe that'll help them loosen up. After a few drinks they might even talk to me about their research."

When the boat docked at Pineland, Marie had long since retired to her room. Jeremy took Alicia to his bedroom for the pleasure he knew she could render so well. No need to let Marie ruin his night.

Max put Jeremy and his games out of his mind. His radio beamed his message to Germany, advising the Abwehr command to order the U-boats to set their course for Jekyll Island, Georgia. He then committed maps of the harbor and river to microdot and affixed it to a letter that he would take to the post office tomorrow. He seethed to think Berlin had told Volker of his plans for the abduction, but it couldn't be helped just yet.

But next morning Mann found a need for repairs on his boat and Max dutifully worked while he fretted to get away to the post office. He missed Marie's return from her ride in early afternoon. She rubbed down Gravedigger and was on her way to her room when Jeremy called her from the veranda where he and Alicia were enjoying drinks. She hesitated, then went to the table, declining his invitation to sit down.

"Alicia has decided to stay with us for a few days," he said.

"That is good, monsieur. I am sure she will be big help."

He smiled and brushed his lips along Alicia's creamy cheek. "You don't understand. Alicia's my guest, not my staff."

"Then I hope she enjoys her stay, monsieur."

Inside her room, Marie sat dazed on the edge of her bed, taking off her boots. She had intended to take a bath and then go walking by the river. Now she wanted only the bath. Just as well, because Jeremy and the comely Alicia had gone down to the river to watch it flow toward the sound and into the Atlantic. Never once did he show dislike of her touch. Marie knew the woman had an attraction that appealed to men. She'd seen women like her in France and England. She sensed, too, that Jeremy knew she was watching from the window.

Rather than be a spectator, Marie skipped dinner and asked Charlie to serve it in her room. But still she heard the sounds of laughter and music on the phonograph, followed later by shrieks from his bedroom.

When she was certain he and Alicia were asleep, she put on her robe and went into the hallway leading to the kitchen. As if he'd been expecting her, Jeremy stepped into the hall with nothing on. He laughed when she turned and scampered back to her room. She locked the door, calmed herself and dressed in her boots and riding pants. From the closet she took one dress and left the house.

Neither of the cars had keys, but the truck sitting outside Max's little cottage had keys. She got in, cranked the truck and drove off into the darkness. At last she came o the road that led to the small house where a light still burned.

Clarke was in his photography lab when he heard her knock.

CHAPTER FIFTEEN

CLARKE REGISTERED bewilderment at seeing a woman at his door dressed for a midnight ride. She glanced back at the truck. "I couldn't ride Gravedigger in the dark."

He could think only to say, "Of course not. Would you like a drink?"

She accepted with a nod of her head. When he pulled out a bottle of French wine he'd found on the chance she would again be in his house some day, she said, "Brandy."

Yes, he told her, he had brandy and would sometimes drink it if he had no bourbon. She drank quickly and he offered a refill, surprised by her obvious need for it. She accepted, violently brushing away the wisp of auburn hair that slipped over her forehead. He poured again and she raised the glass to lips that had no trace of lipstick. Yes, he thought. That's why I thought she was so different. No makeup. He'd heard French women loved their cosmetics, but she doesn't use any.

"Merci," she said and this time drained only half her

glass before slowing to sip it.

He smiled, still shocked to see her here.

"I am sorry to come at such a time," she said, tossing her hair back from her eyes again. "I am disturbing you?"

"No. I was just making enlargements of the photos I took of you the day you were thrown. You asked for copies. Would you like to see them?"

Her green eyes sparkled. "Oui, monsieur."

She followed him into the room he had converted into a lab where prints were hanging on a wire.

"Don't touch them just yet," he said. "They're drying. But you can look at them. See that one there? You're about to fly off the horse. You remind me of a cowgirl in Western movies."

"Would that be good?" she said.

"Could be." He pointed to another print. "That's you just before you swerved away from the truck. You can even see the expressions of surprise on Max and the other fellow. And this is the best one, showing your trusty steed rearing while you sit in the saddle with a smirk."

"I like that one best."

"I agree it's the best one. They'll all be dry tonight and you can take the copies you want. I can make more."

He led her back to his parlor and put more wood on his fireplace. "Even here it's a bit chilly when the sun goes down."

He stoked the fire and turned back to find her looking at the portraits on his walls, as though dreaming. He took in the vision of the green-eyed lady with healthy cheeks, the long auburn hair, the out-of-place riding clothes that accented her trim form. She was so unlike the few women he had invited here after selling off Pineland, women with names and faces he'd already forgotten. And when the desire for those women had passed, he had settled into a life of celibacy in which he sometimes bitterly recalled the woman he had left in Washington, DC. The woman whose treason to him had ended his career at Justice.

"There now," he said. "Cozy as a chateau. I'll pour you another drink if you'll promise to drink it more slowly."

She smiled agreeably and they settled onto opposite ends of his sofa. She sipped and looked around. "Your maid has not redecorated ."

"My maid? No, she hasn't. The interior decorator is all booked up just now. Perhaps she'll find time when the rich people leave the island and move back north."

Marie looked puzzled. "Move? Who will move?"

He sighed, knowing she had missed his jest. "Most of the residents of Jekyll and St. Simons. They come here during the winter months to escape the cold. And to conspire. When hot weather returns, they move back north."

"All of them?"

"Most of them. They'll come back in the fall to hunt. But times are different. Those who would normally go to Europe during the summer won't be going because of the war."

"They'll miss la France this year."

"A few hundred thousand Americans may be going soon. Maybe I'll have to go."

"You? I so hope you don't go to war. If you would see France, I would want you to see her peaceful when her grapes are ripe. Do you know a way I can return to England?"

"It's unlikely. Most transport now is for war material which is the target of German U-boats. You left just in time. I don't think it would be safe for you and Mr. Mann to attempt to return."

"Not both of us. Only me. I can't believe him now as I

did in London. He seemed so gallant, but now he makes business with Germans. They've done so much to France. I want to go back and help."

"Why do you stay with him?"

"Where does a foreigner go in this country? I know no one else."

Clarke sensed a deeper grief than her plaintive words could convey. He instinctively leaned toward her, touching the hand that pressed the cup of brandy to her unpainted lips.

"You could make your way in this country. With your charms. You can't go back to France now. Soon perhaps, if the war turns in our favor. But not now."

"Do you know where I could go? America is strange to me."

She had asked a good question for which he had no answer. "I can make some inquiries. You were at the Sorbonne? You could teach French here."

She giggled.

"You might teach riding. Horses are very special in this part of the country."

This time she didn't giggle and he knew she was having difficulty finding the right words in English to answer. He couldn't help her find words because he could not guess what she was thinking. What was this talk of leaving Jeremy Mann and returning to bombed-out London?

"I have heard how some women can excite men. The kind who want to play in the cinema. Why would such a woman attract Jeremy?"

Her change of pace surprised him. "Does someone like this attract him?"

"Oui. He sleeps with her now."

He stiffened with surprise, then relaxed and studied her. Her eyes dropped to her glass, then looked up again to meet his perplexed gaze. "Last night he slept with this woman. She has life and passion. Joie de vivre. I wish I could be beautiful like her."

He exhaled slowly, beginning to understand her confusion and why she had arrived at his door without the first idea of when she would go back to Pineland. She thought Jeremy Mann's tart was more beautiful than her?

"Is this his first time with her?"

"He had another many days ago. The poor woman fell from Gravedigger."

"Erica Blandford," he said softly at the reminder of his job to prove she was murdered. "And you think he uses these women to anger you?"

"I don't know." She shook her head slowly. "I don't know. I feel I am not adequate for him. I feel his resentment and hold back."

Clarke seethed with anger. He understood. Jeremy Mann wanted to shame Marie into submission. He'd had any other woman he'd ever wanted but couldn't get full commitment from this one. Rich and handsome with everything he wanted except her unconditional surrender. Incredible. Absolutely incredible.

"Some men have a stronger drive than others," he said. "Mr. Mann has a reputation as a womanizer."

"Womanizer? What is womanizer?"

"He likes to be with more than one woman."

She stared into the fire. He knew she saw vineyards and fields in France, remembering a time and place lost to her forever.

Could she be a Gallic version of his ex-wife Liz--who felt life was her own champagne bottle, eager to bend men to her will?

He tapped his glass. "Another?"

She shook her head and stood. "It is time for me to go.

I will sleep outside in the auto."

"You aren't returning to Pineland?"

"I will not sleep in the same house with Jeremy and his woman."

"Not the truck. I have a guest bedroom. We can make plans tomorrow."

"I do not want to be problem, Clock."

"Clock? You sound like Annie with a French accent."

"Annie?"

"My maid. She cooks with the grease that turns your French stomach."

He led her to what served as a guest room and coughed when the door stirred up dust. He'd never had a guest here. The women who had come after he moved back had slept in his bed in his room. They never stayed long because Liz had ruined his desire for relationships.

"I hope you'll be comfortable. You'll' find some shirts and pants and a robe to sleep in."

"Merci. Perhaps tomorrow I can think what to do."

He closed the door and went to his room, aware of desire he hadn't felt since his courtship with Liz. But the very thought of Liz cooled the fire that briefly flared up. Those feelings had led him into disgrace and disappointment no sane man asks for twice.

Still, the gnawing, aching, craving stayed with him like hunger. The feeling made him angry. He had vowed that if ever again he trusted a woman he would voluntarily surrender himself to mental health authorities. In the quiet old house he heard the occasional squeak of springs as she turned uncomfortably in a bed never meant to be used again. At last he could hear nothing more than a baying dog down the river. She had fallen asleep.

Clarke was mistaken. Marie crept down the hall, shivering in his old robe, reluctant to go nearer his door without an invitation from him. He would think she was crazy. He didn't want her tonight any more than Jeremy wanted her.

For several minutes she stood in the hallway outside his room, her arms folded over her breasts. Hearing no movement from his room, she sighed and started back to her squeaky bed.

Clarke heard the sharp squeak of the old floor. He stood quickly and jerked open the door. She stared at him in surprise, as though ready to bound away like a frightened fawn. Then he wrapped her in his arms. He led her to his room, to his bed, where they found the warmth both wanted, both needed. They loved with passion, reviving desires and appetites both thought they'd forsaken. They fell asleep with pleasant dreams, unaware of the rage that had exploded in Max Lewis when he found his truck and precious letters gone.

CHAPTER SIXTEEN

STURMHAUPTFUHRER KARL VOLKER put on his dress gray-green uniform and posed before the dusty mirror in his moldy, uncomfortable room near the docks. He visualized the moment he would leave this rat hole and march into the gold-plated Jekyll Club at the head of half a dozen men with weapons and announce: "In the name of the Fuhrer, you are all under arrest."

Then he would take the scientists and as many rich Americans as he pleased, board the U-boats and depart for the fatherland.

The immaculate uniform contrasted sharply with the dilapidated room. With irritation, he undressed and carefully folded the uniform into his suitcase, locked it and pushed it under his bed. For now he would have to content himself with the dress of an ordinary seaman temporarily ashore.

Herr von Oster was wearing on his patience. Why no communication from him? Even here in this little town he could tell there was unusual activity on the islands. That man would answer severely when they were back in Berlin. Even Admiral Canaris would be unable to intervene for his favorite puppy. Obergruppenfuhrer Heydrich had entrusted von Oster to Volker's surveillance, and Volker was determined to prove his trust had been well placed.

At Pineland Max frantically looked around in the dark, his fury and fear rising. What had happened to the truck? He'd left it only a few minutes to go inside his house. Now it was gone and with it the mail pouch containing the letter to the Arlington mail drop with details of Jeremy Mann's planned reception at Pineland.

What had happened? Could one of the Negro boys at the stables have taken it? He had watched them walk around the vehicles, grinning, their eyes glowing. Every one of them yearned to drive those gleaming chariots, and he knew they'd borrow them when the urge got too strong to resist. Max vowed that if one of them had taken the truck and his precious letter, his ass would be bluer than black. And if the letter itself was gone, well...

The letter actually was of less concern. The message was in code on a microdot, and the Americans still hadn't caught on to the little dots with messages that German agents affixed to letters. But coming just a couple days before the abduction, it was a bad omen. A very bad omen. In commando training he had been taught discipline. Now, despite his training, he slept fitfully, waiting for the sound of the truck in the dark.

He arose at 6 to be ready for the Negro hands who would be arriving soon for work. He personally wanted to greet the bastard who'd taken the truck.

No one had arrived, so he went to the house where Charlie was sleepily preparing breakfast that he might or might not serve to the master and his guest, depending on whether they came out of the bedroom this morning.

"Is Mr. Mann up?" Max asked brusquely.

"No, Mr. Max. Don't know when he'll be up. He might be some tired this morning."

Max grunted and walked toward the wing of the house where Mann slept with his future movie queen. Charlie padded softly behind him and whispered, "You best not disturb Mr. Mann."

"I won't disturb him. I just want to see what condition he's in. I need to talk to him later."

"If he comes through this night in good condition, he's in mighty good shape."

Max allowed himself a smirk. "Go on back, Charlie. I won't disturb him."

Charlie shook his head doubtfully, but turned and went back to the kitchen, muttering something in a local Negro dialect Max couldn't understand. Max slowly turned the handle on the bedroom door and pushed it open. There they were. Jeremy Mann and the blond slept entwined in their stupor. His head lay on a pillow, his mouth open, snoring. The woman was partially on him, her creamy breast across his chest. Her disheveled hair spread over her pillow. They were hardly under cover, as though they would be ready for action when they awakened.

Max stayed only briefly, his nostrils rebelling at the fetid, feral smell of the room. An impulse took him down the hall to the room of the French woman who had refused to sleep with Mann. He was surprised the door opened, then astonished to see that her bed hadn't been slept in. He couldn't have missed her at the stables. Even for her this was too early to go riding. He hurried back to the kitchen where Charlie was still preparing breakfast on the chance the master and his woman would want something this morning.

"Charlie, has Mademoiselle Cardiene left the house this morning?"

"Don't know. She's most likely still in her room. She likes a bit of bread and jelly and some coffee before she rides."

Max left the house on the run. Gravedigger was still in his stable, impatiently pawing and demanding breakfast. Two of the black stable hands had just arrived. They cowered when a very angry Max demanded to know who had taken his truck. No, they hadn't seen anybody drive off in the truck.

Now he understood. The French bitch had taken the truck. She was gone, her bed unused, and her favorite horse was whinnying for his breakfast. She had the truck and his letter. He shot out a torrent of curses in a language the stable hands didn't understand.

But where was she? That, he didn't know. What he did know was that she had unwittingly earned herself the same fate as the pretty rich girl who'd died here weeks ago. Everyone believed she--what was her name, Erica?-- everyone believed she'd fallen off Gravedigger and broken her neck. That story wouldn't wash this time.

He promised himself he'd think of something special for the mademoiselle.

CHAPTER SEVENTEEN

WHILE MAX STOMPED around the stables planning exquisite tortures for Marie, Karl Volker went to breakfast in a dockside restaurant near his rooming house. The plump, chatty waitress had served sailors from all over the world and found nothing suspicious with his German accent.

"Be shipping out soon?" she asked, pouring him another cup of the thick American coffee that he enjoyed for its deep, smooth taste.

"I think yes," he told her. He caught himself before saying "Ja." Even now he was visualizing the moment he would appear in that place over there called the Jekyll Club and order these worthless rich Americans to come with him.

"I don't see how you fellows stand it out there on the water. You're as likely to get shot by the Americans as the Germans. I hear they're even blasting the beach in Jersey, up north."

"Yes. Good for us the Germans are not down here."

"They're already here. They're blowing up ships right

out there offshore. With ships that run under the surface. Submarines, you know."

Volker smiled as though this was new information.

"There'll be lots more action now that we're getting the shipyard. The town will be swarming with new workers to build the ships. Old man Congressman Vinson's the reason. Well, more men with money means more money for me. The harder they work, the more they'll eat."

"Yes. Perhaps the Germans will target your factories."

She put the coffee pot down behind her and gazed out the window. She nodded in the direction of Jekyll Island. "Course, if you was like the rich folks over there, your ship wouldn't have to take to the open seas. They just go up the intra-coastal waterway. No German subs in the waterway."

Volker's ears were suddenly alert.

"This waterway. How often do these rich men in their big boats use it?"

"Usually just a couple times a year. When they come down here in the winter and go back in the spring. Most will be moving back up north in the next few days. No loss to me. None of them ever come in here."

"They're leaving soon?" Volker contained his anxiety.

"Yeah. It's the end of their season here. They spend the winter months here and head back up north when the sticky weather moves in. They don't fancy sweating like us common folks. I'd expect most of them to be gone in a few days."

"Will all of them move?"

"They'll leave a few at a time. Most will probably go this coming weekend. Talk is President Roosevelt's afraid some of them German subs might drop by and pick up a rich man or two. Can't see what loss that would be. Germans can have them, for all I care."

Volker put down his coffee cup, his throat twitching

nervously while swallowing the steaming beverage at the same time. "So they will all be leaving?"

"Yep. Been seeing some of their boats fuelling up over here. You ready for your check, or you want some more coffee?"

He motioned for the check and paid her with the American money he'd been provided for his travels. She rang the register while standing in front of a sign that said "Loose Talk Sinks Ships."

Volker hurried back to his room and pulled out the case containing his radio transmitter. His hands shook so hard he had difficulty opening the case and setting up the radio. He knew the U-boat pack was already sliding through the Caribbean, heading for its rendezvous at Jekyll. But the rich men were leaving this weekend. Neither Berlin nor von Oster had told him this. That could only mean that if von Oster had transmitted this information to the Abwehr in Berlin, it should have been shared with the SD which had seniority in this mission. He relished the thought of Heydrich's fury boiling over and scalding both von Oster and Admiral Canaris when he found the Abwehr had withheld this vital intelligence from the SD.

Before the day was out, he intended to confront von Oster and discipline him for his non-cooperation.

Clarke awakened at the sound of the back door slamming. He knew it was Annie arriving to fix breakfast. She wouldn't start until he had bathed and shaved.

Clarke sat up slowly and gazed at the woman in bed beside him. She was sleeping soundly and peacefully, as though she was dreaming of riding through the French countryside as it had been before the Germans came. He gazed at her, recalling the renewal he had felt with her until they'd dropped off to sleep.

He wondered why did he feel so uneasy about a woman being in his house for the first time in months? He knew it was because of the revulsion he'd felt with himself ever since Liz had betrayed him.

As his feet touched the cold hardwood floor, he vowed again that he would carpet the bedroom. The hot bath cured his chill and he went back to Marie who was awake and waiting for him in bed. Despite the temptation to get back in bed with her, he kissed her with all the fire he could bring and told her the tub was hers. Then he went to tell Annie she would be serving breakfast for two this morning.

Annie had a question before he spoke. "Mr. Clock, I was wondering if somebody stayed here last night. Don't that truck out there belong to that rich man who bought your daddy's house?"

"Yes it does, Annie. I'll have some coffee until my guest is ready for breakfast."

Marie didn't take long. She strolled into the kitchen dressed as though she was going out for a ride. She smiled at Annie's wide eyes.

"Annie, you remember Marie, don't you?"

"Yes sir, Mr. Clock," Annie said softly. "I remember."

"Bonjour," Marie said, sitting down in the chair Clarke pulled out for her.

"What did she say?" Annie whispered to Clarke.

Clarke whispered back. "She said 'good morning' to you. Marie, do you like your eggs scrambled or over?"

"Scrambled or over? What means scrambled or over, Clock?"

"Show her, Annie."

Annie brought a pan of scrambled eggs to the table and spooned a pile of them onto Clarke's plate. He looked at Annie.

"No, Clarke. Do you have bread and jam? And coffee?"

Annie poured coffee for Marie, then piled eggs and ham with biscuits on Clarke's plate. She gave Marie two huge country biscuits with butter and put a jar of jam in the middle of the table with a subdued slam. Clarke complimented Annie on breakfast as she silently stood watch by the stove, her arms folded. When Marie seemed puzzled by her biscuits, he said, "That's bread. Our biscuits are soft on the outside and inside. Not like your French bread with a tough crust. You spread the butter and jam on them."

"What's this?" She pointed to a steaming bowl in the center of the table.

"Grits. Not a French food. It's very popular in this region."

"I never see them when I eat with Jeremy."

"Jeremy's not a local. Here, try some of my eggs and ham."

Annie maintained her silence by the stove while Clarke and Marie ate, then walked onto his porch.

"Do you intend to go back to Pineland?"

"I can't. I can trust him no more. I will get my clothes from his house and move."

He hesitated before he told her what he had decided. "You can stay here with me."

"You don't want me here."

Her blunt declaration shocked him. "Why do you think so?"

She looked down. "You did not come to me last night. I had to come to you."

He detected disappointment in her. He touched her arm gently. "I'm just remembering old hurts."

She pulled her arm from his hand. "Clock, if you want me to stay, I stay. Not forever. I can see you think I am not the one for you."

"I want you to stay. Really I do. If you detect hesitation, it's because of someone else, not you."

Her doubtful eyes softened. She nodded and smiled.

"Come on," he said. "I'll lead you in my car. You follow in the truck." He looked back at Annie. "We'll be back soon."

He opened the door of the truck for her and pushed back the leather pouch on the seat. Two letters partially slid from the pouch. One was addressed to Brazil, the other to Arlington, Virginia. Because he'd lived in Arlington when he'd been with the Justice Department, he studied the address. It was to a post office box number, but the kinds of visitors to Pineland nowadays caused him to commit the number to memory.

Marie followed him up the road to Pineland where Max was detailing the MG in the circular driveway in front of the house. When Marie came to a stop, he dropped his rag and sprinted to the truck. He had the door open and Marie halfway out before Clarke grabbed his arm and pulled him roughly away. Max turned to Clarke and pushed him back. "Theft is a crime," he said angrily.

"So is assault and battery," Clarke said, stepping between Max and Marie. "And I'll see the law enforced if you touch Miss Cardiene again."

"Where did you take the truck?" Max demanded. Clarke saw Max's eyes go to the pouch. No matter how much he blustered, that mail pouch was his primary concern.

"The truck was parked at my home last night," Clarke said calmly. "It was perfectly safe."

"The truck was stolen last night," Max said in his growl.

Jeremy Mann lumbered sleepily down the walkway in bedroom slippers and a blue robe over brown trousers. "What's all the commotion out here?"

Max turned to Jeremy. "The mademoiselle took the

truck for the night without permission."

Jeremy yawned. "Oh? All night?"

"It was completely safe," Clarke said, staying between Max and Micelle. "It was parked at my house."

"Your house?" Jeremy was suddenly wide awake. "You drove the truck to Mr. Deveau's house last night, Marie?"

"Oui," Marie said without hesitation. "I want to take away my belongings."

Jeremy spoke slowly, as though trying to comprehend what he had just heard. "You went to Deveau's home? For what reason?"

"I will not tell you," she said without smiling. "Excuse me. I'll get my things and leave you."

She stalked up the walkway. Jeremy stared after her, then turned to Clarke and grinned with pain. "You must have something that excites her, Deveau."

Clarke didn't answer. He watched Max slowly move to the other side of the truck and look in at the mail pouch.

"What can you offer this hellcat?" Jeremy asked. "When even your old home here isn't enough for her."

"I'm giving her nothing more than a roof and help to get resettled. Or somehow get back to England, if that's what she wants."

"Back to England? With German U-boats all over the Atlantic? Say, are you still trying to prove I killed Erica Blandford?"

"My investigation is incomplete."

"I'll bet. You think the mademoiselle can clue you in on dark deeds here on the old plantation. Am I getting warm?"

"Not even close. She's leaving you for sufficient reason."

"Just because I was paying her no mind? What can you do with a woman so cold she refuses to even have wine with you?"

"I don't find her cold."

He enjoyed the surge of anger in Jeremy's eyes. At that moment Alicia Jackson leaned from a window, her long blond hair fluttering in the wind.

"I think the maid's trying to get your attention," Clarke said. "Looks like she's airing out the house. Say, isn't that Miss Glynn County?"

"You know her, I see. Have you had your eye on her? Understandable. Wonder why she prefers me to a cracker?"

"Must have something to do with what she learned in Sunday School. Will she be going north to clean your house?"

Marie exited through the front door with two suitcases and old Charlie struggling with another. Clarke moved quickly to take a bag from each of them.

"Is that all you're taking?" Mann said. "Never mind. I'll send the rest over. After I see which items fit the maid."

"She can keep the rest," Marie snapped at him, standing with Clarke as he put the suitcases into the back seat of his car.

Max paid no attention to Jeremy Mann's curses as Clarke disappeared down the driveway. He picked up the pouch from the truck seat and relaxed in relief to see the two letters still there. As soon as Mann returned to Alicia, he would take the letters to his cottage and examine the microdot. Lord help the mademoiselle and her man if it had been tampered with.

"I wish the Luftwaffe would bomb this jerkwater town like London," Jeremy Mann said angrily to no one in particular. He stalked back to the house and yelled to Charlie, "Bring breakfast to the patio."

Charlie moved to comply, knowing from Mann's tone that he was to lock the door to the private porch and admit no one. And no one included his giggling guest.

Lordy me, Charlie thought as he put coffee and rolls on the porch table. Lordy me. What is Mr. Mann thinking up?

CHAPTER EIGHTEEN

HER PLUMP ARMS folded, Annie watched sourly while Clarke carried Marie's bags into the house and put them into what he called his guest room. Unaccustomed to having him in the house at noon, she asked him three times if he wanted her to fix something to eat. She thought it strange that he wanted only cheese and bread, having his with coffee while the young woman had hers with wine. Just look at him. That foreign missy's already changing his habits.

When Clarke left Marie to go to the barn to help Jasper saddle a horse she could ride this afternoon, Annie caught him on the back porch. "Mr. Clock, is that missy aiming to stay here?"

"For a few days. Until she finds something to do."

"I'm thinking she's already found it."

"Annie, she's in a strange country. She has no place to go. Be nice to her. Help clean up the guest room."

Clarke left her on the porch and went to the barn. "Which horse is in best spirits, Jasper?"

"I'd say old Sandman. You riding with the missy?"

"Not today. I need to check some records at the court house."

Records pertaining to the deeds to Pineland. Would the records give some insight into whether Jeremy Mann actually was doing business with the Reich? Slim chance, he knew. Mann would keep such dealings secret from public records.

"Will the missy be staying with you for awhile?"

"Just a few days, Jasper. Until she can find a place to go."

Jasper grinned. "If I was you, I wouldn't work too hard on helping her find another place."

He returned Jasper's grin. When he started back toward the house, Annie was striding resolutely toward him.

"Mr. Clock, I got to talk to you." She planted her stout frame in front of him, her hands on her hips. "Jasper, you go on about your business."

"Don't tell me what my business is. I work for..."

She stamped her heavy foot. "Get on, Jasper!"

"I'll go see to the horse," Jasper said.

"Mr. Clock, you expecting to keep that young thing around this house?"

"For a few days, Annie. She'll leave when she finds a place to go."

"Just as I thought. You're planning to keep her here."

" She won't be in your way."

"I'm not worried about my way. I'm worried about yours."

"Annie..."

"Mr. Clock, I remember the women you used to bring here after you moved back home. I understood it because you was upset about your daddy dying. You think your momma and daddy would've let you keep this woman around the house, living like she's your wife?"

"They would've tried to help her."

"Yes sir. I reckon they would've. But this one, it ain't like you're helping her. It's like she's moving in as your wife. She's different from them other women you brought here. I knew you wouldn't keep them around too long. This girl's different. I can tell by the way you look at her."

"You can?"

"I just can't approve it. Your daddy wouldn't either."

"No, I'm sure he wouldn't. But he wouldn't have done lots of things I've done. And I wouldn't have done lots of things he did. But he would've wanted me to help this young woman."

Annie grunted grumpily. "Help her? If she moves in here you're the one's gonna need help."

Clarke controlled his irritation. He smiled at her, dear soul. She'd always felt like a Deveau. The family's honor was her honor. She wasn't afraid of him. She'd spanked his bottom when he was a baby and she'd do the same now if he'd let her. She and her family had been part of Pineland for generations, helping work this land until the depression had sent everyone else away to fend for themselves. He saw her eyes pretend to be angry as she wiped sweat away from her upper lip. She didn't spend time outdoors like Jasper, so her skin was still a milky pink, unlike Jasper's tanned outdoor complexion.

"Jasper," Clarke called. "Can you come here for a minute?"

Jasper came from the barn in as close to a trot as his old legs could manage. "I was just putting the bridle on Sandman."

"Jasper, have you ever heard Annie say I need a woman around this house?"

"Lots of times, Mr. Clock. Sometimes it seems like that's

all she worries herself about."

"Now that a woman's here, why do you think she's so upset?"

"Don't know, Mr. Clock. Seems to me she'd be happy about it. I know I'm happy about it. She's a fine looking woman."

Annie's face clouded for an explosion. "You look here, Jasper. I said he needed a proper woman. I mean like after the preacher tells her she can come here to live."

"Why would he need the preacher to tell him he can bring a woman so fine here?"

Clarke raised his hand to shield Jasper from Annie's sputter. "Jasper, have any of your sons ever lived with a woman before tying the knot?"

"Well, there's James, and Richard, and Sam and..."

"You shut your mouth, Jasper!"

"How about your grandchildren?" Clarke asked, talking to Jasper as though Annie had left them. "Any of them start off without a preacher?"

Jasper grinned. "I reckon a few of them did. There was Bill and..."

"And look what they become!" Annie fumed. "They're carousers and no counts. Mr. Clock, you was raised different. You're a Deevoe."

Jasper adjusted his cap on his bald dome ringed with white fuzz. "Well, it seems to me Mr. Clock got the right to some fun, too."

"Seems fair to me, Jasper," Clarke agreed. "Especially when I'm just giving her a helping hand."

"She had a helping hand over at the big house," Annie said.

"That hand did more than help her," Clarke said softly.

"Well, at least she don't throw herself around like that old Alicia Jackson," Annie said, her mood softening slightly.

"That girl's trash, no matter how pretty people think she is."

Annie knew about Alicia? Clarke felt shocked for a moment before remembering he'd learned long ago that talk spreads among the servants far faster than among their employers. Right now he'd wager half the county knew about Alicia living with the rich stud at Pineland. Of course, that meant they also knew about Marie. Now they would have a new story to spread about the French woman.

Clarke agreed with Annie. "Alicia's doing what Marie refused to do. That's why she had to leave. Be kind to her, Annie. She's lost and scared. A long way from home. She's already lost her mom and dad in the war."

Annie grunted, feigning displeasure. "It's bad to lose your momma and daddy both. Is she going to eat the same food as you, Mr. Clock?"

Clarke grinned. If Annie was wondering if she would have to fix the kind of food a French woman would eat, she had accepted Marie as a resident of the house, however temporary. "She'll have to, Annie."

Annie favored both men with a "Humph" and strode resolutely back to the house.

Jasper laughed. "Maybe we'll have some peace now. I'm sure happy to hear about this, Mr. Clock. You've done good for yourself."

"Marie won't be here long."

"I'm hoping you're wrong. That woman's not like the others. Me, I'd say you got the best of the deal. Alicia's mighty powerful medicine. Got lots of what a man wants. Well, some men. She knows it, too. Talk is, she's laid in some bad beds and laid in some fancy beds. Guess now she's in just about the fanciest she's ever laid in."

"So I've heard."

"Hope her regular man understands."

"Who's her regular man?"

"Sam Betts. Mean rounder works for Mr. Sanford over on St. Simons. Hear tell he used to be a boxer up north. If he gets mean, he might change Alicia's looks some."

"Let's hope not. The world needs more beauty, even Alicia's kind. Maybe Sam Betts will forget about her."

Sam Betts missed Alicia when she didn't show up to clean the Sanford house. When he called her mother on the mainland, she told him Alicia had gone to visit her aunt in Savannah. Sam was accustomed to hearing evasions from mothers of women he pursued, and he reckoned he'd just heard another one.

He knew what it meant when eyes turned away when he asked about her on the island. On the second day, the gardener at the Sanford home said he'd heard Alicia had been seen at the St. Simons dock a couple nights before. The gardener knew, but didn't say, she'd gotten on a boat with a big man with a British accent.

Sam went to the docks though it always disgusted him. He couldn't stand these men caked with sweat and salt, but he was willing to mingle with them to find out what Alicia had been doing on the dock. Nobody knew anything so he went on to the Half Shell Restaurant where he worked on a plate of shrimp, talking with the smelly men off the fishing boats. A big sun-spotted fisherman named Leander allowed as to how he'd seen her getting on a boat a couple nights ago.

"Whose boat?" Sam said in his Jersey growl.

"Boat belonged that that rich feller lives up at the big house on the river."

"You see them, friend?"

"Yeah. I know the woman. Joe here seen her, too. "

Sam's eyes cut to Joe who nodded that, yeah, he'd seen her, too.

Sam growled. "Why'd she get on that boat?"

Leander grinned. "Can't say for sure."

"What do you mean, you can't say for sure?"

Leander's eyes rolled toward Joe and both shrugged.

Sam knew the looks in the eyes of the men at the tables. He knew the laughter in their eyes, knew they were making fun of him. They damned well knew she'd gotten on a rich man's boat, and they knew why. They were laughing at him.

Sam stood and walked to the table where Leander and Joe were smirking. When Leander stood to push back his chair, Sam shoved him backwards onto the floor. Leander bounded to his feet with a straight razor in his hand. "You'll pay for that," he said with determination.

Sam's frown faded into a smile. He motioned Leander to come after him.

The big boatman seemed surprised by the invitation, then obliged with two wide sweeps of the razor. He stepped closer to sweep the razor again, then stiffened from the crushing fist that smashed into his jaw. He shook his head, dazed, then lunged again. Sam sidestepped the blade, grabbed Leaner's wrist and twisted it with his huge hands. Leander yelled in pain and dropped the straight razor to the floor.

Leander swung a roundhouse and hit air, then lost his own air from a hard punch to his stomach. He stumbled backward and caught his balance in time to take Sam's punch to his jaw that put him down.

Sam picked up the razor, stood over Leander and pressed the sharp blade against his sweaty neck. "Let's see how a pig squeals."

His brains scrambled, Leander had enough breath left only for pleading. "No, man, no! Don't!"

"Tell me what happened to the woman, pal."

"She got on a boat belonged to that rich man who lives

in that big house up the river. The old Deveau place."

Leander felt the blade on his neck and stopped breathing. Sam Betts glowered at him for several long seconds, spat in his face, folded the razor into his pocket and left. Outside, he heard laughter erupt inside the restaurant.

"Leander, you shoulda knowed better than mess with that guy. Used to be a real fighter up north. That guy could stomp Joe Louis."

"Leander, man, what's wrong with you? I heard that feller beat up guys for a likker gang in Jersey. Hear tell old man Sanford he works for's in with the gang. Reason he's got so much money. This guy's his bodyguard. You lucky he didn't kill you."

"Leander, you crazy."

For several moments Sam Betts considered how much better he'd feel if he went back inside and beat the scales off every one of those bastards. But he didn't. He had more pressing business. He got into his car and drove to Maude Parker's house. She had the finest moonshine on the Georgia coast. Despite his liking for bottled whiskey, he had developed a taste for the white lightning that was smoother and more potent than the bottled kind. He had drunk enough of it to get what these Southerners called "bust-head."

Today he wanted a full case of bust-head. His woman was up the river pleasing a rich man. Damn her. God damn her. God damn that rich man.

He left Maude's place and went to the room he rented in Brunswick. He chugged down an entire quart of Maude's bust-head, massaging the handle of the razor. He touched the blade. He thought of Alicia and what she was doing with that rich man. He swore a blue storm they could've

125

heard all the way to the docks. How much would she like her rich man if he was a eunuch?

CHAPTER NINETEEN

SOON IT WOULD BE OVER. Max permitted himself
a surge of excitement as he finalized his plans for the
abduction. The winter season on the golden islands would
end when the owners of this country returned to their
mansions in the north to be close to their money vaults. For
Max the real end of the season would be this weekend when
Jeremy Mann hosted his father's friends and those two
gloomy scientists. The time had come to get off his final
instructions to the U-boats and to Berlin and Arlington.

Max heard the master of Pineland calling him from the
back of the house where he was looking out over the river.

"Max, I want you to go to Deveau's house and tell the
mademoiselle I've heard from Free France in England.
That's de Gaulle's crowd. Tell her they say they have news
that her father may still be alive."

Jeremy smiled at Max's look of surprise. "I can tell her
anything I want, can't I? After all, I do have the radio
equipment here to contact London. And Paris. And
Berlin."

"You still intend to break her?"

Jeremy's voice spat bitterness. "She's not going to shaft me for a redneck."

"Do you think this story will entice her to return?"

He smiled coldly. "There's nothing she'd like more than news that her father's still alive."

Max smiled. It was a cruel hoax.

"Go give her the message, Max."

Max didn't like this intrusion into his preparations. This was Thursday and the reception here at Pineland would be Saturday evening. If the mademoiselle came today, she would be here tomorrow, perhaps the day after, interfering with his plans for the abduction. Not to mention the probable distraction of Alicia and Marie screaming at each other.

"Why don't we wait until tomorrow afternoon, sir. She's probably in no mood to even talk to me today. Tomorrow she'll be cooler."

"You're right, Max. I hate to delay it, though. Damn that French bitch."

"Will you keep the wild one another evening."

"Yes. One more night. Though she almost makes me feel inadequate. At least she'll keep me entertained until we get Marie back here."

Karl Volker went to the dock at St. Simons to ask if there was work on the island. He was Polish, he explained, and he had fled the German invasion to find work in America.

"No work till they start building the shipyard," said a man coming off a shrimp boat. "Not even in the big houses."

"This is where the rich people live?"

The man lit a cigar. "Yeah, lots of rich folks live here. The real millionaires live over there on Jekyll. They won't even let you come ashore there. But they're leaving, too."

"When do they leave?"

"Maybe by the weekend. Not much to do now. I do some fishing to get by. Fella, I know you must've been through hell over there. Wish I could help. Like I say, won't be any real jobs till they start up the shipyard. We'll build enough warships here to sink the whole Kraut navy."

"Let us hope so."

Volker left the man and walked back to his car. The rich Americans, not just the doktors, would be leaving this weekend? The strike must be soon. He must let the U-boats know. And the Obergruppenfuhrer.

Why hadn't von Oster let him know their prey was leaving so soon? He had to find him. He delayed his trip to Pineland long enough to send a message to his contact in Berlin to let them know his need to meet with Herr von Oster before the planned abduction. That man's troubles were just beginning.

Marie came in from riding and went to the kitchen for a glass of Annie's tea. She heard the sound of the car pulling up and hoped it meant Clarke had returned. She hurried to the door and stopped when she saw the big man get out of a dirty car. His first stumbling steps told her he'd been drinking. He scowled when he saw her.

"This the Deveau place?"

She barely understood his slurred English. "Yes. Monsieur Deveau lives here."

"I wanna see him."

"He is away."

"Don't fool with me, girl. I know he's here."

The man moved toward her with a slow wobble. Marie recognized danger in his angry glare. She turned and bounded up the steps to the front door where Annie had come to see who was here.

"Oh, my lordy! Get in here, missy!"

The angry man kept coming toward the house. "I want 'Leesha," he said in a guttural growl. "You bring her out here to me."

Annie yelled at the top of her lungs. "Jasper! Jasper!"

Jasper came slowly out of the barn, wondering why Annie sounded so agitated. It was too early for supper and he still had to feed the stock. He walked from the barn with a pitchfork in his hands.

"What you want?"

"Jasper! Get on up here!"

He recognized the alarm in her yell and came toward the house as fast as his old legs would carry him. Sam Betts took no mind of him and kept walking across the yard toward the two women quaking on the porch.

When Jasper realized why Annie had screamed, he came faster, holding the pitchfork before him like a spear. Sam Betts at last became aware of him.

"Old man, I've come for my woman. Don't tell me she ain't here. Everybody seen her get on the boat and come up here."

"Seen who?" Jasper said between heavy breaths.

"Leesha, old man. You know who I mean."

"Ain't no Leesha here." Jasper's voice quivered. "You go on and leave us be."

"I know she got on a boat and come to the Deveau place. Everybody in town seen her do it. This is the Deveau place, ain't it?"

"This ain't the place you looking for," Jasper said, slowing his nervous steps toward Sam Betts. He was close enough to see Sam's eyes were glazed with hate and drink.

Maude Parker made mighty good moonshine, Sam thought. That and Alicia Jackson were the only things he'd found to like down here in Georgia. And now Alicia had come out here to whore it up with a rich man. Through his stupor, Sam remembered Leander's straight razor in his pocket. He took it out and pointed it toward Jasper.

"You've lived a long time, old man. No use in you giving up your life to save a rich man's ass. Go on back to your cows and horses."

Annie pulled Marie inside the house. "Child, you stay here till that devil leaves. You hear me? Don't you move."

"He's going to hurt Jasper."

Annie turned and went to the kitchen and grabbed the two largest butcher knives she could lay her hands on. She rushed her big round body through the door and stomped onto the porch, slamming the screen door behind her. Sam Betts looked back at her and stopped moving toward Jasper who was unsurely holding his ground.

Annie waved her knives. "Mr. Sam Betts, you seen what happens to a catfish, ain't you? We hook him and skin him and gut him. Then we hold him over the flame till he's burned brown. You swipe that razor round again you're gonna be like that old catfish. Whichever way you jump, one of us gonna be on your back. I guarantee you gonna feel like a catfish."

Annie descended the steps to the yard. Sam Betts was between her and Jasper. A glint of understanding flickered in the raging coals in his eye sockets. Where the hell did this crazy old man and woman come from? Holding a pitchfork and two butcher knives. All he wanted was Alicia and that rich man.

"How come you're against me?" Sam growled. "How come you're protecting a rich man in there with my woman?"

"I done told you this is the wrong place," Annie said through breaths coming in rapid spurts. "Ain't no Leesha

Jackson here. We don't let no such trash come around here. She's in that big house up the river. Mr. Clock don't live there no more."

"Then what's that pretty woman doing here?"

"She's visiting. And she's welcome here. You ain't."

"I know you two're siding with that rich man who's got my woman inside there."

"Sam Betts, I reckon you got all your brains scrambled up north when you was fighting," Jasper said. "They's no Leesha here. If you want her, you go on up to the big house up the river where Mr. Clock used to live. That's where you find her and that rich man."

Sam Betts was drunk enough to be insistent. "I want to see inside this house first."

He started toward the steps, then stopped when Annie drew back a butcher knife as though she was going to charge him. Keeping his dark scowl, he began backing up. This was not what he'd expected. "You'd best be telling me the truth, old woman. I find out you lied to me, I'll be back. You hear me?"

"You come back you'll get the gutting I promised you," Annie spat back.

Sam Betts stared at all of them, as though recognition had finally fought its way through the drunken haze in his brain. He stumbled back to his car, fumbled to crank it, and finally got back onto the road. Jasper stuck the pitchfork into the ground and pulled out a dirty handkerchief to mop his drenched face. Annie made do with her sleeve.

"Lordy," Jasper said in gasps. "What come over that man?"

"Like you told him, he got his brains scrambled when he was fighting."

"Is he gone?" Marie called timidly from inside the screen door.

Annie turned to her as calm as if she'd just come back from the mail box. "Sure, honey. No reason to be afraid."

The old woman dropped the act and her heavy body sank down on the steps. "Lordy, I thought that man was gonna come at me with that razor. That's a mean man, honey."

"What we gonna do?" Jasper asked, his handkerchief drenched with sweat he'd mopped from his face. Annie pushed the handkerchief away when he offered it to her. She was still wiping with her sleeve. "Reckon he'll go on up to the big house?"

"That's their problem," Annie said through huffs. "They's the ones brought old Leesha Jackson up there. Always knowed that girl was trash, no matter how she looks. She's the one Sam's messed up over."

"Shouldn't we warm Monsieur Jeremy the man is coming?" Marie called, still inside the screen door.

Jasper continued to mop his face. "They's plenty of young men out there. Maybe they can beat some sense in his thick head."

Annie nodded. "I say we do nothing till Mr. Clock comes home. That's what I say."

"Don't you worry none, child," Jasper said. "We'll stay here with you till Mr. Clock gets back."

Marie sounded contrite. "I'm sorry to bring this trouble to you."

Annie stood up, her eyes wide as though she'd been insulted. "You? Trouble? I don't want to hear it, child. None of this is your fault. That crazy man's looking for Leesha Jackson. It'll suit both of them just fine if he finds her."

Marie smiled weakly. She still thought someone should warn Jeremy that a crazy man was coming.

CHAPTER TWENTY

WHEN KARL VOLKER ARRIVED at Pineland, a black man at the barn told him Max Lewis stayed in the small house over there among the trees. Volker walked across the yard and looked down the sloping hill where he saw Max working on a cabin cruiser at the dock. He turned and went to Max's small cottage and picked the lock.

Volker sniffed contemptuously at Max's spartan parlor furnished with little more than bare furniture, a wireless and a few magazines. Despite von Oster's education, Volker detected a definite lack of taste in the man's lifestyle.

With a practiced hand, he felt the walls until he was convinced none moved or contained hidden vaults. That made the locked room interesting. The lock presented no difficulty and Volker was through it within seconds. He immediately found the suitcase in the closet. He opened it easily and whistled when he saw the radio, photography equipment, and a microscope.

Volker picked up the leather pouch in the suitcase and was curious to see the letter addressed to Arlington. He realized the microscope proved von Oster knew how to use microdots, so he examined the letter for a dot. Strange it would go to Arlington, he thought.

The address puzzled Volker. He opened the letter and found nothing more than news of a circus coming to Brunswick. His trained eyes quickly located the message dot in the lower left corner of the page. He put it under the microscope and caught his breath when he saw the message.

Cursing in his native tongue, Volker put von Oster's radio on the work table standing in the middle of the parlor. He looked around for a chair, and jumped when he heard the squeak of the door. He froze when the big man with ugly scars ambled into the house, looking as sullen as a Russian executioner.

Alicia believed in overkill. Though Jeremy would be in bed with her tonight, still she dressed in the negligee to enhance her appeal. However, he pretended to take his time getting aroused. He paced the parlor, admiring himself in the mirror over the huge mantel. He pretended disinterest when he saw her enter the cavernous room behind him, sweep off her robe, and strike her starlet pose with a hand on her hip and a strand of long blond hair over one eye.

He smiled and silently admitted she had been as satisfying a piece of flesh as he'd ever tumbled with, on either side of the ocean. These cracker girls had their attractions. With luck she would still be down here for his pleasure when he came back from time to time. He watched her in the mirror as she came toward him on cat's feet and put her arms around him. He hummed with satisfaction as she slid her hands down to unzip his trousers and bring his manhood to stiff attention.

She purred and nibbled on his ear. "You ready hon?"

He closed his eyes and moaned his pleasure.

She took his drink from his hand, sipped it and made a face at its unfamiliar taste.

"You're like that drink," he said gruffly as she unbuttoned his shirt. "You don't fit that drink and you don't fit me. It's time for you to make plans to leave."

He enjoyed her shock. "Leave? Me? Has anybody ever loved you like me?"

"Loved? What's the point of being in love?"

"Because, you know, like they say, love conquers all. Nobody's loved you like me. Admit it."

"Nobody's been as passionate, as energetic. But it's time to end it. The season down here is over and I'll be moving back north to the bright lights."

"Couldn't I go back north with you? Pretend I'm your maid or something? I'd love to leave this jerk water town."

He laughed. "Pretend you're my maid? The very thing Deveau called you. How could I claim I have a maid that looks like you? Nobody in the world would believe it. No, tonight has to be our last for awhile, until I come back down for a visit."

She refused to give up. She knew he loved her. She continued to fondle and undress him. "Are you going to take that French girl with you?"

He started to tell her he would if he could, that Marie was unfinished business. But Alicia's moist lips muffled his protest. This country girl was a handful. A bed full. Maybe she could have a place up north with him when he left. Maybe not. They sank onto the deep carpet and he went happily to his last night with her, thinking that tomorrow he would arrange for the repossession of the mademoiselle.

"Did somebody call?" he said, sitting up and rolling off her onto the carpet.

"I didn't hear a thing, hon," Alicia said, exploring the most responsive parts of his body.

"Maybe it was the wind. Sometimes it howls like a gale up here. There! Did you hear it?"

"No," she said. "Only thing I hear is you breathing hard, enjoying it."

"Well, Max is outside. He'll take care of anything that's wrong."

She giggled and pulled him back on top of her.

Volker was not a gale, but he howled.

"Who are you?" he asked the big man with the ugly face.

"You the rich man who took Leesha away?"

Volker had never seen an uglier scowl.

"I want her back. I'm real unhappy about you taking her."

Volker understood nothing about a Leesha or taking her. But he did understand that this simian giant was taking a straight razor out of his pocket.

"You back up over there," Sam Betts said, motioned toward the bedroom with the razor.

Trembling and keeping his eyes on the razor, Volker backed toward the bedroom, looking quickly around the sparse parlor for anything that might give him a chance against this monster. He cursed himself for leaving his Luger in his room, taking no chance the local police might stop him and find it. The sullen gorilla didn't miss Volker's furtive survey of the parlor. With his eyes fixed on the razor, Volker never saw the heavy fist that shot out like a piston into his jaw. Volker landed semi-conscious on his back, knowing his jaw was broken.

Sam Betts looked in the bedroom, then in the closet where von Oster kept his radio and photography equipment. He shuffled back to Volker.

"Leesha's not in there. You tell me where she is."

"Who're you looking for?" Volker stammered in

German.

"What you trying to say? I told you I want Leesha. Tell me where she is."

"She's….she's in the house," Volker stammered through broken teeth and English.

Sam Betts still didn't understand. He pulled Volker up by his jacket with one hand and touched the razor to his nose. "Cut your gibberish. You show me where she is."

On his feet, Volker regained his courage and desperately sent a one-two combination to the big man's stomach that barely brought a grunt. The razor slashed down the front of Volker's light jacket, opening it and his chest. Volker had barely howled in pain before the blade sliced upward under his ribs. Blood flooded into his lungs and smothered his scream.

For seconds, Volker was suspended off his feet until the huge hand on his throat released its hold and let him crumble to the floor in his own blood. His pleas in a language the big man didn't understand increased his fury and brought a hard kick to his hemorrhaging ribs.

"Tell me where she is or your time's up."

But Volker was beyond talk. His words gurgled out in a babble of German that made no sense to Sam Betts. Sensing he'd get nothing more from this bloody mess twitching on the floor, Sam decided to end a razor affair the traditional way by giving the victim a new grin. Another swipe of the blade opened a spurting slit in Volker's throat. He turned and slowly slouched to the door, calmly wiping the bloody razor on his dirty pants. He looked back once at the gory mess on the floor, then looked up at the big house where lights were already burning in the early dusk. He decided the nearest way into the house would be through the side entrance instead of through the front door.

The burning pain of the final slash revived Volker's glimmering senses just enough to make him aware his attacker had left the house. He had barely enough strength to get to his feet and steady himself against the wall. He fumbled out his handkerchief and put it to his throat, immediately soaking it beyond the point of use. He tried to cry out his pain and realized the razor slash across his throat had cut his vocal chords and left him mute.

Volker knew he was dying. For a moment he considered getting Max's radio onto a table to signal Berlin with one last service to the Reich. But he knew he had no strength to set up the equipment. And he didn't have time. His only chance was to get far away from here and hope he could find help that would delay his trip to Valhalla.

But where? Not in the big house where the man with the razor must've gone. And driving was out of the question.

The dock. His lone chance was to get to the dock and into a boat. He'd drift downstream until somebody found him, maybe in time to save him. But von Oster was at the dock. Surely he would suspect what Volker had found in his cottage and would finish the job the big intruder had started. But right now he had to take his chances to get past von Oster. Maybe he would be inside a cabin and wouldn't notice him getting into a smaller boat.

Volker stumbled outside the small house. In the dusk he could just make out the man with the razor entering the big house. Wheezing through blood spurting from his chest and throat, Volker moved faltering legs to the crest of the hill overlooking the dock. He started down the hill, fell, and began crawling.

In the moan of the wind, Volker didn't hear the screams that came from the big house.

CHAPTER TWENTY-ONE

CLARKE FELT UNEASY when he pulled up in his yard and saw Jasper leaning on his pitchfork. It was long past time for him and Annie to go home. What was Annie doing with two butcher knives? For a moment of panic he wondered if something had happened to Marie. He relaxed in relief when she came out the front door behind Annie and bounded down the steps to him. He enjoyed her arms around him.

"Lord, we're glad it's you instead of old Sam Betts," Annie said in heavy breaths, putting her knives on the top step.

"Betts?"

"Leesha Jackson's man. Works over on St. Simons. Used to be a fighter up north."

"Yes, I've heard of him. He was here?"

"For no good reason," Annie said sternly. "He's after Leesha. He thought she was here."

"She's with Jeremy Mann, isn't she?"

"Last we heard," Jasper said.

"He left, didn't he?"

Annie stood as straight as her rotund body would allow and folded her chunky arms across her huge breasts. "Yessuh, he left all right. We seen to that."

"The man thought Leesha was here," Marie said through gasps. "He tried to come into the house."

"He meant harm to missy," Jasper said.

Clarke understood. He knew exactly what Sam would have done with Marie.

"We told him he done come to the wrong place to find old Leesha," Annie said with force. "Me and Jasper told him if he didn't get gone from here, we'd treat him like any other polecat comes on this place."

Jasper pushed his pitchfork into the dirt. "I was on the point of putting him on my fork and carrying him off to the river."

Annie wasn't about to let Jasper seem braver than her. "Nothing I can't carve up with my butcher knife. That varmint came mighty close to ending up on the table."

Clarke grinned despite his alarm. "I doubt even you could've made him taste good, Annie."

Marie kept her arms around Clarke. "They were magnifique. They protected me."

Jasper beamed. "Honey, you family here."

"Should we warn Jeremy that man is coming?" Marie asked softly.

"I say Sam Betts is his problem," Annie said with a huff. "That man brought Leesha over there, she's his problem. He's got plenty of help over there."

"True," Clarke said. "How long ago did he leave?"

"Hour, maybe," Jasper said.

Clarke thought about it. "Plenty of time for him to be there by now. Just the same, I'll give Mann a call. It's getting dark. His men might be gone home now and he's on his own."

Annie was stubborn. "He's got that other big man out there. The one that talks funny. I say any trouble he's got he brought on himself. Old Leesha's the devil's spawn anyhow."

"Just the same, I'll call and let him know."

Alicia had Jeremy Mann on his back in the deep carpet, wiggling her hot body as he thrust. God, was he ready! He laughed and smoothed back her hair, pulling her lips to his. His eye caught a movement in the mirror above the mantel. He stopped his kiss abruptly and looked again in the mirror. The movement took on the form of a man. A huge, scowling man.

Alicia shrieked as Mann roughly pushed her off and got to his knees facing the intruder. She started to whine in protest, then saw the man and brought her hands to her mouth in a shrill scream.

Mann gasped and fumbled for his pants. "Hey, what're you doing here? You're trespassing. Get out of here."

The big man kept his scowl. "I go anywhere I please. Especially to find my woman."

"Your...?" Mann's eyes cut to Alicia who was reaching for anything that she could use to cover her naked body. "Alicia, do you know this...this man?"

Sam Betts sneered. "Course she knows me."

He walked slowly across the parlor toward them, the straight razor in his hand. "You're busting my woman, big man. I don't like fellas who run off with what's mine. Especially rich men who think they can take anything they want."

Jeremy's terrified eyes stayed on the razor. His privates felt exposed. Very exposed. He still shuddered from his most horrible dream--the dream in which his privates were cut off in a sword fight fantasy. He'd never forgotten that dream. That dream gave him cold shivers to this day.

But this was no dream slowly coming toward him. It was a nightmare in ugly human form, holding a blade more menacing than a sword in a dream.

Jeremy's fingers were too paralyzed to handle his pants, to cover his precious parts. He swore at Alicia when she fell against him and sent both of them tumbling to the carpet. She clutched at him for protection and he pushed her away.

"For god's sakes man, take her. I didn't know. She just came up here on her own. You know how women are!"

"Shut up! Sam Betts roared. "I know you took her off St. Simons on a boat. You've been poking her ever since then. I remember that little car parked outside. I remember the day you drove her to the house. You'd already started in on her then, hadn't you?"

Jeremy struggled to think what this man was talking about. Then he remembered. The day he'd fallen into the tall grass with Erica Blandford, there where they'd fought that battle. The Battle of...what was it?...yes, yes, the Battle of Bloody Marsh. Stopped the Spanish, sent them back to Florida. Alicia had seen them and offered herself as a better alternative that very day. He'd driven her home in the MG. This ugly hulk had seen them that day.

Sam Betts spoke calmly in a guttural growl. "You think you can get away with that? Just cause you're rich? I don't allow nobody but the boss to do her. And I don't exactly like him doing it."

The boss. Jeremy thought quickly. The boss. That would be his friend, John Sanford. The liquor man.

"Sam!" Alicia said pitifully. "Sam, darling. I was just about to come home to you, honey. I swear."

"You're lying, baby." Sam Betts took a practice swipe

with the razor, Jeremy and Alicia darted several feet across the floor like crabs.

"Take her, man! Take her," Mann pleaded. "Honest to god, she came here without me knowing. One of my men must've picked her up in town. I just found out about her tonight and she came in here and took advantage of me. I was just about to drive her back..."

Sam was standing over Jeremy, the razor resting against his shaking throat. Sam's eyes went down to his shaking prey's privates. "Damn, man, you don't even lie good! I already cut one man out there. Kind of got me in a mood to cut another."

Jeremy's hope collapsed. The blood on the blade. Another man. It had to have been Max. There was no one else outside except Max. Nobody else out there who would even attempt to rescue him. He felt himself fainting from the terror of knowing he had no hope of rescue from this madman. "Take her! Take her!" he pleaded.

"I plan to do just that, big man. But I want to have some fun first. I can tell you take a lot of pride in how you handle women. I'm gonna take that golden rod of yours for a trophy. That's fair, don't you think, mister money bags?"

Jeremy whined, bathing in his own sweat. How could the full life he had ahead come to nothing under the blade of this crazed brute, over a worthless girl with a hot body?

Betts suddenly reached out and pulled Alicia's long blond hair to keep her from crawling away. "Not yet, baby. I want you to see what happens to men who think they can take you from me. You watch good, honey. You hold still and watch."

"Sam, Sam...please don't hurt him...me...don't..."

He backhanded her across her face, leaving her stunned on the carpet. But he wouldn't let her lie half-conscious on her back, though it crossed his mind that she was in perfect position to crawl on now and show this rich stud how she liked to be treated. Instead, he grabbed a handful of her hair and propped her up against the sofa, facing Jeremy.

"Don't worry, hon. I'll be finished in two swipes. Won't take any more to fix him. Then we can go back home and I'll take care of you."

He playfully patted both her breasts, then turned back to Jeremy Mann. Jeremy was trying to get to his feet to run. But Sam's boot slammed into his ribs and he pinned him on his back. Sam Betts heavily straddled his back, sending him into new paroxysms of cries and pleas. His terror soared as Betts kicked away the pants he'd been trying to get back on. Alicia sat against the sofa, too dazed even to shriek.

Charlie came down the hallway to investigate the strange sounds in the parlor. He stopped at the door and stared in horror, then turned and got outside as fast as his old legs could carry him. His first impulse was to put miles between himself and the house. But Mr. Mann was his employer, and there would be questions about what had happened to him. Who could tell where the questioning would end? They might even blame him.

Charlie quivered, knowing he must do something, but knowing there was nothing he could do. He couldn't fight that giant in there. He didn't have a gun, wouldn't know how to use it anyway.

He stood on the crest of the hill that sloped down to the river, his insides sobbing in desperation. He had to do something, and do it fast. But he knew as well as he was alive that there was nothing he could do to stop that crazy man in there.

In the dusk he saw movement at the dock. Mr. Max was there! Mr. Max might do something. Charlie began waving his arms and jumping.

"Mr. Max! Mr. Max! Mr. Max!"

Charlie saw no sign that Max heard him in the low moan of the wind. Charlie looked back at the house, feeling helpless, knowing the big man was doing his awful work with the razor blade. He screamed again, but when he looked down at the dock, he saw no sign of Max at all.

CHAPTER TWENTY-TWO

GOOD, MAX THOUGHT. The engine checked out, and the below-deck compartments were ready to stow the captives on the first leg of their trip to the U-boat waiting offshore. Yes, the craft is ready, he thought. He looked out the porthole. What a thrill it would be to march his prisoners from the house, down the hill to the boat and on to their new lives on the other side of the Atlantic.

What was that? Motion? Was that a windmill up there on top of the hill? He looked again. Dusk had nearly fallen and he could barely make out more than the lights in the house.

Yes, there it was. Now he was sure of it. Was Mann signaling to him? Why didn't he just come on down here to the dock? Silly question, he realized. The lord of the manor didn't want to stray far from his entertainment.

Max went up on deck for a better look. Yes, someone was up there at the top of the hill waving his arms around. Mann? No, somehow didn't seem to be him. Probably Charlie, he thought. He couldn't be sure in the dark.

Charlie faded right into it.

Max took his time getting off the boat onto the dock. He stopped and listened. He heard faint sounds from the hill. Was it Charlie? Or something from the house? Hard to tell with the breeze blowing. Just the wind, he thought. Just the god-forsaken wind on this god-forsaken coast.

He took a last look back at the boat, then began walking slowly along the dock to the path leading up the slope to the house. Let Herr Mann have some time with his play thing. His carefree life would soon undergo a drastic change. Why was he there waving like a madman?

Max looked again at the agitated figure on top of the hill. Yes, now that he was closer, he could tell it was Charlie. Was he calling to him? The damned old fool was waving like a wild man.

When Charlie started stumbling down the path toward him, still waving his arms, Max stopped. Something was wrong. Charlie never left the house unless he had to. He preferred his job in the house. Max broke into a trot up the hill toward the old man.

"Mr. Max! Mr. Max!"

Now Max was close enough to hear the terror in the old man's cries, desperation in his eyes. Charlie was gasping and coughing, barely choking out some words in his strange coastal accent. He pointed toward the house. "He's gonna kill Mr. Mann!"

"Kill? Who? Come on, Charlie. Tell me."

"Mr. Mann…he's gonna kill him…"

Max sensed he was desperately needed in the house. Without waiting for Charlie to wheeze out his story, he sprinted for the house. Charlie had mentioned Mann, and he was too scared to talk. There was trouble in the house. Real trouble. Maybe Mann's lady friend had taken exception to his games. Was she armed? It hardly seemed likely, but

148

you never know.

Max reached the top of the hill breathing hard, but he was well conditioned and still felt strong. He moved quickly, warily, into the kitchen. Now he could hear the groans and screams coming from the parlor. He recognized the shrill screams, male and female. The most shrill were Jeremy Mann's. His pitiful cries sounded like the wailing of a man being dragged into the depths of Hell.

Max moved quickly and noiselessly to the parlor. He stopped in astonishment at the landscape of Hades he saw there. A huge man with glassy eyes sat on Jeremy Mann, sizing up his grisly work. Alicia was huddled against the sofa, sobbing and covering her eyes from the horrible sight.

"I told you to watch me, bitch!" the big man yelled at Alicia. When he cut his eyes toward her, he saw Max burst across the room on the run. Betts swung the razor with a swipe that Max avoided with a leap that carried him over Alicia and the sofa.

For a moment, Sam Betts seemed to be deciding whether to proceed with his surgery on Jeremy Mann or stop long enough to deal with this interruption. He had always been ready, willing, to accept a fight wherever he found one. No hurry. Plenty of time for his main work. Neither his woman nor this whining rich man would move far away. Just to be sure, he drove a hard blow into Jeremy's chest to immobilize him. That done, he rose to face the tall muscular man with dark blond hair who had disrupted his fun.

"How come so many fools live in this part of the country?" Betts sneered, stepping toward Max. "You Rebel boys bleed so good. Come on, boy. Let's you and me get our thing over with so I can get back to work."

Max motioned for Betts to come get him. "Come on, old chap. Wouldn't want to put your little blade down and try me without it, would you?"

Sam's scowl dissolved into a grin. "Well, son of a bitch. A limey. Anything bleeds better than a Rebel, it's a limey."

Betts could hardly believe his luck. This fool had actually invited him to slug it out. From Brunswick to New York, there were crippled men who wished they'd never taken that chance. Now here's a grinning limey begging for a cracked head and smashed ribs to go along with it.

"How about it, monkey," Max said. "Don't act so scared."

"Monkey, huh? That'll get you extra, limey."

Sam lunged angrily with his razor. He intended to shut up this limey and get back to the real fun. He moved quicker than Max anticipated and the blade gashed his forearm as he skipped backwards. Sam licked his lips at the sight of the blood. Damn, Maude made good moonshine. He still felt good from it.

That lunge told Max something. Though fuelled by liquor, Sam Betts was still very fast and very dangerous. He was not a man to be taken lightly.

Betts laughed as Max evaded a second sweep of his razor. "Come on, limey. No need to prolong it. Get it over with. You ain't getting away. Nobody gets away from old Sam, do they baby?"

Keeping his eyes on the razor, Max slowly backed away, waiting for Sam's next swipe. Sam waved the razor as though it was a sword, and he wasn't ready when Max suddenly closed on him. Max smashed down on Sam's knife arm and slammed a hard blow into his elbow. Max knew he must've torn ligaments in Sam's elbow, but the big man was too strong to release his grip on the razor.

Using both hands, Max used every grain of his strength to twist Sam's knife wrist and force the razor from his grasp. But Sam's ring instincts brought his other fist around with a blow to Max's ribs that sent him stumbling backward.

In disbelief, Sam rubbed his aching arm and stared at his razor on the floor. Now he was irritated. He bent to pick up the razor. Time to finish off this foreigner. He'd already cut up one today, and slicing another would feel good.

Seeing Sam take his time to retrieve his blade on the floor, Max sprang and kicked the razor away. In the same motion he smashed his knee into Sam's massive chest, sending him reeling back against the sofa where Alicia cowered in terror.

"You're better'n I thought, limey." Sam rubbed his chest and went into his boxer's stance. His defiant demeanor changed when Max picked up the razor and switched it back and forth, hand to hand, too fast for Sam's glazed eyes to follow. Sam wanted only to get with arm's reach of this intruder and smash his handsome face. He wanted to see those blue eyes go glassy and blood spew from his mouth as he swallowed his teeth.

In his weaving boxing pose, his hands up, Sam began stalking his prey. Then he stopped in astonishment. The blond man had flipped away the razor to the other side of the parlor.

""Come on, you ape," Sam heard in a British accent. "Show me what you can do without your little blade."

Betts smiled and looked quickly at Jeremy and Alicia, huddled together on the floor against the sofa. "Can you believe this guy? He's gonna let me beat out his few brains."

Sam closed on Max, flicking a jab that missed his nimble opponent. Sam pressed forward, jabbing the air again and following with a roundhouse right that merely stirred a breeze. He grunted with irritation, then yelled with pain when Max shot a quick kick to his stomach.

A smaller man would have crumbled from the kick. Sam Betts was merely stunned. He was immediately stunned again when the flat edge of Max's hand tore into his throat. Sam whirled, trying to confront his elusive target. Coward. Why won't he stand and fight? Suddenly Max was behind him. He powered a knee into his back that sent Sam on a stumbling run into the fireplace. Sam slapped ashes and coals from his shirt and pants, and turned to find Max calmly waiting for him.

"What kind of children have you been fighting, ape?" Max said in that British accent that Sam found more and more infuriating. As though he was laughing at him.

Sam Betts roared curses and charged. Max sidestepped the rush and put his foot out. The house shook as Betts charged head first into the wall. He turned, groggy, his hands up instinctively, waiting to counterpunch. He realized something was wrong. Terribly wrong. This man wasn't fighting by the rules. He wasn't even fighting by street rules he'd learned in Jersey and New York. He was fighting in a way Sam had never encountered. For the first time, the thought flickered through his moonshine addled mind that maybe he'd stepped into the wrong ring.

Sam didn't know it, but his belated instinct was correct. Max wasn't fighting by any recognized ring rules. He was in combat—fighting coldly, with calm calculation, the way he'd been taught in commando training. Where he'd been taught not merely to stop an enemy, but to kill him.

"Come on, you ape," Max taunted him. "Show me how you beat up girls and babies."

Betts pushed himself away from the wall, determined to grab some part of this man and beat him into a mess. Once he had him in a squeeze, he could deliver the killing body blows that had done in so many other unfortunate men. His long, muscled arms in a semi-circle, he moved toward Max, then swallowed a scream in his throat as a foot smashed brutally into his testicles. Sam plunged forward, his arms vainly groping to envelop his elusive prey.

To Sam's surprise, Max again moved toward him, not away. Inside Sam's arms, Max shot precise jabs to the big man's weakening ribs, then upward into his throat. Sam was out of wind and out of strength, unable to parry the rapid chops to his throat.

Max revolted at the dirty, sweaty smell of this brute, a smell that reminded him of the stable hands. Another hard jab to Sam's solar plexus sent him heavily to the floor in a landing that shook the stone-based house. Sam Betts lay on his back, groaning and hardly moving.

Max was breathing harder now. Must get myself back into condition, he thought. His trainers didn't graduate men who would become so winded after so brief an encounter. He looked at Jeremy and Alicia still huddled on the carpet against the sofa, both speechless with astonishment that he had dispatched a brute who, but a few minutes ago, had had their lives at his mercy. And for Jeremy, more than his life had been on the chopping block.

"I trust you are safe, sir? And madam?" Max said nonchalantly, smiling.

Jeremy nodded feebly, as though in a trance, still too paralyzed with terror to so much as move to dress himself. He was paying little attention to Alicia's sobs.

Max seemed amused. Addressing Alicia, he nodded toward the heap on the floor that was Sam Betts. "And you actually have an affection for this gorilla?"

"No, no!" She hugged the negligee to cover her breasts. "I don't like him. I never did. Honest. He scares other men away from me."

""I daresay," Max said, seemingly to himself. "Please relax, madam. Stop trying to cover yourself. A whore is a whore. I've seen them before. So has my master there. We didn't meet in Westminster Abbey, you know."

"We...we have to...get him out...of here," Jeremy stuttered, unsteadily getting to his feet and fumbling to get his pants on.

Max looked at Alicia. "Is there any chance this fellow will want to return?"

When she stumbled with an answer, he raised his voice. "Is there any chance he'll come back looking for you? Or Mr. Mann? Or are you all he wanted?"

She sobbed. "I don't know. I'm scared of him. Everybody is. He's the meanest man on the whole coast. I just wish he'd go back where he come from."

Max saw that Sam Betts was stirring on the floor. "Then we'd best make certain he has no desire to return."

"Max, you can't...kill him," Mann said in a stutter.

"Actually, I can," Max said. "But let's think of something else. We don't want the local constabulary looking for us on a murder charge, do we? Alicia, who is this pile of dung?"

"He's Sam Betts."

"And why is Sam so feared, other than that he's a big, strong bully?"

"He's a fighter. He used to fight up north. In New York and places like that. I hear he's always been in trouble with the law. He's Mr. Sanford's bodyguard. I hear tell he killed somebody up north. Mr. Sanford got him off. He knows people."

"A fighter." Max looked at Sam Betts, still on his back groaning. "Thought I recognized the form. Yes, I think I know an appropriate disposal of our friend Sam."

"Disposal?" Mann was shaking. "I said no..."

"Murder? No. Too many problems. I don't have murder in mind, though I shouldn't think it would bother you, considering his plans for you."

Max chuckled when Mann involuntarily clasped his

hands over his crotch.

The ringing of the phone came as the tolling for an execution. Max picked up the receiver and answered calmly. "Mann residence. What's that? Yes, Mr. Deveau. No, Mr. Mann's taking his bath just now. This is his valet, Mr. Lewis. May I be of assistance?"

Max's amused eyes scanned Alicia and Mann as he talked. "No, Mr. Deveau. We haven't seen Mr. Betts. And he left your house about an hour ago? Well, if he was coming here, I should think he would be here by now. Yes, we'll certainly be on the lookout. He alarmed Mademoiselle Cardiene? I'm sorry to hear that. Thank you for calling. And good night to you, too, sir."

Max smiled. "That was Mr. Deveau. It seems Sam stopped by his house about an hour ago and put a fright into the mademoiselle. That's where he thought Miss Jackson was lodging, poor fellow. After they explained the situation to him he went on his way. I assured him we would keep an eye out for Sam."

Max looked across the parlor to the door where Charlie was incredulously surveying the scene. "Charlie, would you care to retire to your quarters? Everything seems quite under control here."

Charlie grinned nervously. "Yes sir, Mr. Max. Mr. Mann, I'm sure glad you're safe."

Max crossed the parlor and put his hand on the shaking old man's shoulder. "Charlie, you won't tell anyone what you saw here, will you?"

"No sir, Mr. Max. Not if you say so."

"Splendid. You have a good night and sleep tight." Max gave Charlie a friendly slap on his back.

Sam groaned and tried to roll over, unsure where he was. Max bent over him and, without a word, drove another precise punch into his solar plexus. Sam went totally limp, gasping.

Max spoke calmly. He had recovered his breath. "Now Sam, we don't particularly appreciate the way you barged in on us tonight. You've really been a great bother, to tell the truth. Since we can't really trust you to stay away, we have to discourage this kind of impromptu visit. Besides, there's a bit of a score we need to settle for your rather crude behavior toward Mr. Mann and his guest. Pity you acted so rashly. We were just about to return her to you."

Max picked up Sam's limp wrist and examined his hands. "Yes, I suppose you were a pugilist of sorts. Strong hands with all the correct scars. You used this hand rather efficiently, didn't you? He did, didn't he, Miss Jackson?"

Alicia nodded, wide-eyed. She and Mann shrieked at Sam's sudden scream when Max bent back Sam's big fingers on his right hand and broke them. Just as casually, he picked up Sam's left hand. He took the wrist in both hands and twisted it like a stick. The wrist bones crackled like muffled rifle fire. When Max looked back at them, both had hands to their mouths, trying to hold back vomit.

"I think I've neutralized Sam," Max said. "It should be some time before he poses a threat again. Shall I bundle him off to the village?"

Jeremy Mann struggled to keep his stomach under control. "I...I'd forgotten how brutal...how efficient you are, Max."

"It's not the end of the world for him. The last fellow I did this to regained enough control of his hands to take up cooking. He became a passable chef. Perhaps Sam will also learn a trade. Are you feeling well, Miss Jackson. You look somewhat pallid."

She sobbed. "Did you...did you have to do that to him?"

"Couldn't be helped. With his temperament it would've

done no good to send him on his way uneducated. He would've come back again. In time, I'm sure he'll regain his touch, if that means anything to you."

"No, no. I don't want to see him ever again. He'll sure enough be mean to me now."

"Perhaps this experience will mellow him. He has a long recovery period ahead and it'll give him time to ponder his future. Now, would you both be kind enough to get dressed? We need to return him to town."

They both retrieved their clothes, she from her bedroom and he from the floor. Max let Sam Betts regain his consciousness and led him to his car. Sam kept up a stream of moans and curses. Max forced him to lie on the back seat and bound him securely with rope around his arms. Sam redoubled his curses and moans of pain.

Max returned to the house. "Sir, if you and the lady will follow me, we can leave Sam in an appropriate medical facility and return here. I'll lock my quarters and we'll be on our way."

When Max opened the door of his cottage, he froze. He saw the blood puddles on the floor and his radio transmitter on the table. He dashed to the closet in his bedroom and found his photography equipment open. Outside he lost the trail of blood in the grass and darkness. He turned on the outdoor lights and used his flashlight to follow the smell of blood down the hill. When he reached the dock he found more blood and one of the small boats gone. Staring into the darkness of the river, he redoubled his curses. The blood hadn't been here just minutes ago when he'd charged up the hill to rescue Jeremy Mann.

Max bounded back up the hill to Sam's car and shined his flashlight into the suffering man's ugly face. "Did you go into that small house before you came to Mr. Mann's house?"

"I ain't telling you nothing."

Max squeezed Sam's broken hand. Sam screamed. "Lord, yes!"

"Did you see anyone there?"

Sam's slight hesitation got his mangled wrist a squeeze. "Lord yes! They was a man in there!"

"I found blood. Did you attack him?"

"I cut him. I cut him real good. Please, man, no more!"

"What did he look like?"

"He...he was pale. Black hair."

"Was he short as me? Taller?"

"Shorter. Kinda thin."

"What was he doing?"

"Messing with some machine. I don't know."

"Did he say anything?"

Sam went silent, gasping for breath.

"Tell me what he said or I'll break your hands all over again." He touched Sam's broken hand and brought another howl of pain.

"I don't know, man. I didn't understand him. Sounded like some foreign language."

Max's heart sank. Sam hadn't understood the intruder's language. But Max understood. A foreigner had found his radio and photography equipment. Volker was the foreigner. He'd found his equipment and messages. And now he was somewhere out there on that dark river drifting to who knew where.

"Sam, did you hurt the man?"

"I just remember cutting him. He was on the floor when I left. Hell, I didn't know he was your friend."

"He wasn't."

Max wearily stepped back from the car. Jeremy and Alicia had gotten into the Packard. He signaled for them to lead him to the hospital and slid behind the wheel of Sam's old car.

Where in this god-forsaken country could Volker be? The river flowed miles to the sound and into the Atlantic. Volker could be drifting there to rendezvous with U-boats, or he could be holed up somewhere on the river. His most rational move would be to find medical help, but that would give him away and assure an American execution.

He had to be found. He'd had the radio equipment out before Sam cut him short. But how short? Had he gotten through to Berlin before the interruption?

Welling with fury, Max cranked Sam's old car and drove down the driveway toward Brunswick.

Where the hell is Volker?

Chapter Twenty-Three

WITH JEREMY MANN and Alicia leading in the Packard, Max followed them into town to the hospital. He pulled Sam Betts from his car and stood him up in the parking lot before untying him.

"There now, Sam. You can walk right in and obtain all the medical help you require. Don't expect the impossible. I doubt they'll be able to make you fit enough to fight in a ring again. You might have some trouble with those chaps you've slapped around in the past. But I can't always be around to protect you, can I?

"Listen carefully, Sam. It's vital that you remember a couple of points. One, you hurt yourself when you fell off a boat onto the dock. Or, some such. Take your choice of places to fall. Just don't tell the authorities how you were injured, or where. Understand? Two, if you ever threaten me or Mr. Mann again, I won't go so easy on you next time. Understood?"

Sam remained sullen. "I'll kill you if I ever see you again."

"Do you understand me?" Max repeated, reaching for Sam's splintered wrist.

Sam grimaced and stepped back. "Yeah."

"That's a good fellow, Sam. If anyone asks, Miss Jackson drove you here to get medical attention. We're going to send her on home with your vehicle. You can collect it later. And remember, not even a threat to her."

Max walked back and opened the door for Alicia. Her eyes pleaded. "You're not going to hurt me too, are you?"

"Of course not, Alicia. I want you to take Sam's car back with you. If anyone asks, tell them he asked you to drive him here."

Alicia tried to hug Jeremy. "Let me stay with you, hon. I'll go anywhere with you. New York. Anywhere."

"Ask John Sanford to take you with him," Jeremy said calmly without emotion.

"Sam will kill me. Please take me with you."

"Sam will be in no condition to injure you or anyone else,"" Max said, taking her by her arm and firmly pulling her from the car.

Max climbed into the car beside Jeremy and left Alicia outside the hospital with Sam Betts. They remained silent during the drive back to Pineland. Max welcomed the silence and pondered his vital need to find Volker. Jeremy Mann interrupted his thoughts when they drove past the road that led to Clarke Deveau's house.

"Deveau." Jeremy spat the name bitterly. "Max, I want you to go there tomorrow and tell that French bitch I have news of her father. But she must talk to me in person at my house."

"What makes you think she'll come?" Mann's interruption irritated Max.

"She'll go anywhere for news of her father."

"You're still planning your reception for your father and

the scientists?"

"Yes. But first I want to know I've sampled the best of France's vineyards. That's why I rescued her from London. She thought she was to spend time raising support for France. This time she won't walk out on me."

Max chuckled without mirth. "In both our countries, that's known as rape."

Jeremy looked at Max. "As capable as you are, I've underestimated you, Max. I won't forget what you did for me tonight. How on earth you could've handled that monster so easily, crippled him...damn, you scare even me."

"The secret of avoiding a problem is to eliminate the problem. Sam will never bully anyone again. He'll stay quiet because he'll be ashamed to admit what happened to him. He has only himself to blame. A less sensitive man would've killed him with his own razor. Given the circumstances, I'm rather surprised you didn't insist on it."

"Damn! Drop it!" Jeremy instinctively put a hand on his crotch to reassure himself everything was still there.

Max gladly obliged him and turned his thoughts back to Volker. With luck, Heydrich's man had capsized and been silenced forever in the murky river. But Max knew better than to trust to luck. He knew too many men who had trusted luck once too often.

Max and Jeremy briefly bade each other good night when they arrived back at Pineland. Jeremy hesitated in the doorway of the big house, as though fearful that somehow Sam Betts was waiting inside for him. He looked back at Max. "Damn, Max. Where did you learn to fight like that? To break a man into pieces?"

"An old family skill."

"Some family." Jeremy shook his head. "See me tomorrow. We'll plan our invitation to the mademoiselle."

Max hurried to his cottage and examined it thoroughly.

Volker had seen the letters and the microdots, no doubt. The microscope was out, so he undoubtedly knew the contents of the microdots. Had he been able to convey the contents to his superiors in Berlin? If so, the tensions between the Abwehr and SD intelligence agencies in Berlin would explode into repercussions that would reach the Fuhrer himself. Worse, by now the information would soon bring other SD agents with murderous orders to tail him through the Spanish moss.

Max knew he had to find Volker, learn what he knew and what he had transmitted back to the SD. The only way to do that was to transmit to Volker's contact in the Hamburg station. Even though Hamburg was on the other side of the ocean, he felt himself sweating as he made his transmission. He found receivers waiting, as though to receive the completion of an incomplete transmission.

Max thought about his message. He decided it would be best to proceed as though they hadn't heard anything from Volker. Hamburg's response would give him clues about how much they had heard.

So Max affirmed his plan to carry out the abduction this weekend. He confirmed the plan to move the U-boats up the American coast into position off Jekyll. Hamburg acknowledged the transmission. Then came the query: "Advise disposition of Sturmhauptfuhrer Volker."

Max keyed his response. "Sturmhauptfuhrer Volker at ready. Advise."

The reply to await further instructions shocked him. Why await instructions if the plan was still in place? Instructions from whom? Knowing the personalities of the deadly rivals in Berlin, he had the disquieting feeling that Heydrich had hijacked the mission from Canaris. That meant the SD was altering plans, setting him up for capture in a venture they planned to carry out on their own. But he had to find Volker to be certain. He could very well have transmitted with his radio before coming here to be interrupted by Sam Betts. How much had he told them? Had they indeed ordered the U-boats to follow through and proceed to Jekyll as planned?

At daylight Max got into the Chris Craft and slowly cruised the Altamaha River, searching its banks and marshes for the missing boat. He saw numerous abandoned boats, but not the one taken from Pineland last night. The recent floods had washed so much debris downriver that it was impossible to make a thorough search.

At mid-morning he dejectedly pulled back to the dock at Pineland. Where the hell was Volker? He knew intuitively that the SD man had gotten through with information that had led Heydrich to seize control of this mission with plans to leave him to face American guns.

CHAPTER TWENTY-FOUR

MOSES DICKEY SAW the small boat in the flooded marsh grass. The boat had caught in debris that had washed down from the flooded upcountry.

Moses paddled into the marsh toward the orphan boat. He whistled to himself when he got close enough to see the body in the boat. A man, his lifeless hand holding a bloody handkerchief to a gaping slit in his throat. Blood mixed in red and pink puddles with the muddy river water on the floor of the boat.

Moses paddled alongside the boat to get close enough to poke at the man. No response. He looked closely at the man and saw that he had two bad wounds: One under his ribs, the other across his throat. The man clearly had died from these cuts, most likely from a knife. A sharp knife.

Moses tied a rope to the boat and paddled to shore where he began pulling it to him. He called for his two oldest boys who were close enough to hear him yell. They took hold of the rope and helped him pull the boat to shore. Their eyes bugged when they saw the body.

"He's dead?" seventeen-year-old Ezra asked unnecessarily.

"He shows all signs of it," Moses said.

"Cut real bad," said the other boy James. "Reckon who he is?"

"Was," Moses said. "Looks like somebody mistook him for a slab of bacon."

"You going to call the law?" James asked.

Moses stood looking at the body in the boat, his hands in his overalls. "Not sure that's a good idea."

Both boys helped their dad work the moonshine still, so neither had to be told why calling the law might be a bad idea.

Ezra kept his eyes on the man in the boat. "Mr. Clarke Deevoe's a lawyer. Reckon we might tell him instead?"

Moses grunted and Ezra knew he had come up with a good idea. "Let's wait maybe another hour before you run over and let him know. Don't be taking him this kind of story before his breakfast."

They walked around the boat speaking in grunts about who this man might be and why he was here in this boat with two mouths and a slit belly. After an hour, Moses sent Ezra running to tell Clarke Deveau.

Clarke was finishing breakfast and drinking a second cup of coffee when he heard Annie tell someone to wait there at the back door and she'd see if Mr. Clock even wanted to speak to somebody whose daddy made liquor. Clarke went to the door with his coffee and grinned at Ezra. "Morning, Ezra. You got a couple quarts for me?"

Ezra ran his words together telling him what his dad had found in the boat up the river. Clarke put his cup of coffee on a table. "I'll come and take a look. Annie, serve Marie breakfast while I'm gone. I'll be back soon."

"I'd be surprised that girl's up before dinner time,"

Annie said.

"Are you leaving so early?" Marie walked into the kitchen yawning.

Clarke winked at Annie who turned away. "I need to go with Ezra for a few minutes."

"Is something wrong?"

"No, ma'am," Ezra said. "We just found a dead man in a boat up near our place. He's cut up real bad, like a hog. He's bled white as a catfish's belly."

"Get on away from here before you ruin Miss Marie's stomach," Annie scolded. Ezra retreated from the steps and waited for Clarke to get his keys and give him a ride back to the river.

Clarke gagged when he saw the blanched, lifeless body.

"Do you know this fellow, Moses?"

"No, sir. Never seen him before."

The body looked ghostly and Clarke didn't dwell on him long. "I'll tell the coroner where he is and he'll take it from there. Somehow he looks familiar, even drained of blood."

"You don't think the law will think I'm involved, do you, Mr. Deevoe."

"No, you reported it."

"Yes sir, I did sir. But sometimes that puts you in the law's sights."

Clarke slapped Moses on his shoulder and told him not to worry. He went on to town and reported the body to Henry Brogan and the sheriff. Then he went to the small house where he had set up an office. As an afterthought he called David Warren. Mr. Warren was rather busy, said his secretary, and he'd call back if he had any questions. Seems the coroner had just called him.

At mid-afternoon David Warren called. "This guy's foreign. His papers show he shipped in on an Argentine cargo ship that left port days ago. We're checking the waterfront boarding houses to see if he had a room down there. Strange he'd be upriver in a boat bled dry. But it's been a strange day."

"Oh?"

"Guess who the hospital called about? Ever hear of a fighter named Sam Betts? Sort of a handyman for John Sanford over on St. Simons. He won't be handy anymore. Would you believe that fool turned up at the hospital last night with both hands crippled? Multiple fractures in both. Says he fell off a boat onto the dock. Must've been into some good shine."

"Betts? He was at my place yesterday drunk and waving around a straight razor."

Clarke surmised that crime detection was only part-time work for David. It took him several seconds to draw a connection. "The hell you say. Betts was drunk and waving a razor around, and I've got a sliced up corpse. I think maybe he owes me a better explanation."

Go get him, Clarke thought, hanging up. Where have I seen that corpse before?

CHAPTER TWENTY-FIVE

WHEN MARIE RETURNED from her ride in early afternoon, Max was waiting for her under the oaks in Clarke's front yard. Annie had refused to invite him in or even to offer him a glass of tea while he waited. He seemed agitated, pacing the lawn under the oaks. She watched from the window as Marie warily approached him.

Max smiled and bowed in mock civility. "Mademoiselle Cardiene, I'm happy to see you're enjoying your accustomed lifestyle."

She answered with silence.

"Monsieur Mann wishes you to know that his contacts with Free France in London have informed him that reports of your father's death were premature. He's working to confirm the report now. He wonders if you might be interested to be nearby when he places the call. Due to the demand on communications facilities for actual war purposes, such calls can be sent and received only a pre-arranged schedule to selected civilians such as Monsieur Mann."

She was instantly alert. "He has heard from mon pere? What did they say?"

Max smiled to himself at the sudden glow of excitement in her eyes. "He didn't divulge the details to me. He said only that he felt the information would interest you."

"There's nothing more you can tell me?"

He found the plea in her voice amusing. "I'm sorry. He said nothing more to me about his contact."

"How did he receive the message? Who sent it?"

"Mademoiselle, I'm only a messenger."

He saw doubt flash in her eyes. "Monsieur Max, you are not just a messenger. He depends on you. You know all about him. He would trust you with his life."

"You overestimate my importance, mademoiselle. Will you come with me to listen to the transmission?"

Despite yearning for news of her father, she was afraid of being alone with Max. Despite his disclaimer, he was no mere lackey. And there was another matter. "Who is with Monsieur Jeremy now?"

Max laughed. "No one."

"No one?" She was doubtful.

"No one. He tired of the young woman and sent her home. I took her myself."

Marie didn't answer. Max knew she was struggling to decide whether he was lying or toying with her. Finally she nodded. "Tell Jeremy to call me himself. I want to hear from him about mon pere."

"As you wish, mademoiselle. He only wished that you know what he has learned. He'll be making contact again later this evening." Max bowed and got back into the MG. This arrogant bitch will deserve whatever Mann does to her, he thought. Perhaps I myself will partake of her pleasures before returning to the fatherland. It would be small payment for the interruption of his vital quest to find

Volker before he could make contact with Berlin--if he had not already done so.

Annie met Marie at the door. "What did that man want, honey?"

"He told me that Monsieur Jeremy has news that mon pere may still be alive," she said softly, as though afraid to voice the very thought.

"Mon per? Who's that?"

"My father, Annie. He returned to France to resist the Germans and I've had no news of him for months."

"Why, that's good news, honey. How come you look so down?"

"Because he says I have to come to his house when he makes the call to England. That's the only way I can hear the news myself."

"Go back to him? Is that safe?"

"I don't know. There's just something...I don't like Monsieur Max. He scares me. Something feels wrong. Maybe it's because I've already accepted mon pere's death."

"That Mr. Mann's a scoundrel, honey. You right to mistrust him."

Marie fixed a cup of hot tea and took a piece of cake into the parlor to sit near the phone. Her eyes roved over the old room, feeling almost at home in it. Of course, she realized. Some of this furniture had come with the Deveau family from an older France to Haiti and then here. The faces in portraits of uniformed Clarkes and Deveaus could've been Cardienes. She was looking at the old Confederate sword hanging beneath the flags when the telephone startled her. She grabbed it from the wall.

"Bonjour."

"Bonjour, Marie. Jeremy here. Max says you want my personal assurance that I've heard news of your father"

"Oui. What have you heard?"

"That the report of your father's death was erroneous. Free France has received a message that they believe came from him."

"They told me he parachuted into a German area."

"He could've escaped if he knew the terrain better than the Germans."

"Did he send any message for me? Could I return to him in England?"

"The Brits don't need anyone else to look after now. And your father's survival hasn't yet been confirmed."

"You can tell me nothing else?" she said with resignation. "I want to go back to England."

"Come now, Marie. Going to England wouldn't help. But I can communicate directly with Free France. I have the proper radio equipment here. It's necessary in my business. I communicate with associates in several countries. At certain times of the day when frequencies aren't monopolized for state affairs, it's possible for individuals to communicate. Usually between four and eight, our time. That's only a couple hours from now. The sooner we try, the better the chance of getting through. If you can come on up now, we'll learn what we can about your father."

"Why have you not told me before about your radio?"

"I had no news until now. Fortunately, one of the French officers I used to drink with remembered that you left with me and got this message to me. Shall I send Max for you?"

"No," she said immediately at the thought of being alone with Max. But the urge to know about her father was stronger than her caution toward Max. "I must know about mon pere. I'll ride over."

"As you wish."

She hung up the phone and grabbed Annie's plump

arms, vainly trying to pull the stout woman around in a dance. "Annie, I'm going to talk to London. Can you imagine? I'm going to talk to them and find out about mon pere."

"How you gonna do that, honey?"

"Monsieur Jeremy can make calls across the ocean. He's going to talk to Free France today. They may have news of mon pere."

Annie pulled back from Marie's grip. "You mean you're going back to that house?"

"Just for a few hours. I'll ride one of the horses. "

"Mr. Clock won't think much of you going back there, especially by yourself. If that man's got a way to talk to your pa, why didn't he say so before?"

"He hadn't heard anything from them until now."

Annie's frown cut deeply across her face. "Honey, I think you ought to tell Mr. Clock before you go."

"I don't like to bother him. He's busy. Oh, perhaps you're right. I'll call him."

She let the phone ring a dozen times and got no answer at the office of Clarke Deveau, Private Investigator. He was out working, she thought. I won't disturb him.

"Will she come?" Max asked when Jeremy Mann stepped onto the veranda and inhaled the clean country air.

"Of course."

Jeremy sat at a table with a file on an oil proposal drawn up by George Hertle. It provided that Venezuelan oil would be shipped to ports in France and Spain, then to North Africa. Field Marshal Erwin Rommel was pushing the British across North Africa and would soon have control of the Middle Eastern oil fields. But Jeremy knew that for Rommel to completely drive out the British, he and Germany needed every drop of oil it could get from any source.

"Then we'll deal through our contacts in Cairo once Rommel gets there," Jeremy said, more to himself than to Max.

Max wasn't listening. He was more concerned about a wounded man who'd gone downstream last night than about someone who would come riding up the road this afternoon. He cursed at this silly affair between his master and a French woman. He'd had no choice but play along as the faithful servant to hide his cover. Damn Sturmhauptfuhrer Volker. Damn that woman. Damn Jeremy Mann's lust for her. He vowed that he would take his full measure of the beautiful mademoiselle while Mann watched.

CHAPTER TWENTY-SIX

WHEN MARIE RODE UP the lane to Pineland, Jeremy Mann smiled and put down the file he pretended he'd been studying at the table on the veranda.

"I trust you had a pleasant ride, cherie," he said, going to greet her.

"Nice, merci. Spring here makes me want to be outside."

She's in a good mood, he thought. That will make this easier.

Max appeared on cue to take Marie's horse. She noted the tension in his expression and held back a moment when he reached for the reins, then handed them to him.

"Yes, it is a fine day except for this morning. Some of Monsieur Clock's neighbors found a dead man in a boat on the river. He went to see the body and called the police."

Max froze. "Where did they find the man?"

"On the river near Monsieur Clock's house. The poor

man had been badly cut."

"Was he black?" Mann asked absently.

"No. The man told Monsieur Clock he was white as fish."

"Did you see him, mademoiselle?" Max asked.

"No. Monsieur Clock would not let me go with him. I am happy he did not. I have no stomach for such sights. I saw enough death when the Germans came to France."

"Come, come," Jeremy said, gesturing toward the veranda where a bottle of French wine sat on a table. "Enough about Southern violence. This could be the happiest day of your life."

Max led the horse to the stable, feeling a mixture of elation and dread. The dead man in the boat must be Volker. Wonderful. But had he gotten off a message to Berlin before his gruesome demise? If so, avenging replacements were already on the way.

For now Max put aside his anxiety to play his part in Jeremy Mann's scheme. He smiled at the simplicity of the plan. Jeremy would pretend to call London each hour and Max would reply in his proper British accent that all lines were busy. Marie would never guess that the calls were only a few hundred feet apart. Jeremy planned on Marie's anxiety to push her to take one drink after another while they waited for a response from Free France. By evening Jeremy was counting on the wine to leave her susceptible to his suggestion that she continue to wait for a call to be routed to Free France. By then, she would be in his power, willing or not.

The wait gave Max time to ready his last post to the mail drop in Arlington and messages to the stations in the Caribbean tracking the U-boats. He felt relieved that Volker had been removed from the equation, unless he had gotten off incriminating messages to his superiors in Berlin.

But Max was too experienced in the ways of hide-and-seek to feel completely at ease. Some clue to Volker's identity could be traced back here.

Just another twenty four hours, Max thought. Just another twenty four hours. Then the local polizei could investigate all they pleased.

When Clarke returned to his office he called home and Annie told him Marie had returned to Pineland.

"Damn!"

"Sir?"

"Forget it, Annie. Sorry."

"Mr. Clock, she said it was something about her daddy. That big guy that talks funny come and told her."

He sat back wearily in his creaking chair and looked out the window. What could this mean? Was Marie really so naive? Was Mann's lifestyle too much for her to give up? Maybe she'd lied about her treatment there.

Now he was happy he'd controlled his feelings for her, just as he was about to let them rush out from behind the dam where he'd contained them. He had thought for just a few hours that love for someone had somehow come back into his life. If he had let her, Marie could have hurt him as badly as Liz had. No. If she had no better judgment than to go back to a man she had vowed she hated, she was better off gone.

He turned from the window and called David Warren who was back relaxing in his office.

"Anything new on the guy we found up here in the boat this morning?"

"Not yet. But some folks near the docks identified his picture, such as it was. Could take a while to find where he was renting a room. He might've been staying on a ship, or with some whore in town."

"What's the story on Betts?"

"Doesn't want to talk. Seems upset about his girl friend."

"You do know who she is, don't you?"

"No. I just figured it was some whore in town."

"Name was Alicia Jackson. That's who he was looking for at my house."

"The gal who was Miss Glynn County a couple years back?"

"That's her. She and Betts both work for a John Sanford on St. Simons."

"I know of him. Rich guy with shady connections up north. Legal moonshine, as I hear it."

"Betts was looking for her with a razor when he came to my house. Thought she was there. My tenants sent him on the way to Pineland. Now he turns up busted, a corpse turns up gutted, and we don't even know about Miss Jackson. Is she missing too?"

"Damn. I'll get to Sanford lickety split. Wish you'd told me this before."

"Yeah. Could be a connection."

"Let me know if you think of something else you forgot to tell me."

Clarke told him he certainly would. Where had he seen the drained corpse before?

John Sanford told David Warren that Sam Betts had been missing for two days and Alicia Jackson for three. Of the two, he missed her most. No, he didn't know where they were and, truth be told, wouldn't be surprised if they'd run off together. What she saw in a thug like him, he didn't know. What, you say Sam had an accident? No, hadn't heard about that. Sure hope he's OK. Yes, Alicia has an address in Brunswick.

Dave relayed the information to Sheriff Roy Hazel who

was thinking of going home to supper in a couple hours. He turned to a deputy waiting for his shift to end. "Phil, check out the address. See if Alicia's there, knows anything about Betts."

Phil grumbled all the way to his car. When he knocked on the screen door to the small frame house, a gray haired woman cautiously answered. "Like to see Alicia," Phil said.

"She left."

"Where'd she go?"

"Don't know."

Phil heard voices inside the house and took off his hat. The woman looked irritated the speakers hadn't kept their voices down. After a moment of staring at the badge on Phil's chest, she stepped back. Phil followed her into the kitchen and temporarily lost his speech when the saw the beautiful girl with long blond hair. She's mixed up with a Yankee gorilla?

"Lisa, the man says he wants to talk to you."

Alicia's eyes showed fright. "What for? I been here in the house all day."

Phil shook himself from his trance and remembered why he'd come. "You know Sam Betts?"

Alicia's eyes darted to both the women with her. Three generations under one roof, Phil guessed.

"No," Alicia said.

Phil pretended to be embarrassed. "Well, miss, I know you do. Don't reckon you know where he is now."

"Why should I? I haven't seen him in several days."

'How long?"

"A week or two."

"He was looking for you last night."

Alicia's eyes again darted to the two women with her, then back to Phil. "How come you want to know?"

"He threatened some folks up the river last night."

"Who did he threaten?"

"Mr. Clarke Deveau. And the people who live at his house."

"Deveau? You mean that lawyer?" Alicia relaxed. So the complaint had come from Deveau, not Jeremy as she'd feared.

"He used to be a lawyer up in Washington. He's sort of a detective now. Used to own that big house where Jeremy Mann lives."

"Well, I heard Sam got hurt," Alicia said.

"Hurt? How?" Now we're getting somewhere, Phil thought.

"I don't know for sure. Did that lawyer hurt him?"

"No, not Mr. Deveau," Phil said, amused by her evasions. "Sam was threatening the folks at Deveau's place with a straight razor. Said he was looking for you. They sent him on up to the big house. Next thing we know we've got a guy with his throat cut, like with a razor. Happened last night, we figure. Maybe around the same time Sam was out looking for somebody to cut. Did he come on up to the big house?"

"Lord no. Never saw him. Did he kill this other guy?"

"That's what we're investigating, miss. Sam's over in the hospital with multiple fractures, as the doctors say. Do you know how he got that way?"

"No," Alicia said quickly. "I didn't see him last night. I just heard downtown this morning that he got hurt."

Phil sighed in resignation. This girl was going to dance around her story all night. It might even be right, for all he knew. But it was supper time and his shift was supposed to have ended an hour ago. He thanked her for her time and excused himself.

When Phil was gone, Alicia ran to her room and locked the suitcases she'd been packing. "That's it, momma. I'm leaving here."

"You got no place to go, honey."

"Anywhere else is fine. I know how to make out."

Mrs. Jackson nodded with sadness. She knew all too well how her daughter would make out.

Alicia picked up the suitcase from the bed and set it on the floor. "I might just take off to Hollywood. Mr. Sanford says I could make it big out there."

David Warren's voice sounded unusually enthusiastic.

"Clarke, we lucked up and found the room our corpse was renting. Found some interesting items. I wouldn't tell you this, except you were at the Justice Department and may know something about it. One, this guy's got some kind of radio transmitter in his room. Two, he has a couple of pistols, both Lugers. What's really got me is this damned uniform in his suitcase. It looks like it's German."

"German?" Clarke sat alert, remembering the Germans who had come visiting Pineland days before.

"I think it's German. Beats all."

"Would you mind if I swing by and take a look?"

"Did you run across German uniforms when you were at Justice?"

"Briefly. Hitler was going into Poland as I was leaving DC."

Clarke went to the rooming house where David Warren and another policeman stood guard. The radio, pistols and uniform were arranged on the creaky bed. Dave gestured at the uniform. "What do you think?"

Clarke drew in his breath. He knew the uniform. He hadn't spent his entire career at Justice chasing mobsters who didn't pay their taxes. He had followed the rise of the Nazis in Germany and had been moving into espionage investigations when his career had come to its abrupt end.

Though he'd left the front lines, his prior knowledge of Hitler and Stalin was enough to keep him scanning the newspapers and Movietone News for information about the Nazis and Communists.

He recalled that when he'd left Washington, there was the feeling in the town that the world was full of goose-stepping Nazis marching toward America, notwithstanding the Atlantic Ocean in between. But there was also a calm conviction that Hitler's sinister forces would never invade the elegant privacy of Georgetown to disrupt the comfortable lives there. Some even thought they could deal with him as they already were with Stalin.

Yet, there on the bed was evidence that the threat had made it all the way to Brunswick. At Justice, Clarke had learned which branches of the Third Reich were involved in espionage. He knew he was looking at the SD uniform of the Gestapo's espionage arm, an organization hated and feared by Germans themselves.

What was an SD agent doing here? The SD almost always operated within Germany or its occupied territories. Foreign espionage was the job of the Abwehr under Admiral Wilhelm Canaris, not the shadowy Reinhard Heydrich who directed the SD.

David Warren interrupted Clarke's musing. "Think I ought to call the FBI or Army?"

"The FBI. This man was an agent. That's the FBI's business to investigate."

"Who would cut up a spy?"

"I couldn't say."

Dave shook his head slowly. "Wonder why this guy was here. They haven't even started the shipyard yet. Nothing much more than turpentine and lumber going through the port now."

Clarke didn't answer.

"Reckon he was after the millionaires?" Dave said.

Clarke shook his head. "I don't know what good they'd be to Hitler. They're no good to us."

Dave shrugged. "Anyway, most of them are leaving this weekend." Jerry was silent for a few moments. "Reckon he's the only one?"

"Hard to say. Like I say, call the FBI pronto."

"In Atlanta?"

"Wherever."

"Boy, a spy here in Brunswick. Can you beat it?"

Clarke shrugged that he couldn't beat it. He looked at Warren who didn't seem sure of what he wanted to ask.

"Who do I call? FBI people like to keep to themselves, you know."

Clarke hesitated. He knew exactly who to call. But he didn't want to even speak the name out loud, knowing the name on his tongue would taste like manure. He sighed. "Call a fellow named Alex Montgomery. In the Washington headquarters."

"You know this Montgomery?"

"Yeah."

"Might be quicker if you make the contact."

Clarke hesitated. He could just give Dave the number and let him make the call. After all, it was his investigation and, despite what Dave thought, the FBI would take tips from local law officials. Clarke could tell that Dave was awed by the FBI, the agency with great public relations that had been credited with running Capone and Dillinger and Pretty Boy Floyd to ground. Dave couldn't imagine his voice even getting into that big building up in Washington, D.C.

Clarke grunted. "Okay."

"You can call from my office."

"Thanks, but I'll use my phone. I'll call collect."

"You can do that?" David Warren's voice expressed awe. Would J. Edgar Hoover answer? "Shall we leave this stuff here for the FBI to handle?"

"Yes. Post guards and don't let anybody near this room."

Clarke drove back to his office and sat down at his desk. Yes, he'd make the call for good old Dave. But he wouldn't tell him the man at the other end of the phone up there in D.C. was another old Georgia boy.

Clarke sat at his desk with only a small lamp on, not wanting to make the call. Not that he was afraid to call. He just didn't want to. He never wanted to hear that man's voice again. When he had left Washington, he'd sworn that, if he ever saw Alex Montgomery again, he'd shoot him like a coon in a trap.

He jerked the receiver and dialed for the operator.

CHAPTER TWENTY-SEVEN

"M R. MONTGOMERY HAS LEFT for the day," said the efficient voice at the Federal Bureau of Investigation headquarters in Washington, DC.

"Then why are you still there, sweets? That is you, isn't it, Pamela Swift?"

The chirpy voice went icy. "You may call back tomorrow if you wish to speak with Mr. Montgomery."

"Tell Alex his old buddy Clarke Deveau is on the line all the way from Georgia. I'll hold for fifteen seconds. Counting one...two...three..."

"What the hell do you want?" came the familiar growl.

"Sounds like I interrupted you on the way to a good time, Alex. That sounded like Pamela Swift's still doing your stenography. You getting much?"

"You said fifteen seconds? Counting..."

"Then listen closely. I don't intend to repeat myself. Are you still helping J Edgar catch spies?"

"Every day."

"Something strange just washed up on shore. This is the

coast of Georgia, by the way. You ever get down this way anymore? We've found a foreign national with ID that says he was on a freighter that shipped out three days ago. The papers may be fake. We found him on the Altamaha in a boat. Somebody had given him a second mouth for grinning through his pain. Ear to ear. The perpetrator used the same method to tickle the organs under his ribs. Looked like an autopsy.

"The sheriff traced the fellow to his digs and found some interesting items. One, a radio transmitter. Two, an SD uniform. Whoops. I see my time's up. I'll call back tomorrow. Will Pamela keep you out late?"

Montgomery growled. "Come on, Deveau. What's the deal?"

"I just told you all I know. The deceased appears to be German. He has a uniform that matches a German espionage unit. And a couple German Lugers, which he should've been carrying with him, by all appearances. I haven't the foggiest what it means. That's your department. The local man didn't know who to call up there in such a big, important building."

"Thanks."

"Thanks? Damn. I must have the wrong number. Could you pass this along to J Edgar or that Montgomery guy?"

"I've wondered about you."

"You have a full file on me. It ought to answer any questions you have."

"Come off it, Deveau. There was nothing personal. I did exactly what you would've done in my place."

"Too bad I didn't get the opportunity to be in your place. Maybe I'd feel all kissy face about it."

He heard Alex Montgomery sigh. "Have you seen Liz?"

"No. Your file on her should be up-to-date, too."

"Just asking, for God's sake. Okay. What's the situation with the millionaires down there?"

"They're still rich and expect the war to make them even richer."

"Damned fools. They're sitting ducks for a kidnapping."

"They're safe, Alex. It's the end of their season down here in the Southern sun. Most will be back safe in their humble mansions up north in a few days."

"All right. Tell the coroner down there to keep this German stiff on ice. I'm sending a man from Atlanta. I'll have him check with you. He'll..."

"Wrong connection, Alex. I'm not a bloodhound anymore. Do your own legwork. If you could run down me and my ex, you can surely check out a Nazi who's not going anywhere."

"It wasn't personal."

"I know. My case just happened to land on your desk by chance."

"Anything else suspicious you can tell me about?"

"You take it from here. Should be a headline for the Bureau in it."

"One more thing, Clarke. Do you know a fat cat down there named Albertis Mann? Owns Mann Corporation."

"I know him only by name. And by his son who bought my old home place. Mann senior is a member of the Jekyll Club and that's off my beat."

"Okay."

"Say, is Crappie Chesson still around?"

"Crap...yeah, Chuck's still at Justice. Look, if you find out anything else, let me know. Or Theo when he gets there."

"Theo?"

"Theo Stevens. He's the man I'm sending from Atlanta."

"Tell him to look up the sheriff."

"Theo? Alex here. Get to Brunswick double quick. Look up Clarke Deveau. Don't let his grouchiness put you off. He's not on good terms with us."

"What's he going to tell me besides go to hell?"

"About a German they found down there. Got his throat cut in pig sticking style. The guy had a radio transmitter and SD uniform hidden in his room. And a couple of Lugers."

"In Brunswick? Damn. That's near Jekyll. Doesn't that fool Mann have those two scientists down there?"

"You bet he does. My guess is that's why the SD man was down there. I knew we should've been monitoring those mush heads in that club."

"How does Deveau fit in?"

"It's a long unhappy story that started when we roomed together at the university. Call if you need back-up. Don't try to play Texas Ranger on this one. Those millionaires are supposed to be gone by this weekend. Why Roosevelt's concerned about them, I don't know. Maybe because he's related to most of them."

"And after I talk to your friend Deveau?"

"You play it from there. Damn. I told them we should've assigned a couple men to watch that bunch down there. Everybody up here thinks all they need to do is let the Navy blow up a U-boat now and then. Which the Navy hasn't done much of, news reports to the contrary."

"If this Deveau's so hard to get along with, how will I get anything useful from him? Maybe he won't like my New York accent."

"That's why you were assigned to Atlanta. And I'm here. Don't worry. The people you talk to on the island are mostly from New York, too. It all has a logic."

"Maybe it'll become clearer to me when I get there."

"Get on down there, Theo. Deveau has no idea what he has stumbled into."

For minutes after hanging up, Clarke did a decent job of forgetting that he had actually allowed himself to talk to Alex Montgomery. And forgetting that day in 1938 when Assistant Attorney General Charles Chesson had summoned him to his office. To rid his mind of both memories, he called Annie on the chance Marie had returned. No luck.

"You and Jasper go on home, Annie. I'll eat here in town."

He went to the Oglethorpe Hotel for a plate of shrimp, oysters, fries, slaw and biscuits. But the hearty fare did nothing to banish the thought of that morning he'd marched into Chuck Chesson's office. Clarke called him "Crappie" behind his back because he maintained a demeanor that bespoke a perpetual urge to go to the can. Crappie had maintained his seat behind his big desk and didn't invite Clarke to sit.

"I have the report, Deveau." He held up a folder and threw it back on his desk.

"What does it concern?"

"Your wife."

"Liz? You have a file on her?" When he reached for the folder, Chesson pulled it away and leaned back in his leather chair.

"You've no idea what's in this file?"

"I don't read your files. Do you have one on your wife, too?"

Crappie glowered. "This file details your wife's relationship with several persons who are under your observation. In particular, she had a rather close relationship with one Ted Shultz of New York City. Mr. Shultz is familiar to you, I believe."

Clarke waited.

"Did you know of their relationship, Deveau?"

"Of course not. Where did you get this slander?"

"You're not aware of it even though your office has Shultz under surveillance? You are aware of his association with mobsters?"

"What're you saying, Chesson?"

"I'd like to know if you've discussed official business with your wife."

"You're implying I passed on information to Shultz through Liz?"

"I'm merely pointing out the possibilities for vital information to fall into the wrong hands. I never want there to be a reason for anyone to even question the integrity of my team."

"But now that integrity is in question?"

"Yes. This report on your wife is not public, nor need it be. I can understand innocent people feeling the need for thrills. Bad men have a certain attraction for the naive. Does Mrs. Deveau continue her association with Shultz?"

"I don't believe you, Chesson. Why are you asking? Doesn't that file in your hands have all the answers?"

"Have you thought about your next step?"

"My next step?" Clarke felt the sickness welling in his stomach.

"Yes. I can't...we can't abide questions about our honor. This raises questions in spades. You should see that."

"You want me out of the round table."

"That decision is yours. I hope you will think it over carefully and do the honorable thing."

"Really? Who compiled that file in your hands?"

"The Bureau, naturally."

"The Bureau. Naturally."

Chesson leaned back in his big leather chair with that look of extreme need to evacuate. Clarke turned and left, slamming the door in a way no one ever dared slam Chesson's door. After an hour collecting his wits in his office, he knew he had to talk to someone in the Bureau. Alex Montgomery. His old roommate at the University of Georgia. He'd know who was at the bottom of this.

Without calling, he went to the FBI building and presented himself to the receptionist outside Alex's office. Her name plate identified her as Pamela Swift.

The pert brunette smiled sweetly and asked, "Is Mr. Montgomery expecting you?"

"In a way."

"In a way?"

"Yes, he is," Clarke said firmly. The adorable Pamela scanned the appointment list on her desk and saw no Clarke Deveau there. She stood and lightly rapped on the door behind her. She stepped inside and, after a few seconds, emerged and smiled. "Go right in, sir."

Alex Montgomery had just passed thirty and looked well on his way to forty in his dignified pin stripes. The receding brown hairline topped an ordinary face holding brown eyes that did not twinkle. His thin lips did manage a suspect smile as he took his pipe in his left hand and extended his right.

"Good to see you again, Clarke. Strange we've seen so little of each other, working in the same town."

"Alex, you know why I'm here. I just had a discussion with Crappie about the Bureau's report on my wife."

"Your boss would be..."

"Crappie Chesson."

"Chuck. Yes, I've heard good things about his department. That reflects well on you."

"He wants the good news to continue."

"I don't understand."

Clarke knew Alex understood well enough to nervously relight his pipe for the first of half a dozen times over the next five minutes. Clarke suppressed the urge to comment on the inanity of engaging in an activity that fizzled every few seconds. The capital was full of pipe smokers, all relighting them in that thoughtful manner they believed befitted their image as statesmen-philosophers.

"Alex, I think you do understand. Your division heads up investigations into the New York and New Jersey mobs. Information on my wife Liz turned up in your reports. That means I'm also in your reports. I'd like to know exactly what you have on us."

"Clarke, surely you know I'm not at liberty to discuss our investigations. We gather information and then it's up to the authorities to act on that information. You yourself have been the recipient of our investigations."

"Of course I have. As you've said, the information you gather is shared with responsible authorities who decide on how to proceed. I'm in Justice. What you tell me will be in the strictest confidence."

Montgomery relit his pipe. "Really, Clarke, you know..."

"Dammit, Alex, you saw no danger sharing it with Crappie. Why didn't you come to me first? This is a serious mater here. And a personal one. That report can injure innocent people."

"Clarke, in strictest confidence, we found no incriminating evidence on you. Or Liz, for that matter. She has done nothing to warrant prosecution."

"Then why's Crappie so upset? Alex, what's with you? Why didn't you let me know I was under suspicion? Surely I'm the best authority on whether I've misused my position."

"Really, Clarke, it's unworthy of you to suggest I should've cleared our investigation with you."

Clarke stood as Alex relit his pipe. "Alex, we roomed together and you didn't even have the decency to let me in on this. Still rankles you that I got the scholarship and you didn't."

Alex couldn't answer before Clarke slammed his second door of the morning.

Clarke cancelled his appointments for the day and went home to his Arlington apartment to find Liz just arising, though it was late morning. He poured two coffees and handed one to her. Without more than a "good morning" he told her: "I may have to start making an honest living."

"Please. Anything but that."

"I'm on the department's hit list."

She looked puzzled. "What hit list?"

He took a deep breath. "Liz, you know about hits, hit men. How well do you know Ted Shultz?"

The coffee cup stopped near her lips, then she lowered it back to its saucer. Her eyes were suddenly sharp.

"Ted Shultz?"

"Ted Shultz." He set his coffee down. His stomach couldn't take it now. She knew Shultz. No doubt in his mind she knew him. "The Bureau has investigated him. You're in their file. That makes me a part of it."

"Who told you this?"

"The Bureau by way of Crappie who brought it to my attention rather forcefully. You know Shultz, don't you?"

"I've met him, darling."

"Met him? You do know what he is, don't you?"

"A businessman."

"Businessman! Like Al Capone's a businessman. Shultz is a hood, likely a murderer. How...how close are...were you to him?"

"Are you asking if I spied on the Justice Department for him?"

"Did you?"

She sipped her coffee, staring over the rim of her cup at him.

"Liz, how could you get mixed with a gangster? How?"

"I met him through friends in New York."

"Friends," he said bitterly. "Those long weekends in New York with your sorority sisters. Did all of you pick up mobsters?"

"You mean, how could a sweet upstanding Vassar girl do it?"

"If you want to put it that way."

She giggled. "Isn't this great? Making the most wanted list."

"It's the joke of the year at Justice. I'll wake up at three in the morning in hysterics."

"Darling. Do you mean I could actually cost you your job at Justice? Come on. You're a bright Georgia boy and you're going to become at least Attorney General."

"What happens if I don't?"

"Maybe Ted could give you a job. He needs bright lawyers."

He stomped to the window and slammed his fist on the sill. "Dammit, Liz. Maybe you can afford to take this lightly. This is no laughing matter."

"You're right, darling. I apologize. You know how much I want you to succeed. You came off that Georgia plantation and now you've worked your way this far. But Ted is just an old acquaintance."

"Acquaintance." He considered his next question before asking, wondering if he really wanted an answer. "Were you his mistress before I met you?"

"Whose mistress?"

"Ted Shultz's! Or anybody else's?"

She lit a cigarette and blew a ring of smoke toward the ceiling. "Bet you didn't know I could do that, did you?"

"Do what?"

"Blow smoke rings."

He slumped back against the wall, his tension and fight gone. She obviously felt no regret that she hadn't told him about her good friend, Ted Shultz.

He left the apartment and returned to his office to find Chesson off limits. Chesson and Liz competed to see which could be iciest over the next week. It took him that week to sort out his thoughts from the rubble of ashes that had been his dreams.

So he had made the decision Chesson hoped he would, to resign from Justice while the department was chortling about the hot shot who had married a mob moll. Not even his Princeton credentials were enough to get him even one offer from a law firm in the nation's capital.

After two months of rejections, he left Washington for good. His decision to leave came one evening when he followed Liz to the Mayflower Hotel where she met another of her old friends who was under investigation. That's when the .38 revolver came out. He didn't fire it, and still wondered why he didn't. He had them in his sights. But the judge understood "these passion things" and elicited his promise to leave the capital for good. Soon he was back at Pineland alone, explaining to his father why his son was unlikely ever to become the first President of the United States from Georgia.

He and Liz settled the divorce by long distance. A year later she married the honorable Lawrence Wills of New York, a publisher whose newspapers tended to be critical of police investigative methods. Ted Shultz was rumored to be a close acquaintance of Mr. Wills.

In the three years since he'd left Washington, Clarke had rarely thought about Crappie Chesson or Alex Montgomery, except for an occasional regret that he hadn't used the revolver on them. But the Washington police had kept his .38, removing his temptation to use it again. He knew only that Alex and Crappie had received promotions to deal with the increase of espionage brought on by the war.

"The U-boats are on schedule?" Oberguppenfuhrer Reinhard Heydrich had Abwehr director Admiral Wilhelm Canaris on the phone.

"Precisely. They're north of Cuba, on course for the target area."

"And the agents in the area?"

"Herr von Oster reports that all is in readiness."

"Good. Keep me informed." Heydrich slammed down the receiver.

"Something is wrong?" asked Brigadefuhrer Walter Schellenberg, ever sensitive to the moods of Heydrich.

"Obviously. Else Volker would've reported back to us."

Both men knew an SD officer would not dare go on a mission of this sensitivity without regular reports. Heydrich's men were trained that way. They knew that any deviation from duty would bring at least demotion, at worst death by a method that Heydrich felt would fit the dereliction.

"Could some mishap have befallen Volker?" Schellenberg suggested.

Heydrich spread his hands. "I fear so. This was his mission to carry through to execution. It presented an unequalled opportunity to gain glory for himself and the Reich. He knows he would've been lavishly rewarded by the Fuhrer himself. No, an SD officer would not defer to an Abwehr agent on such a mission as this."

"Will you allow the mission to proceed?"

Heydrich nodded glumly, his blue eyes full of anger and frustration. "We must retrieve von Richter. He's too important. For the moment we have no choice but to go along with the little admiral and his very questionable agent. How I wish we'd had his file before Canaris assigned him to America. Scheisse!"

"His file does raise suspicions, as you've pointed out."

"We would've determined the truth about him. This must not happen again. Once I make the Abwehr part of the SD, I'll deal with the admiral."

Schellenberg knew Heydrich would get what he wanted. Heydrich always got what he wanted. After all, he had the utmost confidence of the Fuhrer himself, and would eventually succeed the Fuhrer. Schellenberg approved Heydrich's determination to consolidate the two espionage agencies, though he did feel some regret that his friend Canaris would suffer in the process.

Jeremy Mann spent the evening pretending to reach Free France by radio in London. At last Marie fell asleep under the combined force of anxiety, exhaustion and wine she had sipped nervously since arriving here. He smiled and called Max to tell him his role in the ruse was completed. He lifted her in his arms and carried her to his bedroom.

CHAPTER TWENTY-EIGHT

A FTER DINNER, CLARKE went to the Ritz to see "The Apache Kid" starring Don Red Barry before going home to early bed. Now he ate breakfast silently as Annie talked non-stop. She thought he should call Jeremy Mann to see if Marie was well. He refused. Admittedly, he had hardly slept, waiting to hear her return. Now he felt tired and irritated for letting another woman get inside his defenses.

He picked up the Brunswick *News* in town and a quick scan told him that Karl Hermann Schroetter, a convicted Nazi spy, had hung himself in the Atlanta federal pen. Shroetter's ashes would be scattered over Biscayne Bay where he'd run a charter boat business for several years. And there was a photo of actor Lew Ayres having a meal in a conscientious objector camp in Portland. Clarke grunted with satisfaction to read that the danger of more flooding on the Altamaha River from melting snows in the uplands had passed.

When he reached his office , he found a thirtyish man in

a blue suit with black slicked back hair parted in the middle waiting outside.

"Theo Stevens," the man said in an accent that Clarke identified only as northern.

"I figured. Come on in."

Clarke pointed to a chair and Theo Stevens stretched into it while taking out a Camel and lighting it. He was all of six feet with bulk that looked strong, had gray eyes and a pallid complexion that demonstrated he had avoided the Southern sunshine.

"Alex Montgomery sent me."

"I don't know why. Didn't he fill you in on what I told him?"

"Only that you found a man, probably German, in a boat on the river near your house. And that the man had some serious incisions on his person. And that his papers traced him to a ship that left port days ago. And that you found a radio transmitter and an SD uniform in his room. That about it?"

"That's about it, except for the two Lugers we also found in his suitcase. You'll want to view the corpse and the room's contents for yourself."

"Yes. Any idea how this fellow met his fate?"

"Some. A former fighter from Jersey named Sam Betts came to my house two evenings ago."

"Betts? I saw him fight. Mean bruiser. He had champion potential, but he had trouble with the bottle. When he was sober, nobody wanted to fight him."

"He's still on friendly terms with the bottle. He'd patronized a local distillery and was waving around a straight razor. He was looking for a girl he thought had come to my place. She'd actually gone a few miles upriver to the Mann house that used to be my family's plantation. My tenants chased him off. He left saying he was going on up to the plantation. When I got home, I called Mann to warn him about Betts. Mann's valet answered and told me Sam hadn't been seen. Then next morning our corpse turned up in a boat grounded near my house with his throat and stomach cut open. So, by deduction, you'd have to conclude the deceased met his fate somewhere upstream, was put into the boat, and drifted downstream to where we found him."

"What does Betts have to say?"

"You'll need to talk to the county attorney. Betts turned up in the hospital. I don't know if he's still there."

"The girl?"

"She was a county beauty queen a couple years back. Claims to know nothing more than rumors about Betts getting hurt."

""Why did he land in the hospital?"

"Both his hands wee broken."

Theo Stevens whistled. "Rather disadvantageous for a boxer. I think I'll have a chat with Sam. The girl is in protective custody, I presume."

"Nothing to charge her with."

"She's linked to a murder suspect."

"That link isn't strong enough to hold her."

"Good grief. She could've left town."

"Yep."

"This plantation. Would that be the residence of Mr. Albertis Mann?"

"No. It's junior's place. The old man prefers companionship with his fellow money changers. He appears to shun his son's lifestyle there on the plantation."

"The beauty queen was with the son up there?"

"Yes."

"I'll want to talk to little Mann. Give me directions to the old plantation. Does he have a harem of slaves there?"

"None ever lived there." Clarke hesitated. "Might be another woman there now. French."

"He likes variety."

Clarke grunted sourly.

"I'll talk to Betts and the girl, unless she's flown the coop. Can't believe you guys didn't hold her. Can you direct me to the sheriff's office?"

"Thought you'd never ask. Why did Alex send you to me?"

"He explained you have company experience."

"I'm not with the company. You'll find the sheriff down the street."

Though the FBI man's accent put him on his guard, Sheriff Roy Hazel greeted him warmly and took him to see David Warren. The county attorney took Stevens to the room where the deceased had spent his few days in Brunswick.

Theo Stevens whistled when the saw the uniform and transmitter. There was nothing else that gave a clue as to the man's identity or purpose in being here, though Theo could easily guess the decedent wasn't a tourist.

"Still no clue why this guy was killed?"

"None from Sam Betts yet," David Warren said. "We may get something out of the girl. We picked up both of them last night at the bus station yelling at each other. Betts left the hospital without going through the usual checkout. Witnesses said he was telling the girl he'd kill her if he'd been in a condition to do it."

Theo Stevens perked up. Maybe these crackers could do something right after all. "You have both in custody?"

"Yes. Phil...one of our deputies...got a little suspicious about the girl's story when he talked to her yesterday. Said he had a hunch she was going to run. So he went by her house when he got off duty. Saw her leave and go to the bus station. That's where Sam Betts turned up and started yelling. He took both into custody. We even showed them our man in the morgue. Neither claimed to recognize him."

"Not surprising. I'd like to talk with both."

"Be my guest. I'd like to sit in. I've got a murder to solve. What you've got to solve, I don't know."

When the deputy led Betts into the interrogation room, Theo sensed his anxiety. He took a chair across the table, turned it backwards and saw down facing Sam.

"You say you never got up to the plantation?"

"No. I came on back to town. I'm really sorry I upset the folks at Mr. Deveau's place."

"That was maybe five in the afternoon?"

"Guess so. Sun was starting to set. I don't remember too well. I was drinking some."

"Yeah, that'll affect your memory. The hospital says you checked in there about ten at night with your hands broken. What happened between five and ten?"

"Like I said, I was drinking. I come on back to town and went to the docks. I was upset about Leesha. The guys on the docks got on me about it. I was so drunk I bet I could knock a hole in a wall with my fists. So we took the bets and I whammed the wall."

"Do you mean to tell me you were so drunk you threw the second punch when you felt the first one break your hand?"

"I was drunk, man. When you throw a one, the two just naturally follows. Automatic like."

Theo shook his head. "A professional fighter and you can't control your punches? Let's review your stories, Sam. First you said you broke your hands in a fall from a boat. The hospital's report is that fractures in one hand were caused by fingers broken, like in bent back. In your other, you wrist was shattered. Neither is consistent with throwing punches or falling. Can you explain that?"

"My hands are broken."

"Listen, Sam. It looks like somebody bent your fingers back and broke them. What happened to your wrist is anybody's guess. Not the sort of injuries you get from a fall. Or punching a wall. Who made the bet with you?"

"Several guys. I was too drunk to remember."

"Sam, I'm not drunk and I'm not stupid. Neither is Mr. Warren here. We can check the docks and see if you caused a ruckus. But we know you didn't break your hands using a wall for a punching bag. Now, it's very important that we know what happened to the fellow who got cut up. He had to have been up the river there when it happened. You were up there the same time, threatening to cut the folks at Deveau's house. You were mad enough to kill that man. Did you?"

"Why would I want to kill somebody? If I'd wanted to kill somebody, I'd of used my fists, not a knife."

"But you threatened the people at Deveau's place. Said you were going to rape that girl there. Another man had taken your girl, so some other man's woman would do just fine. You following me?"

Sam blinked, confused by Theo's logic.

"Sam, after you left Deveau's house, you had plenty of time to get up to the plantation, or any place in between, and do your work with the razor."

"I told you I'd a used my fists if I wanted to hurt somebody."

"Then why did you have that razor? Sam, where did you find that man in the morgue?"

"Never seen him before."

Theo suddenly switched his line. "Sam, how did you get to the hospital after you broke your hands?"

"I walked."

"Walked? Nobody offered you a ride?"

"Don't remember. I was drunk."

If he says that one more time, Theo thought, I'm going to break his legs, too.

"How did you know Alicia was at the bus station?" David Warren asked. "Did you follow her?"

"I just happened to be by there."

"Why? The hospital didn't discharge you. Your injuries are serious and they wanted to keep you under observation."

"I don't like hospitals."

Theo stood up and walked outside the room with David following.

"The guy's lying through his tonsils," David said.

Theo nodded. "Let's talk to the girl. Alicia's her name?"

"I don't know why Sam was at the station," Alicia said. She was irritated at being detained without her makeup kit.

"How long did you and Mr. Mann shack up?" Theo asked.

"What? You've got your nerve, mister."

"Don't lie, Alicia," David Warren said. "We know you were up there with him. And for more than one night."

"Well, I just did some part time work for him. His maid had the week off."

"Yeah, it's hard to get good help out there on the plantation." Theo Stevens exhaled heavily and shook his head. "Alicia, why were you there? Making some extra money off your charms? That in itself is a crime, isn't it, Mr. Warren?"

"That it is," David said sternly while suppressing a chuckle.

"But the charge might be waived if you cooperate with

us," Theo said

Alicia's eyes shifted back and forth between the two dour men facing her. "Like how?"

Theo smiled. "Just help us, Alicia. Did Sam come up to the plantation house?"

"I didn't see him."

Theo sighed. "How did he know you were at the bus station?"

"Guess he was leaving town, too. There's plenty of guys around Brunswick who'd love to get hold of him if they knew his hands were broken."

"Why were you leaving, Alicia?"

"I was going to visit my aunt."

"Where?"

"Savannah."

"Your ticket is for Los Angeles."

"Okay, yeah. I was going out to Hollywood. I'm going to be in the movies. But that's after I stop off in Savannah."

"Mr. Warren, looks like you'll just have to go ahead and charge her with unlawful cohabitation."

"With what?"

"Sleeping around," Dave said helpfully.

"I'm not the only one in town who does it. Ask the sheriff. He's done it. And Mr. Mann, too."

""Yes, we know about Mr. Mann. He's very important."

"Sure he is," she said. "He's rich. The law protects those rich folks. Even if he lives here just in the winters."

"Alicia, remember, we have to arrest Mr. Mann, too," Theo said. "He'll have to tell us why you were there. Of course, we already know. Sam knew, too. That's why he came there looking for you. Was the dead man at the plantation, too?"

"I didn't see him if he was. Please, mister. That's the gospel truth."

Theo turned to David Warren and pretended to forget Alicia for the moment. "Are there other houses upriver from Deveau's place where our deceased might've found a boat?"

"No. The entire stretch belongs to Mann. He bought it from Deveau. Mann has several boats."

"So the most likely place for the deceased to find a boat was at Mann's house."

Dave nodded. "Most likely."

Theo turned back to Alicia. "You were up there with Mann that night."

"I don't remember the night I came back home."

"If you'd come back earlier, Sam wouldn't have been up there looking for you. What time did he get to Mann's house?"

Alicia resumed her denials that she had seen Sam Betts two nights ago, but realized these two men would keep laying traps for her. She began to sob. "Sam got there about eight."

Theo brightened. "What did he do?"

"He came in, like he was wild. He was drunk. He had a razor blade and was threatening to kill us. It was awful, what he tried to do to Jeremy. The other man stopped him."

"What other man?"

"His name's Max. He works for Jeremy. He was the one who picked me up and took me up there. He talked funny."

"Funny?"

"You know, he didn't sound like he was from around here. He sounded like some of the guys off the boats."

"Mann has an English valet," David Warren explained.

"And how did this Max stop Sam?" Theo asked.

"He beat him up and broke his hands."

Theo's eyebrows went up. "Bet him up? A heavyweight

professional fighter? The sheriff said nobody in Brunswick would've thought of crossing him. And this limey just beats his ass and breaks his hands?"

Alicia cradled her head in her arms on the table. "Sam was crazy. He was going to hurt Jeremy bad. Like, you know, like the way they cut cows and pigs. He said he'd already cut one man."

Theo and David snapped to attention.

"He said he'd already cut a man?" Theo pursued.

"Yes," she said through sobs.

"Who?"

"I don't know. I never saw anybody else."

Theo leaned back in his chair. "Yeah. He'd already cut a man. And if that man crawled into a boat trying to get away, he had to have been up there at the Mann place. You say the English fellow broke Sam's hands. How did Sam get to the hospital, Alicia?"

"Jeremy and Max drove him there. Me, too."

Theo and David stood up and went to the room where Sam was trying to hold a cigarette, an impossibility with his hands in casts. Theo sat down at the table in front of Sam.

"Okay, Sam, we know you made it to Mann's house. We also know Mann's valet showed you how tough you really are. You didn't mess up your hands hitting a wall, or falling off a boat. That limey just flat whipped your ass and then broke your hands."

Sam tried to stand and the deputy guarding him kept him from rising. "I'll kill that bitch! She's caused me more trouble..."

"When you came into the house, you told Alicia and Mann you'd already cut a man up. It was the guy laying over there in the morgue, wasn't it?"

"No way. I didn't see nobody. If that bitch says I was at the Mann place, she's lying. Ask anybody round town if she don't lie like a dog."

"Sam, we're going to ask Mr. Mann and his valet what you did up there. We'll put them under oath. We know you got there and that's where you got smashed up. I'm more interested in the man you cut up. Where was he at the house?"

Sam shook his head and started to deny it all. But the stony faces staring back at him told him it was no use. "I found him in the little house off from the big one."

"What was he doing there?"

"I don't remember. I walked in and caught him unawares. He said something I didn't understand."

"What do you mean?"

"He sounded like a foreigner. Didn't talk like nobody round here."

"Do you mean he talked like me?" Theo said. "I don't talk like people around here. Neither do you."

"You sound like the rich folks on the islands."

"I'm insulted. Did Mann and his valet know this guy?"

"Don't know. The fellow that tricked me and hurt my hands looked in the little house and come running out and asked what the man had said. I couldn't tell him no more than I told you."

"Was the man still inside the house when the limey looked there?"

"I don't know. I was in the car when this guy came running back, crazy-like, wanting to know if I cut somebody."

"Wanting to know? So the man you'd already cut had got out of the house? Maybe looking for help. Maybe to a boat at the river."

Theo stood up. "I think you have what you need for your murder charge, Mr. Warren. But keep this quiet until I've talked to Mann and his valet. I want to know why the deceased went out there."

Outside the room David Warren offered to send the sheriff and a deputy with Theo Stevens.

"I'll take this part alone. I need to know more about our dead man. Having uniforms tagging along could complicate my inquiry."

"The valet sounds dangerous."

"Valets are dangerous by nature."

David Warren had already experienced the FBI's possessiveness toward its cases. He didn't like this agent's brusqueness.

"This is still in our jurisdiction, Stevens. Mann and his valet may be material witnesses to a murder, and they'll likely be moving north this weekend with their friends. Aren't you wondering why Mann didn't report any of this to us?"

"Could be he didn't want his name linked to Alicia."

"That wouldn't bother him. He's linked to every whore from here to Brooklyn. But his valet knew somebody had been cut and he didn't report it."

"That's why I'm going out there to talk to him."

Theo put on his gray hat and found a telephone in an adjacent office where he could call Alex Montgomery in the Washington headquarters. Alex agreed it was curious that an SD agent had gone to a plantation owned by the son of the man who owned Mann Corporation.

CHAPTER TWENTY-NINE

THE U-BOAT PACK encountered the American destroyer north of the Bahamas that Saturday morning. The journey from the L'Orient base in France had been so uneventful the crews had been joking and asking themselves if a war really was going on. They'd been skirting the Caribbean where the major portion of America's anti-submarine firepower had been allotted.

According to plan, the U-boats scattered when the destroyer was sighted. The destroyer concentrated on Kapitanleutant Kurt Mohr's U-boat. With some luck, Mohr thought, we'll outdistance the destroyer and regroup for the rest of the journey to the American coast. But the destroyer was coming fast and Mohr quickly realized he had to dive and hope to escape its depth charges. Shock after shock rocked the U-boat. Then came cheers from the deck of the destroyer at the sight of oil, then the broken hull of the U-boat. The destroyer happily radioed news of its hit and headed back to its Jacksonville port. The United States Navy congratulated itself on its kill and began the search for other U-boats suspected of prowling Atlantic waters.

Marie emerged from her stupor that Saturday morning to discover herself lying in bed with Jeremy Mann. He smiled at her.

"Where am I?" she said groggily.

"Please don't tell me you don't remember. What a fantastic night."

"Night? I remember...we were waiting to...hear from mon pere in London...the radio..."

"We waited, dear. When it became clear it was useless to keep trying, you came to bed with me. You tasted even more wonderful than the wine. You're a natural at pleasing men."

He grabbed her arm as she tried to roll from the bed. "Come, come. Relax. You were wonderful."

"I didn't...I don't remember..."

He lay back with a sigh of resignation. "No. Please don't tell me that. The greatest night of my life and you say you don't remember it?"

"I didn't do anything."

"But you did, cherie. You were positively wonderful." He lied. He knew she had gone limp and had passed out from nervously drinking wine while he pretended to reach Free France in London. But still he had had the pleasure of exploring ever inch of her body while she slept.

"You tricked me. There was no call. You tricked me."

"You forced me. But why should you be forced? It's so much more pleasure when two people willingly share with each other."

Again he grabbed her arm as she tried to escape the bed. She managed to slap him. He responded in kind. "All right, cherie. Cry out all you like. Struggle. There's no one to hear you except ghosts who haunt your Mr. Deveau's old house. But before you leave here, you're going to know me intimately. You can't ignore me. And I'm going to enjoy the fruit your father raised."

"You're a beast! This country has laws against this."

"Laws against love? Well, maybe down here in the deep, dark South there are. But there are no witnesses. And in a couple more days, I'll be on back in New York free from the claws of Southern justice."

"Monsieur Clock won't let you escape."

Jeremy Mann laughed. "Your Monsieur Deveau is a discredited wretch who can do nothing for you. Why not enjoy yourself? This will be your last opportunity with me. Unless, of course, you choose to move with me. You would make such a wonderful impression on New York society."

"You savage. Barbarian!"

"No, no." He held to her firmly. "Now, listen to me. You can cooperate and we'll both enjoy ourselves. If you don't, I have other plans for you."

She remained silent, barely able to struggle against his grip.

"Max. Max," he called.

Within moments Max opened the bedroom door, grinning at the sight of two naked bodies in bed.

"Max, my guest seems reluctant to enjoy the pleasure I offer her. I've been trying to explain how much happier we'd both be if she'd simply act as a woman should."

Max nodded, his grin in place.

"If she refuses, however, she'll just have to take her chances."

"Chances?" she barely managed to say.

"First, Max will realize his dream to have you."

Max smiled. She closed her eyes.

"Then," Jeremy continued, speaking softly into her ear, "after Max has had his pleasure, I'll let the Negro boys at the stables have a turn with you. What a frenzy they'd go into. They have the vitality of...well, Gravedigger. There are, let's see...three, four stable hands."

"Five," said Max.

"Five? That many? Heavens. That would take most of the morning. Max, after you have your amusement, where would be the best place for the stable boys to take their pleasure with Marie?"

"In the barn, sir. They'll all be here helping mate Jericho and Dolly."

"Splendid. She can enjoy herself the same as the horses. Sound good, cherie?"

Her eyes teared up, and she was too weak even to turn away when he wiped them with a corner of the sheet. This man was no better than those who had driven her from France and probably killed her father. He would've looked comfortable in a Nazi uniform.

"Come, come," he said, stoking her hair. "Perhaps you're a bit too tired to go through so many fellows in one morning. Maybe I'm all you need. Wouldn't that be better?"

He read submission in her helplessness. "There, there. I'll keep the others away. Max and the boys at the barn will just have to find their own sport."

Max left Marie and Jeremy to go about his preparations for this evening's finale. Most residents of the islands would be going north this weekend, leaving Jekyll vacant except for caretakers who would look after the island and ready it for next winter.

Max went to the dock to assure himself the cruiser was fuelled and ready to go. He put Jeremy Mann out of his mind and waited for him until he came out of the bedroom for coffee and rolls. "I should be preparing for the reception," he said, smiling with satisfaction. "I gave sleeping beauty some pills to keep her out the rest of the afternoon. You can take your choice. Stuff her into the car and return her to Deveau, or keep her for yourself this evening. She's really superb, Max. Despite her unwillingness. If she was more willing, I'd take her back home to brighten up New York society."

Max, in fact, had already made plans for Marie. She would leave with him this evening when Jeremy Mann's reception came to its surprising conclusion. She would find a most enthusiastic welcome among the friends he would be rejoining. He returned to the bedroom, lifted her limp body, and carried her to the truck for transport to his cottage.

David Warren called Clarke just after noon to tell him Sam Betts had confessed to cutting the dead man he'd found in the boat near his house. Clarke took the news with shivers, realizing Betts had intended to use his blade on Marie. And Jasper and Annie. He felt more grateful than ever that Jasper and Annie had stood their ground against him, bless their hearts.

But why had the dead man been at Pineland? His uniform proved his connection to German intelligence. Was Jeremy Mann actually dealing with the Germans? Perhaps he was even more sinister than Harold Blandford thought. Perhaps Erica's death tied in with his business dealings.

David Warren interrupted his musing. "That FBI agent went up there to talk to Mann and his valet. He refused to take along backup, even after hearing what the valet did to Betts."

Clarke hung up, thinking about Max and how much he had scared Marie. Yet, she'd still gone back out there. Damn. He called Annie. "No, Mr. Clock, she ain't come back. You oughta go see to that girl. You oughta."

He dismissed her suggestion and went home. Annie had left supper on the stove for him. Despite misgivings about letting Marie slip inside his defenses, he felt worried about him. He didn't feel angry she hadn't returned Sandman to her. He'd go to Pineland himself and retrieve his horse, the best that remained of the proud stable that used to roam the pastures at Pineland.

He slumped into the chair in his study, looking absently at the volumes lining the walls. Some were his old college and law books, a few went all the way back to his great-great-grandparents who had fled the slave uprising in Haiti.

He contemplated sampling some of Jasper's fine moonshine when he remembered the photos he had enlarged for Marie. He went to his darkroom and looked at the enlargements still hanging from a wire. He liked them. They showed her grace, feistiness, arrogance, undeniable allure. What a pity she had left. And there was the one on the rearing Gravedigger, just before she hit the truck that Max had carelessly poked into her path. He looked at the enlargement, admiring her poise, regretting again that she'd chosen to leave him. Good action shot, he smiled. Even the faces of Max and his passenger were almost clear.

Max. His passenger. God! Max's passenger was the man lying in the morgue with his stomach open and his throat slit. Killed upriver. Where Pineland sat on the banks of the Altamaha. Why was a man with an SD uniform in a truck with Max? At Pineland where Sam Betts would've found him?

Clarke took the photo back to his office. He hesitated, then found Alex Montgomery's home phone number and called collect.

Alex feigned indignation. "This better be good, pardner."

"The stiff with the Nazi uniform? I have a photo of him I took a few days ago. Guess who he's with?"

"Albertis Mann!"

"Who? Hell no. With junior Mann's English valet."

Clarke explained how he'd come to take the photo. With his German camera.

Alex paused, as though considering whether to divulge anything more to Clarke. He relented slightly.

"Theo called to tell me he was on the way to talk to Jeremy Mann and his valet. He hasn't reported back."

"How long ago?"

"Three, four hours."

"Call Sheriff Hazel and tell him to get up there. Your man needs backup."

"He's okay. He'll report back."

"And there's a girl up there. She could be in trouble."

"Theo didn't mention a girl. Did you tell him about her?"

"I'm going up there to see if something's wrong."

"Look, Clarke, I'd rather you stay out of it. The Bureau likes to handle its own investigations."

"Yeah. I know."

Five minutes later Clarke called Alex Montgomery again. "Yes, I did have to call collect. Something else you might check out. This valet sent some letters to a post office box in Arlington. A lady acquaintance took his truck without permission and I saw the letter on the seat."

Clarke gave him the number, having been suspicious enough to write it down that morning he'd driven Marie back to Pineland. Max had clearly betrayed anxious interest in it when he saw it still on the seat of his truck.

"We'll check on this," Alex said. "Could lead to something. That it for now?"

"If I think of something else, I'll call. Collect."

Alex Montgomery contacted the Bureau as soon as Clarke hung up. Within minutes an agent reported back that a Walter Dreeling rented the post office box in Arlington. However, records showed no Walter Dreeling at the address given to the post office. Nor did the couple at the address know anything about the box or anyone named Dreeling.

Alex assigned an agent to watch the box and tail whoever turned up to collect its contents. He pushed away his Scotch, his stomach upset that he had heard nothing from Theo Stevens.

Clarke tried to calm his jitters after talking to Alex Montgomery. His irritation with Marie had flipped to anxiety. She was with one, maybe two men, who'd had direct contact with an SD agent who'd met a gruesome death. He realized he was searching for a reason to go looking for her. He consoled himself with knowing Theo Stevens was personally checking out Pineland.

CHAPTER THIRTY

THEO STEVENS PARKED in the circular driveway at Pineland. A tall man with dark blond hair walked toward him from the house.

"Is Mr. Mann in?"

"He's preparing for a reception this evening. Perhaps I can help."

From the man's English accent, Theo surmised this was the valet who'd treated Sam Betts like a pile of kindling.

"I'm Max Lewis. You're a policeman? You don't sound like a local."

"That's what I'm told every day. I came down with one of the Jekyll residents for security work and decided to stay on. Met a girl here, you know."

"Understandable. I've seen women I wouldn't mind staying with. How can we help?"

"I'm trying to clear a case that dropped in on us yesterday. Do you know a Sam Betts?"

"No sir. Sorry."

"Darn. He claims he was assaulted here a couple nights

ago. Said he came here to see his girl friend and Mr. Mann had him beaten up. Said whoever did it took a poker and broke his hands."

Max laughed. "A poker? Had the fellow been into the local spirits? The natives make some rather potent elixirs."

"That they do," Theo agreed. "Now, the girl he said he was looking for was…" he opened his notebook as though searching for the name, "let's see, yes, Alicia Jackson. Was she here Thursday evening?"

"Not that I recall. Of course, I don't keep track of Mr. Mann's guests. Especially the female ones."

"Right. Anyone else work here that she might've been visiting?"

"Not unless she likes them black. Anyway, none of them live here on the premises."

"That right? This checks out with Sam's reputation. People around town say he's something of a liar. Well, since I've come all this way, I really would like to speak to Mr. Mann. It would help me clear the case. Fact is, I don't even know why we're investigating. Seems like a lover's quarrel between Betts and Miss Jackson. That girl must've taken up with some bad company."

"Agreed. I'll see if Mr. Mann is free for a moment."

"Thanks. I won't take much time. Say, mind if I walk with you? No sense in him coming all the way out here to see me."

"Suit yourself."

Theo took in the layout of the estate. He noted the barns stood some hundred yards away and the house at the crest of the hill overlooking the river. A cottage sat off to the side of the house. "Nice place here. You must hate to leave it."

"It's most pleasant here."

"Do you live here?"

" Yes. In the small house there. Hardly the domain for a lord of the manor."

But ideal for a murder, Theo thought.

They found Jeremy Mann lounging at a table on the veranda with coffee and some papers in front of him. Theo guessed he hadn't been out of bed long.

"Sir, Mr. Stevens is a policeman. He has a complaint by...what was his name, sir?"

"Sam Betts."

"Mr. Betts asserts that he was assaulted here a couple nights ago."

Jeremy registered disbelief. "Really? Preposterous. Say, Max, do you think it could've been that fellow we heard got beat up on that plantation north of here?"

"I'd forgotten about him, " Max said. "Over a woman, wasn't it?"

"I believe that's what the lads said. And this Betts fellow accused us of doing it?"

"Yes," Theo said, enjoying the evasions. "He was beaten up and his hands were broken. Quite a feat against a man who used to be a professional fighter up north."

"Up north," Jeremy Mann said. "I thought I detected a kindred voice in your accent. So you're working with the locals now, eh? It sounds like several men jumped this Betts chap. Damn. I'm glad none of our crew was involved. We need every hand here to help with the move this weekend. We want to get away before your heat and mosquitoes become unbearable."

Theo laughed. "Can't blame you for that. I'm going to have trouble adjusting to them year round. Say, you have a terrific view of the river. Are those your boats down there at the dock?"

"Yes they are."

"Lost any of them lately?"

"Not that I recall."

"You're lucky. We've had lots of reports about boats broken from moorings by high waters. Glad the water's starting to recede."

"Yes. That'll make it easier for my guests to travel upstream tonight."

"Friends from town?"

"The islands. I don't have friends in town. It's the last party of the season for us."

Theo nodded that he understood. He shook hands with Mann, then Max. "Sorry to have bothered you. But we have to follow up when we get a complaint like this. Hope you have a nice going away party tonight."

"Sorry we couldn't help more."

Theo drove away from Pineland knowing Max and Jeremy had lied through their pearly whites.

"That big chap actually complained about us?" Max said.

"Yes. Curious, Stevens and his accent. The locals usually have native yokels. Maybe the sheriff wanted somebody on staff who can communicate with those of us who have bought up the county. Is the mademoiselle sleeping soundly in your cottage?"

"Quite soundly. I'll keep her out of sight should any of your guests wander into my quarters by mistake."

Jeremy smiled and stretched. "Hmm. Smell that beef roasting. Sure hope our guests arrive before dark."

Max watched Jeremy go into the house, then went immediately to his truck. Stevens didn't fit. Something about him didn't fit, not just his accent. He drove to the paved highway and turned south toward Brunswick, looking for signs the man called Stevens might've pulled off the road.

Max saw Theo Stevens' Ford parked back off the road under the trees. He drove past it until he could turn around without alerting Stevens that he was doubling back. He drove back to Pineland and posted himself in trees near his cottage. Within minutes he detected movement in the trees beyond. He saw Stevens hesitate, look around, and run to the back door of the cottage. Within seconds he picked the lock and entered the small house.

Not your ordinary local polizei, Max concluded.

As soon as Stevens was inside, Max sprinted for the back door. He wanted to get inside before his visitor had time to search the house where his first discovery would be Marie. Through a window he saw that Stevens had found the girl already. But curiously he paid her no attention. He was looking for something else. He went to the parlor and concentrated on the floor. Max had replaced the carpet that Volker's blood had soaked, and Stevens was lifting it to view the stains.

Max slipped into the house as Stevens let the carpet fall again to the floor. Stevens went to Max's bedroom and opened the closet that hid the radio equipment. As Stevens concentrated on the radio, Max rammed his Luger into his back. He shoved Stevens against the wall, made him spread eagle and removed the Smith and Wesson .38 from his shoulder holster.

"Your work must be very hazardous to necessitate this," Max said, hefting the revolver.

Max reached into Theo's vest pocket and withdrew the wallet. He opened it and read aloud, as if in disbelief. "Federal Bureau of Investigation. You're one of Mr. Hoover's bloodhounds. Why are you here, Mr. Stevens?"

"I'm investigating a missing person."

Max stabbed a crushing punch into Theo's kidney that sent him gasping flat on the floor. "No, Mr. FBI man, that won't do. Let's come to an understanding. If you can't make your story believable, I'll break one bone for each evasion I hear. Just like that big bloke you pretended interest in. You're a greater danger to me than he was, so I'm prepared to be rather more severe with you. Who sent you here?"

"My superiors."

Theo screamed as Max's boot shot out and sheared a chunk of flesh from his cheek."

"Your purpose in coming here?" Max rammed the Luger against the back of Theo's neck.

Theo hesitated. "Mr. Betts is suspected of assaulting someone here. I'm checking out his story."

"You're not even coming close. What could you possibly learn simply by walking up and asking about Sam Betts?"

Theo's mind was too blurred to frame evasive answers. He was wishing he had taken David Warren's offer of a deputy. Or two deputies.

Suddenly the Luger exploded behind his head, tearing a crimson gash down the side of his neck.

"I can place shots anywhere I like," Max said. "Where would you like the next one?"

Theo was talking rapidly, desperately. "I don't…I wanted to see if there was a connection with the dead man in the boat. " Theo felt blood gushing from his neck. The bullet must've torn an artery. God, why hadn't he brought along backup?

Max was instantly alert, knowing what this FBI dog was talking about. "What dead man in a boat?"

"A dead man the big guy cut up."

Theo felt Max put the Luger against the other side of his neck. Instead of the shot he was expecting, he felt his hair grabbed and his face slammed into the floor. He closed his eyes rather than see his broken teeth in a bloody pile beneath his face.

Marie moaned in the next room and, in the instant Max looked toward the sound, Theo rolled onto his back and hooked his foot in front of Max's neck, sending him sprawling. The big man was up like a tiger, shooting precise blows and kicks that put Theo face-down on the floor. Max straddled him, twisted Theo's right arm behind him and calmly broke two fingers. Theo cried out, recognizing the pain Sam Betts had endured.

"What else about the dead man, Mr. Stevens?"

Theo gasped through his pain. "We traced him..we traced him to his room. He had a German uniform there."

Max cursed. That damned fool Volker! "How does that connect to Mr. Mann?"

"We figured he'd been out here cause Sam found him here."

"So you expected to find a German spy ring." Max gripped another of Theo's fingers and began bending it. "Who else knows you're here?"

"The sheriff."

"Is he coming?"

"Yes..no, no, God..no..the sheriff left it to me…"

Max believed Theo. He broke his finger anyway.

As Theo cried out, Max stuck he Luger into the back of his head and ordered him to stand. Theo marched out ahead of Max, his mind and wits suffocated in pain. Max pushed Theo toward the trees along the river. Once under the trees , Max prodded Theo along for another hundred yards. He put the Luger to the back of Theo's head, pulled the trigger, and watched bones and brains explode.

Max rolled Theo into a culvert. Knowing the body wouldn't be found for days, if ever, he covered it with dirt and leaves rather than roll it into the river where its discovery might come too quickly.

Max returned to Theo's car and drove it farther into the

trees. It couldn't be seen here before daybreak, and only then if someone knew where to look for it.

Now he had only to await the arrival of the guests and send his signal that all was ready. Relieved, he returned to his cottage to prepare for the evening. Remembering the moan he'd heard from Marie's room, he looked in on her and froze.

Her bed was empty.

CHAPTER THIRTY-ONE

WHEN MAX DASHED outside his cottage, he saw only Jeremy Mann strolling on the back lawn of the big house. No, Marie had not taken refuge with him. Then at the barn he saw her on horseback, galloping for the driveway. He fumbled with the handle of his truck door and spewed a stream of curses in four languages when the truck hesitated to crank. When at last the engine roared to life, he tore down the driveway after the rider who now was out of sight.

He saw her as soon as he reached the highway. She was riding at a trot on the shoulder, looking behind her. At the sound of the truck, she spurred the horse into a gallop. Under the lingering influence of the sleeping pills, she rode unsteadily in the saddle. Max hoped she would fall off and end this chase immediately.

But Marie had grown up with horses and her natural instincts kept her mounted. Max accelerated, easily gaining on her.

Suddenly Marie turned the horse from the road into the

trees where the truck could not follow. Max stopped the truck and jumped out, then realized pursuit on foot would be futile. Where was she going? Of course. She was trying to get to Deveau's house. To get there she would have to follow the only route she knew, a path parallel to the road. Just ahead, the trees would open on a field of tall grass. When Marie got to the open area, Max turned the truck into it.

Marie looked around, surprised at the roar of the truck plowing through the grass toward her. She turned back toward the trees and urged the horse into a gallop. In past days cotton had grown here, but now it was grass and broom straw.

As she rode the open field toward the trees, Marie guided the horse in a zigzag pattern. But Max always corrected course and stayed with her until he could pass her and herd her back toward the center of the field. Her head was spinning and not even her riding skills could counter the effects of the drugs. Worse, the horse was Clarke's Sandman, not her familiar Gravedigger who would've responded to her slightest touch.

Suddenly Max blew the horn. The startled horse broke out of Marie's control. When she landed in the grass, the truck had to slide to avoid running over her. Jarred by the fall, she got up and attempted a dash toward the trees.

Max easily caught up with her, preferring to bring her down with a tackle rather than grabbing her from behind. They rolled over and over until he pinned her. Without a word, he brought a backhand across her face, carefully placing the blow to the side of her head to avoid damaging the beautiful lips that he intended to taste when he completed his mission.

"I don't know why you attempt to escape me," he mocked her. ""Don't you see how much I care for you?"

She kicked and shrieked in helpless fury.

"Come, come, cherie. Time for you go back to sleep."

She was sobbing. "Where is the man you hurt in the house?"

So she knew. Whatever slight inclination he'd had to leave her behind unharmed had to be abandoned. He could leave her here in this tall grass and she would remain hidden until long after he cruised down the river. But he had promised himself that this Gallic princess would be his final reward for a mission accomplished. Taking her would be even more delicious because she had rejected the favors of a wealthy heir. Yes, he thought, I like her attitude toward Jeremy Mann. Too bad I don't have time to strip her down right here. She's enraged and full of fire--a wonderful treat right now.

Max laughed, thinking his position on top of her somehow amusing, a prelude to the pleasures to come. After tonight he would no longer be in this strange country with its decaying mansions and haunted moss, its strange natives and their strange food. She would disappear with him and no one would ever know she had fallen into the most exciting adventure of her life. Yes, she was a trophy. A trophy he would decline to share even with his most ravenous superiors at home.

But for now she had to go back to sleep and cease being a bother on this most crucial day of his life. His expert hands pressed the pulses in her neck to put her into a deep sleep. As a covey of marsh hens exploded from the grass, he carried her to the truck and put her into the cab.

When he put her back into the bedroom in his cottage, he bound and gagged her. She would stay here this time.

Kapitanleutnant Ernst Schmidt's sour mood deepened. Losing Mohr and his U-boat crew was rotten luck, and now this. He heard the alarm from his lookout and quickly scanned the horizon. Damn! An American destroyer bearing down on the two U-boats. With an entire ocean to roam, how could he have happened into the path of two destroyers in two days?

Schmidt gave the order to dive. But the destroyer was already crossing over Kapitanleutnant Albert Iobst's U-boat. Within minutes the U-boat's shattered hull lurched upward to the surface and its few surviving crewmen were taken aboard the destroyer.

Schmidt, now the lone survivor of the original pack of three, morosely maneuvered away from the destroyer and kept his course for Jekyll Island, Georgia.

Clarke finished supper and returned to his darkroom, bothered by the photo showing the murdered man in the truck with Max. He admitted uneasiness about her, but she had made her choice in returning to Jeremy Mann. She hadn't said goodbye before leaving and hadn't even bothered to call him since then.

He walked outside on the back porch and looked toward the Altamaha River where a yacht was moving upstream. On the way to Pineland, he guessed. No one but the millionaires could afford yachts. He stepped into the yard and walked slowly toward the river. He looked toward the barns when he detected a sudden movement and heard the sound of a horse refreshing itself in the water trough. It took a moment before he realized it was Sandman, the horse Marie had ridden to Pineland yesterday. Sandman was breathing heavily. He'd been running hard. And he was still saddled.

Clarke dashed into the barn, hoping Marie would be there. No sign of her. He unsaddled Sandman, quickly rubbed him down and put him into a stall.

He sprinted to his house and called Jeremy Mann. Charlie answered and took what seemed half an hour to get Mann on the phone.

"When did Marie leave?"

"I didn't know she had, Deveau." Mann's tone of amusement infuriated Clarke.

"Isn't she still there? Who saddled my horse and rode him?"

"I wouldn't know, old fellow. Hold on. I'll check with Max."

Clarke breathed in short puffs and waited. He heard Mann yelling, then his faint footsteps returning to the phone. "Sorry. Max doesn't know anything about her. We're both rather busy in preparations for my reception this evening."

"Her horse just got here sweaty and breathing hard. She could've been thrown and injured."

"Possibly. Look Deveau, I have a great deal to do before my guests arrive. If you like, I could spare one or two of the stable boys to help you search."

"Do that. I'll start searching immediately."

Clarke cursed and hung up. He hurried to his car and drove the main road toward Pineland. He saw no trace of Marie. He quickly deduced that Mann had not dispatched any of his hands to help him search. Fuming at Jeremy Mann's indifference, he returned to his house and saddled his other horse. Since he hadn't seen her on the road, she had to be somewhere in the trees or brush where the horse could go.

As an afterthought, he took down his great-great-grandfather's sword from above the mantel and strapped it on. It would help him hack through brush if it came to that. Or he could hack at snakes who were becoming more numerous with the coming of warm weather. He shivered to think he would have to find her and avoid snakes in rapidly diminishing sunlight.

Damn her. She had pulled out feelings he had folded up and put away years ago. Now she had left them crumpled in the sand. Damn her.

CHAPTER THIRTY-TWO

IN THE LAST GLIMMER of dusk, Clarke found the tracks where Max's truck had left the road to run into the tall grass. And he saw the horse tracks that he knew were Sandman's. Farther up the road toward Pineland, he found the tire tracks leading into the trees where he found the FBI agent's obscured car. But no Theo Stevens. He didn't have to be told this was bad news.

Clarke reached the long, dark driveway leading up to the main house at Pineland where lights flickered like lightning bugs. This was wrong and ominous. Marie was missing and so was Theo Stevens. This was after a dead man with an SD uniform had been here with the caretaker of this estate. For a long moment, Clarke considered charging to the big house the way his great-great-grandfather had done in the service of General Longstreet. But he recalled that those brave charges had often come up short in the face of overwhelming odds.

Clarke turned the horse and urged it into a fast trot back to his house. His call wasn't the one Alex Montgomery was expecting.

"I found your man's car hidden in the trees off the road near Mann's spread. I didn't see him or the missing girl. Her horse came to my house sweaty and breathing hard, still saddled."

"I'm sending more men down there."

"Your man and that girl need help right now. I'll call the sheriff and get him out here."

"No, Clarke. This is Bureau business."

"You handle the Bureau's business. I need to find out if that girl needs help. I'll let you know if I come across your man."

"Clarke, don't involve the local officials. This concerns national security."

"Then handle it." He saw no need to add that Marie wasn't a matter of national security.

Clarke called Sheriff Roy Hazel's office and found he'd gone home for supper. Clarke knew the number and dialed him. Mrs. Hazel answered and wouldn't call her husband to the phone. He heard the sheriff's growl in the background before he came on the line.

"Sheriff, I've found that FBI agent's car. It's parked off in the woods close to Mann's house."

"Maybe he's snooping around, Clarke. That's what FBI agents do."

"When did he leave town?"

"About noon. Just before I went to lunch. Several hours ago, come to think of it. You'd figure he'd done enough snooping by now, wouldn't you?"

"That's what I'd figure. Something else. That French girl is missing, too."

""I thought she was with you now."

"Where'd you hear that, Roy?"

"Just heard, that's all. What about her?"

"Her horse came back to my house a couple hours ago, saddled and sweating. I can't find her, and Mann says nobody at his place has seen her. I've already searched the road. Mann's not overly concerned about her. How about helping me look through the woods and fields for her? Might check out Stevens, too."

"I don't know, Clarke. I don't like poking round in the FBI's business. But it's right strange about your...that, girl. Tell you what, soon's I finish supper, I'll come on up with one of my deputies."

"Eat fast."

After he hung up, Clarke wondered if he should've told the sheriff that the gutted dead man in the morgue had been with Max.

But Marie was first on his mind. She had to be out there somewhere. Alone, scared, probably hurt. Had she been trying to come back to him?

He still had the sword strapped on. This time he would ride the river bank and work his way toward Pineland.

Twilight had settled over the coast and he knew seeing Marie would be next to impossible. He rode slowly, occasionally calling out her name. His only answer was the mournful answer of night fowl. Right now he wanted to ride up to Pineland, as casually as his ancestors would've done when the home was theirs. He dismissed the thought, knowing he'd feel ridiculous if she came tripping out and asked him just was all this fuss about, Clock.

Almost within sight of Pineland, Clarke dismounted and started walking. He stumbled on the strangely soft form in the shallow culvert. On his knees, he discovered why no one had heard from Theo Stevens. He got nausea when he shined his flashlight on what was left of Theo's head. He had no more doubt about Marie. She was either in terrible danger, or she was somewhere in these woods crumpled and shattered like the FBI agent.

Clarke led the horse almost to the cottage and tethered it to a tree. Sounds of laughter drifted down from the party in the mansion. He saw no sign of anyone at the cottage and crept toward it. On the dark side away from the house, he moved to the window and looked in. He could just make out a bulk on a bed. Risking the flashlight, he shined it toward the bed and gasped. Marie.

The back door was locked. But it was the same lock he could jiggle twenty years ago to get in. He tiptoed to the bedroom door where he'd seen the shape in the bed. It was locked. He remembered something else. The old key was still up there on the door sill. Max hadn't thoroughly checked out his house.

Inside the bedroom he shined his flashlight into terror-filled eyes of the gagged girl. He turned the light on his own face so she could see. "Shh! It's me."

He ripped off the gag, then struggled to untie the ropes around her arms and legs. Frustrated, he used the cavalry sword to slice through the knots to free the sobbing young woman. She forced her numb arms around him, burying her sobbing eyes in his chest.

"It's all right," he kept saying, trying to convince himself as much as her. "Who did this?"

"Max," she said through sobs. "I know he's done something terrible. I heard him hurting a man. Then they left. I don't know what happened then."

Yes, Clarke knew she had heard Max hurting Theo Stevens. He would say nothing about the FBI agent's fate just now. Right now she needed to stay calm, and he needed to get her away from here.

But outside he heard voices coming toward the cottage. He relocked the bedroom door and coaxed her to get back under the covers. She whimpered but he had to make her do it. The voices were louder now, then the front door opened and closed. The voices were gruff, in language he didn't understand, though one of them clearly was Max. Clarke stationed himself by the door, the sword raised and ready to slash down on the first man through. What he'd do about the second or third or fourth man he didn't know.

The door knob to the bedroom turned and rattled. Clarke remained as motionless and heavy as a statue, holding the sword above his head with both hands. He exhaled in relief when the door knob stopped rattling and steps retreated from the door.

Clarke heard the voices in the house and understood nothing in the language they spoke. The voices faded and the door slammed closed. Clarke resumed normal breathing and replaced the sword in its scabbard. He moved quickly to the bed and touched Marie to reassure himself she was still there. She responded to his touch with a tight hug and held to him while he felt his way to the phone. He wanted to tell the sheriff to bring an entire battalion of deputies with him. He wasn't surprised to find the phone disconnected. Max meant to leave no tracks.

"Marie," he whispered. "My horse is tied to a tree just outside. Follow me out."

"What's wrong, Clock?"

"I think there are German spies here. Max almost certainly is one."

"Germans? In America?"

"It has something to do with this party at the big house. Do you know who's here?"

"I know only that it's for Jeremy's father and some of his friends."

That confirmed Clarke's suspicions that Mann Senior and Junior were more deeply involved with Germany than he'd ever imagined. Max was among compatriots.

When they reached the horse, Clarke boosted her into the saddle. "Stay here for a few minutes while I see what's going on in the house. If anything happens, ride back to my house. "

She protested, but he calmed her and promised to be back within moments. He questioned his sanity in leaving her, however momentarily, to go back, but he knew he had to report as much as possible to his former cohorts who allegedly were defending the nation from its enemies. This would be one last collect call to Alex Montgomery.

Marie sat silently on the horse and watched Clarke disappear into the darkness. She still felt weak from the pills and being bound the past several hours. Something kept pricking in her brain, something about the voices she'd heard in the cottage. So strange, yet...something was familiar about them.

She stared intently into the dark, praying that Clarke would re-emerge and they could ride away. But she saw only the lights from the big house. Afraid she might lose contact with him again, she nudged the horse in the direction she thought he had gone.

Clarke felt his way along the boxwoods he had played around while growing up here a quarter of a century ago. Now they rustled in the breeze and shielded him from a guard at the front door as he crept toward the side door where he let himself into the house. Sneaking in from dates, he had learned about all the creaks in the house.

When he was inside the house, he moved silently toward the parlor until he realized the party had fallen silent. He stopped in the hall, then edged forward toward the only voice audible. Perhaps someone was proposing a toast.

From a darkened side room, he could look unseen into the parlor where a dozen guests were assembled. But the

speaker was not proposing a toast.
Clarke listened in astonishment.

CHAPTER THIRTY-THREE

JEREMY MANN AND HIS GUESTS huddled in the large parlor facing Max and a man holding what Clarke recognized from his Justice days was a Thompson submachine gun. Gangsters loved the Tommy gun and, consequently, law enforcement officials needed it to even the odds.

Make spoke calmly with complete authority. "We'll make the passage down the river on Mr. Mann's yacht. Any attempt to escape will be dealt with severely."

Jeremy Mann's voice quivered. "Max, old fellow, why this joke? You're making this up to amuse us, aren't you?"

Max mocked Mann's attempt at familiarity. "No, old chap, this is no joke."

"But why us? We've been very cooperative with you."

Albertis Mann was less timid than his son. "Surely you don't think the United States government is going to allow you to abduct us. They'll hunt you down and deal with you."

Max laughed. "The United States and Russia are allies now, thanks to the Fuhrer's miscalculation."

"See here," Albertis Mann persisted, "this really is a

fantasy. Is Russia trying to tell us to give them more trade? More aid to fight the Nazis? We can do that. Easily. In fact, we're already doing it. You should know that."

Max smiled. "Yes, I'm aware our agents are already active in your government. So you yourself should have no objection to working for the glory of the motherland. The best way you can do that is encourage the two doctors to help us crush the Nazis."

Doctors Neil Harris and Gunther von Richter stood stiffly with the group of captive rich people, their ashen faces twisted in forlorn looks of haunted souls who thought they've escaped Hell, only to be pulled back into the flames. Dr. von Richter dared to speak to Max. "I will not serve a regime of murderers. I did not flee Hitler to produce research for Stalin."

"Your attitude will change," said the beefy heavily-accented man with the rifle.

Clarke knew he had heard the man's voice minutes ago in the cottage. Now he understood. The man with the automatic was Russian. Max was in league with this man from the Kremlin.

"We must make rendezvous," said the Russian.

Clarke retreated carefully, hoping there were no creaky boards he'd missed when he was growing up here. He had vital news for Alex Montgomery but it would have to wait. Marie was waiting for him near the barn where he'd left her. Please lord, make her stay away.

In the dark, he could barely make out the movement of a man down at the dock. He could see just well enough to know that the man had a rifle slung over his shoulder. Clarke surmised he was guarding the craft that would convey Max and his guests to their rendezvous offshore. The man was pacing the dock, looking at the big house up the hill, then across the dark river.

Praying Marie would stay hidden in the trees at the barn, Clarke went down the incline to the dock, skirting the lawn to avoid the lights along the path. At this distance the guard could not see him. But Clarke knew that within moments the group in the house would come marching down to the dock.

Clarke reached the dock without a plan. The old sword was in his hands when he bounded onto the planks. The guard turned toward him and briefly looked surprised, thinking his passengers had already arrived. His hesitation allowed Clarke to cover several precious feet between them before reaction.

Fumbling to bring the rifle from his shoulder, the guard was off-balance when Clarke reached him. The man lifted the rifle and its stock blocked the sword that slashed toward his face. Completely taken by surprise, the guard stumbled backwards while Clarke paused with momentary paralysis in his hand. He recovered to grip the sword firmly and charge the man again.

This time the guard rammed the butt of his gun against Clarke's chest and sent him reeling backwards. When the man rushed him, Clarke regained his balance in time to lunge toward him with a thrust aimed at his stomach. The sword got the man's trigger arm instead, bringing a scream of pain in another language--Russian, he guessed.

Clarke lunged again and drove the blade into the man's abdomen. The man screamed in his unfamiliar language, clutched his stomach and dropped the rifle. He fell backwards off the blade. He dropped to the dock, clutching for the rifle, and shrieked again when Clarke slashed the sword down on his shoulder, like an axe chopping wood.

The man rolled off the dock into the water, dragging the rifle with him. For a few seconds his good arm clawed at the side of Albertis Mann's yacht. He went under and resurfaced once as the current pulled him out into the river. He disappeared and Clarke never heard him cry out again.

Clarke felt sick. He hadn't meant to kill the man, much less gut him like a deer on a hunt. The blood and tissue on the old sword nauseated him, even though he realized the man lost out there in the dark river would've happily dealt him the same fate.

He looked back up the hill to the house and remembered why he was here. That helped him regain focus and quiet his nausea. Too bad the man had knocked his rifle into the water when he rolled off the dock with his sidearm still in its holster. Clarke had only the bloody sword for a weapon which would be useless against the firepower of Max and his compatriots.

He knew his only means to thwart Max's plans was to set the craft adrift, deny him the means to deliver his prisoners downriver to other craft waiting to take them away. What craft? With all the talk of U-boats offshore, he suspected one was awaiting Max at the mouth of the sound. He began hacking through the ropes that bound Jeremy Mann's cruiser and the senior Mann's yacht. As the yacht squeaked against the dock, moving away into deeper water, Clarke saw a body slumped at the railing. Probably Albertis Mann's pilot, he thought, shot by the gutted Russian who was now somewhere out there in the dark water, drifting for Altamaha Sound. The sword's blade was holding sharp despite the heavy chopping.

Exhausted by swinging the sword, Clarke watched the cruiser and yacht disappear into the dark. His arms ached but he knew more of Max's fleet waited to be set adrift. He looked back at the big house on the hill, the lights in its windows staring down the dark slope like piercing eyes. He knew time was running out, that soon the parade of prisoners and captors would come trooping down the path to the docks where they would stare in disbelief to find their getaway craft gone. Max and his compatriots would know an intruder was nearby. Then Max and the other man with the Tommy gun would search furiously until they found the invader and disposed of him.

He shuddered when he heard shots at the top of the hill outside the house. The guard was shooting at something. Someone. Outside the house.

He knew of only one person outside the house.

CHAPTER THIRTY-FOUR

A CHING WITH ANXIETY that she'd lose Clarke again, Marie nudged the horse closer to the house and strayed into the lawn lights. She backed the horse up but the guard had seen the movement and yelled for her to stop. She spurred the horse into a gallop, just missing the guard's shots at her as she disappeared into the dark.

Max was at the door within seconds. "Why did you fire?"

"I saw a rider."

"Damn!"

Could it really be her? How could she have escaped the knots he'd tied very securely. Max ran to the cottage and confirmed his worst fears. She indeed was gone. He picked up the sheared ropes. Yes, someone had cut through them. Someone who had to still be close by. He ran outside and looked down at the dock. Even in the last glimmer of sunset, he saw something was missing. Where were the damn boats?

Clarke had run from the dock into the dark before Max came to look. He dropped into the tall marsh grass by the river. Max ran down the hill to the dock where he found the ropes sheared, saw the blood on the dock. He looked about, as though expecting a bullet to come screaming out of the dark.

Max sprinted back up the hill to the guard in the front yard at the house. Both had flashlights and they first began searching around the house. Clarke knew that they would realize within seconds that their prey was still near the dock. With their flashlights, they would find him crouched in the grass and dispatch him without asking questions.

Max and the guard took little time searching the perimeter of the house before running back down the path to the dock. The guard went upstream while Max proceeded cautiously downstream toward Clarke. When the flashlight found Clarke he jumped to his feet to run for the trees. The temporary silence told him Max was taking aim at his back. He dived just as the Luger spat a streak of flame that creased his left arm. His cry told Max he had scored, and he sprang forward to finish off his quarry.

Unable to run farther, Clarke rose to his knees and used his good right arm to unsheathe his sword. He prepared to rush Max, hoping a surprise counterattack might catch him off guard.

But Max was too much the soldier to rush blindly into the darkness for his wounded prey. He stopped and swept the tall grass with his flashlight until he saw Clarke raise his sword and prepare to charge.

Knowing he would never get close enough even to wound Max, Clarke flung the sword at him like a spear in the instant the Luger flashed again in the dark. The bullet tore into his chest above his left nipple. He knew only that he cried out as the force of the shot flung him backwards into a bed of tall, soft march grass at the river's edge. He didn't know his sword had sliced Max's bicep without disabling him.

Max cried out in pain and dropped to his knees holding his gashed arm. Cautiously he shined his flashlight toward the dark grass where he'd seen Clarke go down. He cursed and crept forward until he was certain there was no movement where Clarke had fallen. He found him lying face-up, motionless, spread-eagled in the watery marsh. Max smiled with grim satisfaction to see the blood oozing from Clarke's chest.

"So it was you, Herr Deveau."

Max called to the other guard that their prey had been run to ground.

The guard at the top of the hill guarding the party yelled. Had the mademoiselle returned?

Max hesitated. He wanted to leave his mark on the inert body of this troublesome detective. But he was satisfied that Clarke was forever out of his way. He turned and trotted up the hill to the house. Inside he went to George Blandford's wife, Nancy.

"Your wrap," he ordered her. "Tie it around my arm."

Nancy Blandford moved nervously, shaking as she inexpertly wrapped the bleeding arm. Max knew his arm was weaker but far from disabled.

"The man at the river is dead," he said simply.

"What man?" George Blandford asked, pulling his wife to him.

"Herr Deveau. He cut several of our boats adrift. And freed the mademoiselle."

"Deveau?" Jeremy whispered. "Marie?"

Max sneered. "I hope she appreciates his last good deed."

The man guarding the group spoke to Max in Russian. "So how do we transport our prisoners now, comrade?"

"We don't," Max said in Russian. "We still have a small fast boat. It can easily hold us and the two scientists. The others are of little value."

Max went to the heavy window drapes and ripped them down. He and the Russian guard cut the drapery cords to tie up all in the group except Doctors Harris and von Richter. Max motioned to his bewildered prisoners.

"Outside. We can complete our task out there."

"Max, old fellow," Jeremy Mann pleaded., "Surely you won't shoot me. Remember all the good times we had together?"

"Are you going to shoot him?" Harold Blandford suddenly blurted out.

Max looked at him, surprised by his outburst.

"Before you do, make him tell me how he killed Erica," Blandford pleaded.

Max looked at Blandford. "Who?"

"Erica. My daughter. How did he kill her?"

Max spoke calmly. "I killed her. She knew too much." He looked at Jeremy Mann and smiled. "And it didn't bother you at all, did it? You had a new plaything before the young lady was buried. The mademoiselle somewhere out there in the dark. And the movie queen."

Blandford growled at Jeremy. "You bastard! I knew it!"

Max and the guard herded the group onto the front lawn where all, except for the two scientists, were made to lie on the grass. Max walked among them, his Luger ready. The other guard went back into the house and piled the drapes into the center of the parlor. With a poker, he rolled a flaming log from the fireplace onto the drapes. They roared into flames as though gasoline had been poured on them. The Russian came running out to Max.

"A fitting monument to capitalism," the Russian said.

Maxed grunted his agreement. "Now, Herr Harris and Herr von Richter, let us be on our way. The motherland eagerly awaits your services."

"And the others?" one of the Russian guards said. "Why should we leave witnesses?"

Max smiled. "Witnesses? My friend, you don't know the Americans very well. They'll refuse to believe Russians came here and burned this mansion. All these good people on the grass won't be able to convince their government that's what happened. The Americans will insist that Germans did it."

"We should leave them in the burning house," the guard persisted.

"Enough. We don't want a mass murder that would shock the Americans into a more thorough investigation. Let them believe these fine capitalists got intoxicated and burned their own house. Who would believe such irresponsible people, eh? Let's be off with these two gentlemen who can help win the war."

Max whirled toward the driveway when he heard the siren. He saw the car with a flashing light on top and knew what it meant. He motioned to the two guards who moved quickly to the shadows at the edge of the lawn. They readied their weapons as Sheriff Roy Hazel's car sped up the driveway toward the burning house.

CHAPTER THIRTY-FIVE

I'M WHERE? Swimming? Wet. A pain. Dull and getting sharper. Sleeping with pain. I like to sleep. I'm wet. Sleeping wet.

That pain. Why do I feel pain? It's there, no there, left side of chest. Above nipple. Is that the side the heart's on? Can't remember.

The flash and flame. Someone shot at him. Darkness. He'd lost consciousness before going to bed. Here in the grass and the water. The water. Yes, that would be it. In the marsh on the bank of the river.

The flash. The boom. Yes. The man shot at him. Then came a shock, like morphine. Put him to sleep. Now morphine is wearing off. Pain spreading all through my chest. Burning pain. Even here in cold river water. Yes, that's it. Lying here in cold river water, pain growing.

Yes. The man had shot him. Put a hole in his chest. He had fallen here in the marsh by the river. Lying half submerged in water. Water rising. Tide raising water inch by inch. Water will soon wash over me and ease the pain.

Darkness. Had it been dark when he fell? Yes, yes. Now he could remember. The man had stood outlined against the light shining from the big house at the top of the hill. He had shot him. It had been dark. It's still dark, getting deeper. Were his eyes even open? He was looking skyward, saw only darkness. No stars.

Perhaps it's a dream. But the pain is increasing. Pain is not a dream. Burning pain in chest. Perhaps I'm breathing through the hole in my chest. Now. Open eyes again. See beyond the dark.

Clarke's eyelids strained to open. There. What's that? A probing nudge on his neck.

Was someone knocking? No. Nobody. There's the nudge again. Something cold and slick sliding up his neck, over his cheek, toward his eyes. He knew that feel. A water moccasin. With enough poison in its fangs to leave him still forever in this watery bed. Against every urge to cry out and raise himself, he kept his eyes closed.

Heart pumping like an engine. Was his blood pumping out through the wound in his chest? Could the snake hear it too? Maybe the pounding would alarm the snake and it would strike at the noise. Maybe it would try to find the noise, find the wound, try to squirm into it.

The snake took its time. Its tongue shot out, seeming to taste his skin. It slid its belly slowly over his face, inch by inch by inch. He ached to open his eyes, to see how big the snake was. But he willed his eyes to stay closed, knowing the least movement would startle the snake, cause it to strike out at his face, his eyes, his throbbing neck.

Inch by inch by inch. An eternal wait until the reptile moved again. Time enough for fear to revive his senses and his memory of the man who had shot him. Of the girl he'd left mounted on the horse. Of that first day he'd gone to Jekyll Island to talk to a man. Who was it? Oh yes, a Mr. Harold Blandford. Who thought the man in the big house had killed his daughter. And there was a French girl on a big horse. And then...then he was here. With a hole in his chest and a snake crawling over his face while he lay in marsh grass in the rising waters of the Altamaha River.

The wound burned in his chest. Must've missed my heart, he thought. Burning. Even in cold river water, he burned.

That damned snake is still on my face. Need to move soon or the water will drown me. Damn! Move, snake! Is it coiling, preparing to strike? Coiling on my nose, waiting for the movement that would tell it where to strike? It'll strike at the wound. At the oozing blood.

Clarke sized up his chances of sweeping the snake from his face. No, he thought, the snake could react faster, much faster, than any movement he could make. It would sink its deadly fangs into an arm moving toward it. He knew he hardly had the strength to move his arm, much less out-punch a snake.

The water inched higher, covering his body as it sank deeper into the muck under the grass. Sinking into a world inhabited by snakes. Lord! What if this snake's family decides to hold a reunion on my face? To enjoy my blood?

Suddenly it seemed he could see, though his eyes remained closed. There was light. The snake suddenly slid off his face into the water. Was the man with the pistol back, shining a light into his face? He had to open his eyes, see the light that had scared the snake. No flashlight beamed into his eyes. Why the light? He stayed in the grass and cold water. That light. It's coming from the house at the top of the hill.

Had outdoor lights been turned on? No matter. Move before the snake returned with his family and his friends. Before the water covered his head and flooded his lungs. He pushed himself up, gagging and coughing blood.

Was the man with the gun still there? No. The man.

Max. He was nowhere in sight.

The light. Now he would see the light at the top of the hill. Pineland was burning. Again!

He crawled from the grass to solid ground, fighting searing pain. The light reflected on something in the grass. Yes, yes! The sword he'd hurled at Max. Where is Max? The blade must've missed him.

He got the sword back into its scabbard. He berated himself again for not having brought at least one of the revolvers his forebears had bequeathed him, some already proven in battle. Now he'd love to have just the .38 he'd pulled on Liz and her boy friend in the Mayflower Hotel in Washington, D.C.

He limped to the trees lining the walk to the docks and leaned against one. He knew his legs wouldn't support him for long. He knew that he had to get back to Marie and the horse. Riding the horse into the dark back to his house would jar his wound and hurt like hell. No choice. If she was there. Please let her be there, he repeated over and over to himself. Please Lord, let her be there.

Why is the house burning? Why is Pineland burning again?

Clarke stumbled and crawled toward the top of the hill. Outside the ring of light from the fire, he saw the front lawn where two men were walking casually among what looked like sacks of sand on the grass.

Sacks of sand? Maybe horse feed?

But no sign at all of Marie and the horse. She hadn't stayed. He couldn't blame her. She had heard the shots and had saved herself.

All Jeremy Mann's vehicles were in plain view of the men on the lawn. No way to get to one of them and drive away. He knew only one place to find some transportation. In the barn. If he could get there and somehow mount a horse, he could ride to his house and call the sheriff for help. Wait. He had already called the sheriff. He was already on the way. No. Have to call someone else. Maybe Jasper. Jasper would go get help for him.

Clarke wheezed and limped and stumbled to the barns, grateful that the chaos at the house occupied the attention of whoever was there. Soon, he knew, the fire would turn the horses frantic and make them impossible to handle.

He fumbled along the walls in the dark, hearing the horses already stomping and whinnying. The glow was getting brighter, the horses more restless. In the glow he saw the saddles on rails. He chose an English style saddle because it looked lightest. But when he tried to lift, its weight send him screaming to the ground in pain.

He was unconscious for several seconds. When his senses revived he pushed away the saddle that had fallen on him. The fire in the house could be no hotter than the fire in his chest. Perhaps he could just lie here and wait for Max to go away. But maybe he'd want to burn the barn, too.

Grabbing stall slats, he slowly pulled himself up. That bay there looked less agitated than the other horses. He entered the bay's stall, dragging the saddle with him. Gravedigger was snorting and kicking in the adjoining stall, and he longed for the strength to saddle the powerful thoroughbred and break for the road. But he knew Gravedigger was too much to handle.

Fighting pain, he got the bridle on the bay. Twice he tried to lift the light saddle to the horse's back, twice it tumbled from his weakened hands.

Bareback. He would have to ride bareback. Without stirrups. Using the stall slats as a ladder, he fought through pain to climb onto the horse. He held the reins weakly, knowing he would lose them if the horse so much as shook its head. Gently nudging the horse with his knees, he urged it toward the entrance away from the house to lessen the impact of the fire on its fright. He prayed that just one more time his body would meld with the horse's and they would move in one rhythm.

To his horrified surprise, he exited the barn and saw the sheriff's car screech up in front of the house, its light flashing.

For a moment it appeared the sheriff was so astonished to see Pineland ablaze that he was glued in his car. When he and his deputy got out of the car, automatic weapons exploded in unison, splattering the sheriff's chest. He died without drawing his revolver. The deputy was quick enough to dive to the ground and come up shooting. Clarke knew he scored because one man screamed and dropped his gun. Another burst of automatic fire flung the deputy back against his car. He fired twice more, then went flying across the hood of the patrol car, perforated by automatic fire.

Clarke briefly wondered if he knew the deputy, then realized he had to leave fast. He kicked the horse into a gallop. He had gotten the sword from its scabbard with his good arm and emerged from the darkness into the light of the fire just as one of the gunmen leaped toward the patrol car to confirm his kill. To his horror, the horse ignored the reins and bolted toward the fire, not away from it.

The man who had killed the deputy stopped short of the sheriff's car, his legs apart, staring intently at the two slain lawmen. His concentration on the two corpses and the roar of the fire muffled the hoof beats of the horse until it was only feet from him. He whirled, too startled to bring up his rifle. He never saw the sweeping path of the sword that glanced off his rifle and sliced into his neck. He never screamed as the blade sliced through his voice box. He dropped into the sand, his head hanging to his body by a slim chunk of vertebra.

The charge was Clarke's last stand. The sword left his weakened hand with its victim. Without stirrups, he lost his balance on the galloping horse and tumbled to the ground as the gunman fell back in his headless death.

A merciful unconsciousness blotted out the pain that flooded through Clarke when he landed. He dimly knew steps were coming toward him at a run, knew Max was coming to complete his execution.

"So it's you, Herr Deveau." Max aimed his Luger, determined to complete the job he'd left unfinished in the marsh grass down by the river. He even liked it that the lawyer was on one elbow, watching him, waiting for the burst that would be the last thing he would see in this life. "You're a brave man, Herr Deveau. Almost a shame to kill a man so brave. But brave men die every day, don't they?"

The two men were concentrating on each other so intently that neither heard the hoof beats of the horse that shot out of the darkness and crashed into Max and sent him tumbling across the sand onto the lawn. Clarke first felt relief at his reprieve, then horror when he realized that Marie was the rider. Now Max would get up and kill her, too.

Marie dismounted in one motion. Whimpering and crying, she pulled Clarke to the dark side of the sheriff's car.

Looking under the sheriff's car, Clarke saw Max groggily get up, look around, and pick up his decapitated comrade's Tommy gun . He sprayed the car with a burst of fire, then began to circle around it.

"The gun," Clarke gasped. "Get the gun."

"Gun?" She was confused. He pointed to the deputy's revolver lying several feet away.

"Get it," he gasped.

"But..."

"Get it!" His command was little more than a gasp.

She cautiously reached out and pulled the revolver to her, then fell back, holding the gun in both hands like a bowl of hot soup. He reached for it but had no strength to take it.

Looking under the car, Clarke saw Max's boots coming slowly toward them. Marie had been around guns on hunts in France, with soldiers in France and London. Reading Clarke's desperation, Marie knew what she had to do. She pointed the revolver under the car at Max's approaching legs and fired. The recoil threw the gun from her grip. Max sprinted away in surprise. She retrieved the gun, aimed and pulled the trigger again. This time it only clicked.

The deputy was lying near the front wheel and Clarke tried to pull one...two bullets from his belt. Marie saw his fingers fumble weakly as he fought to stay conscious. She pulled the cartridges herself and looked at him helplessly. He could barely show her how to swing out the chamber and insert the cartridges. He motioned for her to get more ammunition, but Max was coming around the front of the car. Marie pointed the gun at him. It clicked on an empty chamber. Max smiled.

"Cherie, cherie."

She pulled the trigger again. It clicked uselessly. Max seemed amused. He lifted the Tommy gun and aimed at Clarke. "You first, Herr Deveau. You've earned it."

Marie's revolver boomed, the hammer hitting on one of the two chambers containing a bullet. The shot hit Max's trigger hand and sent him cursing in pain into the dark, leaving his fearsome gun lying in front of the car.

Marie cradled Clarke's limp body, taking no heed of the blood that soaked her clothes. "Clock! Clock!"

He made no answer. His mouth was open and his eyes closed. She found only a weak pulse in his neck.

She looked toward the house in disbelief. The roof had collapsed and only the original tabby walls remained. For the first time, she saw the shapes on the lawn, rolled up like logs ready to be thrown on a fireplace.

She eased Clarke from her arms and stood, then ran when she realized the logs on the lawn were people. They called to her as she walked among them, bewildered. What were they all doing here?

"Marie!" Jeremy Mann called her. She looked directly at him, then at the others. They were all well. Clarke was dying. Max was somewhere out there in the dark. He would undoubtedly return.

She ran back to Clarke. Hoping he wouldn't die of the pain as she moved him, she helped him rise to his feet, then pushed him into the back seat of the sheriff's shattered car. He lost consciousness before she slid behind the wheel. Somehow she had to drive to the town to find care for him.

The car didn't start when she turned the ignition key.

CHAPTER THIRTY-SIX

MAX WAS STILL somewhere out there in the dark. Marie knew it. She frantically pushed the gas pedal and turned the ignition. Nothing. She pumped the pedal some more. She smelled gas and vaguely thought "It's flooded." The engine gurgled uselessly. Though she had driven ambulances during the bombing in London, she knew nothing about mechanics, how to make balky cars start. She had the vague realization that the numerous bullets fired at the car could have, probably did, damage the engine.

There! She saw Max on the edge of the lawn, trotting from the darkness toward her, a Luger in his hand.

She pushed the pedal down and held it there while turning the key. Nothing. Pump again and turn the ignition. Nothing. Max was close enough now to take aim at her. Suddenly the ignition cleared the gasoline in the fuel line. The engine popped and coughed and chugged to life. She shifted into gear and the car jumped forward. She stopped when the car hit a lump. She backed up, feeling sick, knowing she'd hit the body of the dead deputy whose gun had saved her life. Saved it until now.

Max broke into a run across the lawn and fired a shot that went wild because he had to aim with his weak hand.

Marie got the car free of bodies, praying for forgiveness for damaging these good men who had come to help. She pointed the car down the driveway, extending her prayers to plead that Max wouldn't score a lucky shot that would stop her forever. She reached the highway without feeling a tell-tale stab of pain and turned down the highway toward Brunswick.

She pulled off the road twice to see if Clarke had revived, then pushed on with renewed terror when he showed no sign of life.

She reached Brunswick with no idea of where to go for help. She knew nothing about the town. She stopped in front of the Sims Super Store as a man was exiting. He stared in disbelief at the sheriff's bullet-riddled car and was startled to hear a feminine shout from within it. "Doctor! Where is doctor?"

"What say?"

The man cautiously walked to the car where the woman was yelling. Damn, the car was a mess. Looked somebody had used it for target practice.

"Doctor?" the woman yelled again. "Where is doctor?"

"Doctor? You say doctor?"

"Oui! Doctor!"

"Doctor? Well, I don't know this time of night, ma'am. Reckon they'd be home. You could call one."

"Man is hurt! Doctor!"

"Man? Say, ma'am, how come you're driving the sheriff's car?"

"Doctor!" she screamed. "He is dying!"

The man moved closer to the window and saw the bloody body in the back seat. "Say, is that Mr. Deveau?"

"Where is doctor?"

"Well, I'd say your best bet is to take him to the hospital. Now, you go up two, no three streets, take a right..."

"Show me!"

"What's that? Well, uh, yes ma'am. Reckon I could. Let me just put this bag there in the front seat and..."

The man fumbled getting his bag of groceries into his lap in the car. He looked back at Clarke motionless in the back seat. "He hurt bad, ma'am?"

"Hurry! Where is doctor?"

"Yes ma'am. Right straight ahead and..."

She jerked away from the store with cardboard signs advertising Georgia hams for twenty four and one-half cents a pound, ground beef for eighteen cents a pound, and eggs for twenty-nine cents a dozen. The man directed her through several turns to the hospital where he got out and hurried inside. Moments later two men with a stretcher came running out. She pleaded with Clarke to show some life and not be another victim of tonight's carnage.

She followed him into the hospital. Inside two men met the stretcher and opened two swinging doors. A woman in white stopped Marie at the doors. She stared at the doors, her heart sinking. She became aware that he man who'd guided her to the hospital was standing beside her. "Can I get you something, ma'am?"

She shook her head, trying to force a smile. She sank into a chair, then stood up quickly when a man in a white coat emerged from the swinging doors at a run. "Just to be sure, ma'am. Gunshot?"

"Oui. Yes."

"What kind of firearm?"

"Je ne sais pas."

"Ma'am?

"I do not know."

"I see. Thanks." The man turned abruptly and

disappeared through the doors.

Marie sat back down and sobbed silently while the man who'd guided her paced about nervously. They both looked at the desk when a man in uniform hurried in and spoke to the receptionist. The woman nodded toward Marie and the man hurried to her. "Ma'am, I'm Jim Reavis. Deputy. I was told you brought a wounded man here in the sheriff's car. It's all shot up. Who's the man you brought here?"

"Monsieur Clock Deveau."

"Mr. Deveau? The lawyer...uh, detective?"

"Oui."

"Where's the sheriff?"

"At the grande maison of Monsieur Mann. The house by the river. It burned."

"The Mann place? Pineland? Is the sheriff up there now?"

"He is shot."

The deputy sat down beside her. This made no sense. The fire, the sheriff shot, lawyer Deveau here in the hospital."

"You say the sheriff's shot? Dead?"

"Oui, I am sure of it. Poor man shot so many times."

"Do you know who did it?"

"Some strange men. They spoke German. And Russian."

The deputy plainly was bewildered. "German? Russian?"

The deputy went to the receptionist and whispered something. He left quickly without speaking again to Marie. She continued to stare at the doors through which she'd last seen Clarke.

The man who'd guided her to the hospital asked her once more if he could get her something and said he really ought to be getting on home because they'd be wondering about him. She smiled and touched his arm in thanks.

Deputy Reavis drove recklessly to the station to make sure another deputy was there to cover for him. The deputy was happy to stay in town. "Oh yeah, message here from the FBI," he said. "Wants to know if you know anything about that agent who was here this morning."

"No. I'm on the way to Pineland. That's where the agent was going. Get him back and give him directions to get there."

Deputy Reavis saw the glow of Pineland long before he reached the driveway. When he parked, his first discovery was Sheriff Roy Hazel, his body caked with blood from several wounds. Nearby was the deputy who'd volunteered to come along because Reavis had stopped by to check on his grandmother before coming to the office. That girl in the hospital was right. Both were dead. He wanted to cry, vomit, hit something, anyone to relieve the sickest feeling he'd ever had.

Germans, the girl had said. And Russians. Russians? The girl must've meant Germans. She sounded foreign herself. Probably didn't know the difference. Did this have anything to do with the FBI agent who'd come up here today? The sheriff hadn't talked about it other than saying you don't mess in federal business because they want to do things their own way.

Reavis walked toward the group of people standing on the lawn. They were gathered around a woman who was crying. The crowd parted and he went to the woman sitting on the grass.

"Who're you, ma'am?"

She hesitated and choked through her answer. "Nancy Blandford, officer."

"Are you hurt? What happened here?"

"He took Mr. Mann. Both of them. Albertis and Jeremy."

"Who took them?"

"That man. Max. He worked for Jeremy. I'm not sorry he took Jeremy."

"Where'd they go?"

"Down the river in a boat."

"Did this man Max shoot the sheriff?"

"He and the other one."

Reavis knew he would get little more useful from this woman. She was in even more shock than he was. He helped her stand and looked at the glow that had been Pineland. But he had to go back to his car and radio for help. He finished and was trying to talk to the others when another car came up the driveway traveling fast. A man in an unpressed gray suit got out.

"George Slayton. FBI. You Reavis?"

Reavis wearily told him what he knew. Slayton listened incredulously, hardly bearing to look at the sheriff and deputy. He had something else more important on his mind. "Where's agent Theo Stevens?"

Reavis shrugged and Slayton know he'd get no more from him. Slayton checked the cottage and found the phone line had been cut. He'd learned how to cut and reconnect lines in his surveillance training and soon had Alex Montgomery on the line with news he didn't want to hear.

"Germans? Russians? How about Theo?"

"No sign of him. We'll scour the area come daylight."

"And the two scientists?"

"This Blandford woman says they ran off into the dark. We'll look for them."

"Damn. And Deveau's as good as dead?"

"That's what the deputy says."

"Russians." Alex Montgomery snorted bitterly. "Damn it, we knew they were up to this. Good allies. Stalin's got more friends in this town than J Edgar. Lowery and Nelson are on the way from Atlanta. Theo and the scientists get priority. And keep tabs on Deveau. He knows something."

Slayton returned to the lawn and helped Reavis shoo away the crowd. They had seen the glow of the fire and had gathered from nearby farms. Reavis agreed with Slayton's instructions to avoid any questions about what had happened. He wearily leaned back against his car and accepted a Camel from Slayton. They smoked in silence, neither wanting to look at the shattered bodies of the lawmen. They wanted the bastards who had done this.

Max came upon a welcome sight soon after leaving the Pineland dock in the Chris Craft with the Mann father and son. There, its nose stuck in the marsh off Broughton Island in the Altamaha, was Jeremy Mann's cabin cruiser, provisioned and fuelled for the trip Max had originally planned. He herded the Mann men onboard. Max found the propeller free of obstructions and maneuvered the large craft into the river. He locked his prisoners in the cabin and took the controls.

For the first time in hours Max allowed himself a sigh of relief. The two rich men would be his hostages if it came to that. The elder Mann's chemical industrial knowledge in particular would be valuable. He deeply regretted he wasn't delivering the scientists, but they had escaped into the dark. Now, if only his contacts would know some first aid for the wounds inflicted by the sword blade and the mademoiselle's lucky bullet.

Soon after George Slayton hung up, the agent watching

the post office in Arlington called Alex Montgomery to tell him the alleged Walter Dreeling had turned up to check the postal box. He had taken the fake letter placed there by the agent and now was being tailed across the Fourteenth Street bridge. Dreeling had stopped at a restaurant and passed the letter to a man coming out. An agent had stayed with Dreeling and another followed the second man to the Russian embassy.

Federal Bureau of Investigation Director J. Edgar Hoover was spending a quiet evening reading and he answered gruffly when the phone rang. He grunted several times while he listened to Alex Montgomery.

"Fine. Do it," Hoover said and hung up.

Thirty minutes later District firemen rushed by the startled guard at the Russian embassy to answer the fire alarm. Among the firemen were three FBI agents who quickly removed documents from the small room next to the ambassador's office. At the time, the ambassador was attending a reception celebrating Soviet-American cooperation in the war against the Nazis.

The firemen disregarded protests that no one had raised a fire alarm. In fact, there was a small fire outside the embassy, started just before the firemen swarmed in. When agents found letters bearing a Brunswick post mark addressed to a postal box in Arlington, they left with the firemen, apologizing for upsetting the furniture in their efforts to bring the fire under control.

Within minutes FBI technicians located the microdots. By early morning Alex Montgomery had the translations. Director Hoover was having early coffee when Alex called.

"Of course they'll lodge a protest," Hoover said. "The Russians always protest."

When Alex hung up, Hoover sat for a moment thinking

how he'd tell the President. He knew President Roosevelt would be most displeased that the Russians were upset.

Kapitanleutnant Ernst Schmidt had watched two cargo ships pass in the early dawn, holding his fire in adherence to his order to do nothing to draw attention to his presence. But the loss of the two other U-boats rankled him, all the more because he knew he'd been kept in the dark about the true purpose of this mission. The more secrecy the greater the risk to his craft and lives of his men.

"Herr kapitan! Craft sighted!"

Schmidt strained his eyes into the early dawn. No moon to help. Then he saw the small white craft. A pleasure craft, he reasoned. Strange, these Americans. They're in a war and they use their fuel on pleasure craft. But he knew that some pleasure craft were used for military purposes, especially for spotting U-boats and reporting to naval forces. Yes, this innocent-looking pleasure craft likely was in the service of the American navy. The navy that had sent two U-boat crews to watery graves. They were just north of Jacksonville, Florida. The craft likely was returning to its station there.

Schmidt remembered the fine officers and crews of his two lost U-boats. He made a decision.

"Ready torpedo."

Onboard the cruiser Max felt relaxed for the first time in days, though his superiors wouldn't be happy that the scientists had escaped. The two hostages were below. Now to find the inlet where the car would be waiting to take them to the plane. The rising sun raised his spirits.

Max smiled. He knew Admiral Donitz had ordered U-boats to cease operations in these waters until after this weekend so as not to arouse the Americans about the kidnapping taking place under their noses. Somewhere out there were idle U-boats waiting for a rendezvous that would never take place. These waters were particularly safe.

He felt nothing when the torpedo blasted the cruiser into splinters.

The next evening Kapitanleutnant Schmidt declined to approach the island called Jekyll. Why all the naval activity around the island? Surely not because of his attack on that small craft off Jacksonville early this morning. A radio message from base agreed he should depart the area immediately.

CHAPTER THIRTY-SEVEN

"WHY DON'T YOU invite me down to hunt quail?" Clarke hadn't heard from Alex Montgomery since that night in 1942 when he had gone looking for Marie and ended up mostly dead for weeks.

"Because I don't want you near me with a gun. And you'd be crazy to let me near you with one."

"I see you're feeling fine."

"Does that mean you're sending your goons to finish me off?"

"I'm coming down to visit our Atlanta office next week. I neglected my folks during the war. My dad's in failing health now."

October, 1946. Clarke realized he hadn't given Alex Montgomery much thought since his last brush with the Bureau.

"Sure, come on by. I'll hide the ammunition. You can meet Marie. She's starting a riding school now. Putting her Sorbonne education to good use. She and Annie are taking care of the two kids. Lord knows what kind of accent they'll end up with between them."

"I've looked forward to meeting Marie. Our agents were

very impressed with her."

Montgomery met Clarke at his office in Brunswick and went with him to Pineland. "We've restored it on a smaller scale. We don't need a mansion. It came back on the market after Jeremy Mann disappeared and it was sold at auction. Nobody realized the debt he was in."

When Marie met them in the foyer, Montgomery realized the reports of her beauty and bearing were not exaggerated. Her French accent had absorbed a tinge of Southern softness to give her a refinement he wished was contagious. She excused herself to attend to horses in the stable.

Clarke let Alex choose his drink and pretended disgust when he chose Scotch to emphasize his distance from his Georgia roots. Clarke stayed with reliable bourbon. Montgomery sipped and walked to the mantel where the old sword was hanging under the crossed Georgia and Confederate flags. "So that's the singing sword of Glynn."

"From Bull Run to Brunswick. You'll notice it's clean now."

"Yes, it did create a mess back there in '42, didn't it?"

"I wasn't totally successful. Had Marie not been there I would be out there next to my dad with the other Deveaus."

"Marie is a peach".

"Fortunately I convinced her to become a Georgia peach, thank the saints."

Montgomery grinned in agreement.

"It was good in another way," Clarke said. "Getting shot kept me out of the war. Even if I have a permanent pain in my chest. And my law license was restored. Seems there was some kind of recommendation from somebody in DC that carried weight with the bar. I never found out who was responsible."

"Brunswick needed another attorney. Military camps

and shipyards just naturally breed lots of clients. Gives you the chance to forget old scars."

"Marie helps me forget them. Her father is still unaccounted for. We have to assume the worst."

Montgomery seemed to hesitate. "Do you ever hear from your first wife?"

"Liz? No, thank God. I occasionally read that she and Mrs. Roosevelt are cleaning up some blight or another. Keeps them off the streets."

"And in our hair."

Clarke chuckled when Montgomery rubbed his thinning pate.

"Why did you come, Alex?"

"Beg your pardon?"

"You didn't detour all the way from Atlanta just for a Scotch and water. Or to ogle Marie."

Montgomery coughed. "Okay. I thought you deserved to know what you were up against that night. You interfered with a plot to kidnap two nuclear scientists. Fortunately, we found them hiding in a barn and they helped us win the war."

"Who was behind the attempted kidnapping?"

"Russians, for sure. Probably Germans, too."

"Russians. I'd always suspected it, even though we found the German uniform. The official story was that Germans were responsible for the kidnapping attempt and burned Pineland. Who was Max?"

"Our British friends helped us piece it together. His real name was Max von Oster. His father was assigned to the British embassy between the wars. He fell in love with a British socialist who was a staunch Stalinist and married her. He was recalled to Berlin and killed in a street riot, we think on orders of the Gestapo. Max and his mother had stayed in England, so his father's death was what pushed him to contact the Soviets and become a double agent.

"Max grew up in England and got an English education complete with socialism, courtesy of his mother. He spoke the language perfectly. He joined the Abwehr, Germany's military intelligence service, and was assigned to England. His English education and manners made it easy for him to survive when so many other German agents were flushed out.

"He attached himself to Jeremy Mann and followed him here to America to get inside the American chemical industry. He fed one set of facts to Germany and another to the Russians in DC. Getting that information put Mr. Hoover in Dutch with Roosevelt, by the way. But he stood up to it. After all, he knows secrets most of DC is desperate to keep hidden.

"Max's mission was to kidnap the two scientists and fly them to Russia. The Germans thought he was going to do the same thing for them. We can only surmise, but we believe the German agent you found dead had been sent to keep tabs on von Oster. Apparently the Germans themselves didn't trust him."

"What became of him?"

"We never knew for certain. Fragments of Albertis Mann's cruiser were found north of Jacksonville. We believe it was torpedoed and everyone aboard killed. We do know that von Oster never appeared at his rendezvous near Jacksonville. The Mann Corporation was absorbed by a pharmaceutical corporation."

Clarke shook his head. "So we developed the bomb and won the war, no thanks to our Russian allies."

"Yes," Alex said. "A few months after von Oster and the two Manns disappeared, the bomb research was consolidated into what they called the Manhattan Project. Under a general named Leslie Groves. Harris and von

Richter were part of it. They might've done the work for Stalin if you hadn't ridden into their party that night waving your sword like JEB Stuart. I've always wondered if you were drunk at the time."

"Unfortunately, no. I was feeling plenty of pain."

"From which you recovered, thanks to your Marie. We lost a good man in Theo Stevens."

"Agreed. The sheriff and his deputy did their duty, too. To me the bravest man that night was the deputy. Even after the sheriff was cut down, he stood up and got off the shots that took out the Russian guard. If it hadn't been for him, there would've been an extra gun coming after me and Marie. The least I can do is to give his son free rein to hunt on Pineland the rest of his life."

"Ever give any thought to getting back into government work?"

"Not once. I resolved to go straight. I like it here. It's a real shame you didn't get that scholarship to Princeton. You were the one who wanted to cut your roots. A Princeton skin would've shot you to the top in DC. Of course, you're going to make it anyway."

Alex snuffled softly. "Keep it up, Clarke. I'll send Liz and Mrs. Roosevelt down here to reform you of things you didn't even know you were doing wrong."

"Hand me that bottle of bourbon, will you?"

EPILOGUE

THE JEKYLL CLUB never reopened after the season of 1942. The older residents lost interest and the younger socialites found livelier diversions in the post-war resurgence. In 1947 the state of Georgia purchased the island and operated it as a vacation retreat. In 1950 the Jekyll Island State Authority took control of it. Today a causeway connects the island to the mainland, and it is no longer a preserve of a wealthy elite.

* * * *

Admiral Wilhelm Canaris brooded over the lost opportunity to snare Drs. Harris and von Richter for Germany's nuclear research. Never knowing the fate of Max von Oster or Karl Volker, he sought to infiltrate America and, along with general sabotage, learn the truth about his brightest agent's disappearance. Pressured by criticism fomented by Reinhard Heydrich, Canaris dispatched two groups of saboteurs to America. In June, 1942, one group of four men landed at Amagansett on Long Island, and another group of four landed at Jacksonville, Florida. All eight were captured. Six were executed.

* * * *

Obergruppenfuhrer/Reich Protector Reinhard Heydrich did not live to gloat over the discomfiture of Canaris. On May 27, 1942, Heydrich was wounded in an attack on his car in Prague by Czech resistance fighters. He died a week later.

* * * *

Heydrich's goal to absorb the Abwehr into the SD was accomplished in 1944 after Canaris was implicated in plots to murder Adolph Hitler. Dismissed in February, 1944, Canaris was arrested in July, 1944. He was hanged naked by piano wire suspended from meat hooks at Flossenburg concentration camp on April 9, 1945. Three weeks later on April 30, Hitler committed suicide with his Walther PPK-765 in the Fuhrerbunker in Berlin.

ABOUT THE AUTHOR

 MARTIN WILSON has written on a multitude of topics ranging from history to financial services to agriculture. He grew up in the North Carolina foothills where his ancestors settled before the American Revolution. He lives in Mechanicsville, Virginia, and draws upon his Southern agrarian heritage to produce a garden laden with the earth's bounty. He enjoys reading Poe, Faulkner and Twain—stop by to enjoy a Hanover Tomato sandwich and swap tales with him.

GOLD-BUG MYSTERIES

SHOTWELL PUBLISHING mysteries appear under the imprint name "Gold-Bug Mysteries." The first detective story, *The Gold-Bug* was written by the great Southerner Edgar Allan Poe and set near Charleston, South Carolina.

www.ingramcontent.com/pod-product-compliance
Lightning Source LLC
Chambersburg PA
CBHW060525260626
47161CB00003B/767